Praise for BETWEEN A WOLF AND A DOG

'Blain just gets better and better. The clarity and precision
of *Between a Wolf and a Dog* brings to mind the formal beauty of an
exquisitely cut gemstone. Blain looks at the big questions — mortality,
grief, forgiveness — through the lens of one family's everyday struggle
to love each other. This portrait of marriage and work, of sisterhood,
mothers, and daughters is resolute and clear-eyed; so commanding and
beautifully written it made me cry.'
Charlotte Wood, author of *The Natural Way of Things*

'Heartfelt, wise, and emotionally intelligent, *Between a Wolf and a Dog*
is a beautifully tender exploration of the complications of family love, self-
knowledge, and the struggle for forgiveness.'
Gail Jones, author of *A Guide to Berlin*

'What a marvellously clear eye Georgia Blain has for the ways in which
we love and harm one another. Whether she is observing a "coconut-ice"
grevillea or meditating on everyday consolations and sorrows, Blain is a
quietly profound writer and this is a remarkable book.'
Michelle De Kretser, author of *Questions of Travel*

'*Between a Wolf and a Dog* is an elegantly told story describing the
ambiguities within human relationships. Each evening, when my children
slept, I would enter the world of this book — coming to know a flawed,
courageous, and creative family of characters, as they struggled to be good,
to be whole, and finally, to let go.'
Sofie Laguna, author of *The Eye of the Sheep*

'Picking a favourite Georgia Blain novel is like picking a favourite
child … Blain intelligently asks the big questions — about mortality,
grief, forgiveness and how hard it can sometimes be to love those we're
supposed to.'
North and South

'[A]n elegant novel, written in lucent and, at times, luminous prose. It is a work of delicately detailed emotion and beautiful balance, and it is so well paced that its narrative is utterly compelling. It is a remarkable portrayal of family relationships, and the complex and often competing desires and sensitivities that drive them, but it is mostly a book about love and forgiveness, and holding on to our good fortune and our loved ones, even and especially in the face of loss. It is heartfelt and resonant, and a remarkable novel that lingers long after its final page.'
Fiona Wright, *Weekend Australian*

'Captures the elusive moment when it's time to forgive, when it's time to stop fighting.'
Australian Women's Weekly

'Blain writes enchantingly about the interstices of life, the places where morality and meaningfulness blur, and characters try to justify their actions or deal with their emotions … lyrical and lucid.'
Herald Sun

'Blain is a writer of such lucidity and strength that her characters speak, undeniably, for themselves … What makes it possible to contain tragedy in words, so that the reader enters into the experience and passes through it, cleansed? The Greek playwrights had their own answers to this question; but the question, I suspect, is far older than their version of it. Each generation of authors must find the right words for writing about death. Part of the reason *Between a Wolf and a Dog* succeeds so well is that everything in the novel is heartfelt without being in the least sentimental.'
Dorothy Johnston, *Sydney Morning Herald*

Praise for THE SECRET LIVES OF MEN

'Many adjectives have been used to describe Georgia Blain's work, including evocative, powerful, atmospheric, haunting, rich, thought-provoking, skilful, uncompromising, and finely detailed — all of which apply to this collection of short stories.'
Bookseller + Publisher

'Subtle, beautifully paced stories ... a finely tuned collection, thoughtfully written and arranged, with profound and unsettling things to say about love, loneliness, and risk.'
Denise O'Dea, *Australian Book Review*

'Richly imagined characters ... told with lovely restraint. The authenticity of the writing is such that you feel you are standing in the shoes of these characters whose lives are at a particularly intense point.'
Herald Sun

'[A] skilled, disenchanted reckoning of the way we live now.'
Peter Pierce, *The Saturday Age*

'There's a quiet, understated quality to her prose, an introspection in her narrative that makes her words glow dully with slow-burning intensity ... Relationships in all their combinations and permutations are skilfully dissected by an author with a keen eye and a firm grasp.'
Thuy On, *The Age*

'Blain's achievement with the short story form is to render it a mid point between the overt artifice of fiction and the covert artifice of life-writing ... her stories fill up with ambiguity ... characterised by an irresolution that mimics the resistance of experience to shape and comprehension.'
Stella Clarke, *The Weekend Australian*

BETWEEN A WOLF AND A DOG

Georgia Blain published novels for adults and young adults, essays, short stories, and a memoir. Her first novel was the bestselling *Closed for Winter*, which was made into a feature film. Her books have been shortlisted for numerous awards including the NSW, Victorian, Queensland, and SA Premiers' Literary Awards, the Stella Prize, and the Nita B. Kibble Award. Georgia passed away in December 2016.

Also by Georgia Blain

Closed for Winter
Candelo
The Blind Eye
Names for Nothingness
Births Deaths Marriages
Darkwater
Too Close to Home
The Secret Lives of Men
Special

BETWEEN
A WOLF
AND
A DOG

GEORGIA BLAIN

SCRIBE

Melbourne • London

Scribe Publications
18–20 Edward St, Brunswick, Victoria 3056, Australia
2 John St, Clerkenwell, London, WC1N 2ES, United Kingdom

First published by Scribe 2016
Reprinted 2016, 2017 (four times)

Typeset in Adobe Garamond Pro by the publishers
Printed and bound in the UK by CPI Group (UK) Ltd, Croydon CR0 4YY

Scribe Publications is committed to the sustainable use of natural resources
and the use of paper products made responsibly from those resources.

9781925321111 (Australian edition)
9781925228540 (UK edition)
9781925307481 (e-book)

CiP data records for this title are available from the National Library of
Australia and the British Library.

scribepublications.com.au
scribepublications.co.uk

For Rosie and Anne, Odessa and Andrew

NOW

This is the dream: Lawrence is alone. It is not quite dark, between a wolf and a dog; a mauve light is deepening like a bruise, the cold breath of the wind a low moan in his ear.

He stands on what feels to be the highest point in a landscape that he knows to be desolate and barren, although it is too dark for him to see. Hills roll away, dry grasses beaten low by the weather; pocked boulders, dappled with creeping lichen, appear to tumble, heavy, down a steep slope.

Is it breathing he hears? Or just the night sigh?

Fear tickles the back of his neck, the hairs on his wrists bristle, his eyes widen, and the darkness is thickening.

He should not be here.

There must be somewhere he can go, a light in the distance.

Perhaps if he calls out … and he opens his mouth, but his throat tightens.

It is like an elastic band pulling in, a peg clip on his vocal cords.

He tries to speak, but his mouth is drying, the palate hard like bone, the trachea clenching, and he cannot utter a sound.

In his dream, he panics, and he tries to wake himself, aware at some level that this is only a dream, but he can't rise from the

1

depths; there is a weight keeping him down, the pressure — like an ocean — above him. He needs to breathe.

Calm, he tells himself. It will be all right. *Calm*. And so the clamp loosens, his mouth opening, his throat a little less clenched as he finally speaks.

'Hello.'

Unable to utter more than that, a single word whispered in all that emptiness, as around him the wind builds, and he feels the cold, sour breath of night, and the rain like sharp pins slashing the clamminess of his skin.

Sitting up in the darkness, Lawrence lets his eyes adjust. He has left the window open, and it is raining, damp and miserable, seeping down from the sill onto his bed. He reaches over to close it, the swollen wood bringing the sash to a standstill, so he has to jiggle the frame, slot it into a new groove before it will slide all the way down.

He hates that dream. It leaves a rusted aftertaste, ferrous flakes in his mouth, and a panic like poison — the hollowness of sadness and despair coursing through him as he lies back down in the bed. He hasn't looked at the clock — years of insomnia have taught him the foolishness of doing so — but the sound of the first suburban trains lets him know that he is at least on the right side of the darkest hour for those who don't sleep. Outside the rain continues, softer now that the window is shut, and he closes his eyes, hoping he at least will find a sense of calm before morning comes, although he knows that this is unlikely. He has had that dream before, and it always leaves him, mind awake, trying to rid himself of the last vestiges of that man: a man alone, exposed, and afraid; a man he knows more intimately than he would like.

ALL THROUGH THE NIGHT it continues to rain; heavy, relentless, 'malevolent' a client had called it yesterday, and Ester had looked at him across the space of her consulting room and smiled. 'That's a strong word to choose,' she'd commented.

She wakes at four to a brief pause in the downpour, a stillness that descends over her house, and she sits up, her feet on the cold, bare boards, reluctant to leave the warmth of her bed, but also disturbed by the quiet. Outside, a car turns off the street, the hiss of its tyres on the wet road soft in the silence. The branches of the she-oak scrape on the roof, a familiar groan of bark on tin, and then the rain begins again, not gently but with full force, torrential sheets of water running down the windows, pouring out of the downpipes and into the streets, rising and falling with each obstacle in their path, gushing up around the wheels of parked cars, bubbling over the rubbish blocking the drains, scooping up the soil and mud and leaves and sticks and plastic, all in a rush, until they are dumped against the next obstacle, the flow continuing, unstoppable, on and on to the lowest point.

Sitting on the edge of her bed, Ester listens.

As a child, rain had made her anxious. She remembers nights by the river, the room where they slept leaking like a sieve. Whenever it rained, Maurie would put all the pots and pans across the floors, rolled towels under windows and doors, the constant drip, drip, drip of water on metal keeping her awake, along with her worry that the pots would fill and overflow, or the towels would fail to stem the leak between sill and frame, and everything would just float away.

Rain still makes her unsettled.

In the darkness of the corridor, the dog lies pressed against her door. He began sleeping there shortly after she moved to this house, disturbed by the change and wanting to be as close to her as possible. She lifts his body with her foot, the warmth of his coat soft against the cold of her skin, and he jumps, nails scratching on the bare boards, only to stand just in front of her so that she walks into him again, blind in the dark.

'Otto.' She doesn't want to wake the girls. Clicking her fingers and pointing towards the kitchen, she tries to direct him to where his mat is, never used, but he ignores her.

'Move.' She knees him again, and he shifts slightly before sighing heavily and slumping to the ground once more, eyes open and glittering white-blue in the darkness, making sure she doesn't leave his sight.

The door to the girls' room always creaks when she opens it. She turns the handle slowly, attuned to the shift, and when that doesn't work, she twists it as quickly as she can. It doesn't really matter. Once they are asleep, they don't wake.

The streetlight shines in through a chink in the blind. Lara hated this when they first moved here. She couldn't go to sleep with any light on, insisting that the room was totally dark.

'I can't fix it,' Ester had told her. 'The light is there and I can't make it go away.'

She remembers. She had sat on the edge of Lara's bed and she had wept. In all the preceding months, she had gone into the bathroom to cry, or into her bedroom, once even hiding in the pantry cupboard, while they ran around the house calling for her, over and over again. But that night, she had just given in.

'You're going to have to live with it,' she'd said.

Lara hadn't uttered a word, not calling out as she usually did, not getting up and rubbing her eyes as she complained she couldn't sleep. She had stayed where she was. And she had never mentioned the light again.

Standing at the entrance to their room, Ester sees the slope and curve of their bodies, the slow rise of their chests, the golden tangle of their hair, the loose abandonment of a limb, the soft pad of Catherine's heel, and the smooth muscle of Lara's calf. They always end up in the same bed, curled into each other; two beautiful bodies, alike to everyone but their family.

They are hers, and they are not hers. They are growing to become unique, distinct beings who will lead lives of their own in places of their own.

She loves them.

And the warmth of that is a blessing in the night, at an hour when no one should be awake. Ester breathes it in, a great draught of it, full and rich, while outside the rain continues unceasing: silver sheets sluicing down, the trees and shrubs soaking and bedraggled, the earth sodden, puddles overflowing, torrents coursing onwards, as the darkness slowly softens with the dawn.

Ester's appointment diary is open.

9.30am: Louisa

11.00am: The Harcourts

1.00pm: Daniel and Sarah

2.15pm: Chris

4.00pm: Hannah

In her head she sees the structure of her day: post-natal depression, school aversion, relationship crisis, death, and loneliness. Lawrence used to call her diary 'The Happiness Book'.

'Ho-ho,' she'd respond. 'What a wit.'

But she hadn't been averse to teasing him about his own work. Lawrence conducted polls and surveys. *He measures dissatisfaction*, she would say when people asked her what he did. A state he was fond of indulging in himself.

She closes the diary. When the girls are with Lawrence, the client hours can continue well into the evening — but not tonight. Tonight, she is finishing early. And this morning, she is up before they are awake, her yoga mat laid out in the lounge room. It is only just light, and the rain is continuing, no longer torrential, just steady, plastering wet leaves against the cold glass — crimson, brown, and green.

Each time she tries to go into dog pose, Otto licks her face. She puts him out in the hall and he whines, scratching against the wood, the noise harsh and insistent.

She hates it when the girls go to Lawrence, but where the girls go, Otto goes, and the break from him is always welcome. Breathing in, she tries once again, the stretch easier this time, the knot in her back unfolding as she lowers her hands to the floor, ignoring the dog as she exhales and inhales, slowly, deeply.

Her phone chimes. The text message on the screen is from her mother: *Cold Men*. She can only assume this means 'Call me', as this is what Hilary usually wants, but as she never wears her glasses, and her phone has an old form of predictive text that she uses in an unpredictable way, the words that she sends usually bear no relation to what she means.

'Why don't you just call me?' Ester asks.

'Because I didn't know if you were up yet,' Hilary replies.

Hilary sleeps badly, although she has always ignored any suggestions Ester gives to try and help, telling her daughter that insomnia gives her more time to work. Ester knows she frequently gets up before dawn and goes to the studio Maurie built for her — a room that leaks a lot less than the river house, his first project all those years ago. She sits at a desk in the corner, computer screens in front of her, the surrounding walls covered in images: cards, letters, scraps from newspapers, old family photographs, a piece of flimsy fabric, shiny wrappings from Easter eggs, ribbons, drawings from Catherine and Lara, and there in the centre of it all, Maurie's horse: beautiful, wild, the charcoal lines black and sure, the strange mixture of panic and pride in its eye enough to stop everyone who entered Hilary's room.

'It's his portrait of me,' Hilary would always say.

She tells Ester her film is ready, and will have its first screening at the Pompidou Centre in a month.

'I want to show you before I send it off,' she says. 'And they've sent the program notes for my approval, but I can't understand a word of them.'

Ester and Lawrence had lived in France until just after the girls turned one, and although her French is rusty, she has enough to get the gist. 'I can't today,' she says. 'Tomorrow?'

Hilary wants to know if tonight is possible.

'I'm going out,' Ester tells her. 'I promise I'll come tomorrow.'

She doesn't want to say anymore, to tell Hilary anything about her plans for the evening. It is too fragile, and she needs to keep it close for the present.

But Hilary rarely gives in. 'It will only take an hour.'

Ester is silent for a moment. She sighs, relenting with reluctance. She will come after work. 'But I can't stay.'

Outside, the streetlights have turned off and the first watery wash of morning colours the sodden sky. The rain continues. Across the road, Ester can see her neighbour getting into his car. He sits with the door open, trying to close his umbrella, the drops soaking into his suit and splashing onto his shoes, and she watches as he shakes the now closed umbrella into the gutter.

Catherine and Lara are awake. Their room is still dark, and

Ester pulls up the blind. The grevillea presses against the window, coconut-ice flowers and fine feathery leaves.

'Up,' she tells them.

Catherine ignores her, continuing to whisper to Lara. She is using the language she and Lara shared for the first four years of their lives, a secret language that neither she nor Lawrence could ever understand. He used to worry about it, to try and get them to use English only; Ester was always less concerned. 'They'll drop it in their own time,' she would say, which they had, although they still occasionally liked to revert.

'We don't want to go to school,' Catherine tells her. 'It's too wet.'

'And we don't want to go to Dad's,' Lara adds.

'We just want to stay here. In bed.' It's Catherine's turn now.

She smiles at them, and pulls back the blanket.

'Please,' Lara persists.

Catherine whispers something in her ear, giggling as she does. Lara replies in their language.

'Enough,' Ester tells them. She had made the mistake of succumbing to this request in the early days of the separation, and they still try, prying for the chink.

'I'm being bullied,' Lara tells her.

Ester laughs. 'You are not.'

'We don't like Dad.'

'That's not true either.' She resorts to a bribe. 'Hot chocolate if you're up by the time I count to twenty.'

They like school. This occasional reluctance to go is something new. She wonders whether they do this with Lawrence as well. She knows Lara was recently in trouble for setting off the fire alarm, with Catherine initially taking the blame. It was Lawrence who had dealt with that one, although the school informed her as well. She also knows they don't like their teacher this year. She is one of the old ones; a woman who has been there for years and only shows enthusiasm for the classroom footy-tipping competition and describing re-runs of *Judge Judy* episodes to the wide-eyed seven-year-olds who love the shameless airing of conflict. If the homework they bring back is any indication, the actual schoolwork is boring and repetitive, so much so that she offered to write them both a note to say she didn't want them doing it. Lara leapt at the chance, but Catherine was more nervous. 'She ignores those notes,' she said. 'She still shouts at the kids who don't do the work.'

She imagines asking Lawrence how they are with him, whether he too has noticed a slight shift in their attitude to school, whether he thinks it is a matter that should concern them.

In her sessions with Victoria, she is working on her communication with Lawrence — on her forgiveness, really. Because that's what it all comes down to, always. Can you forgive?

'You *have* to forgive,' Hilary would urge her, too often and too soon. 'We all have to forgive.'

As children, Ester and April rarely fought, but when they did, Maurie would make them apologise to each other. He hated conflict around him, although he was never averse to arguing his own point, loudly and frequently. She remembers the time she ruined April's new shorts, wearing them into the river and tearing them on an overhanging bough that she used to haul herself out. They were flared blue gingham, April's pride and joy, and Ester had been jealous because April looked so pretty in them. Despite being two years older, April was the same size as her, slender and delicate with long legs and thick golden hair. Looking down at the shorts, Ester knew she would be in trouble. She took them off and hid them under the verandah.

Denial was useless. When she was discovered, she didn't want to apologise. They always shared clothes, and what had happened had been an accident. She'd hung them on the bush so that they would dry out, she lied. They'd blown off.

April cut up her favourite T-shirt.

It took Maurie two days to get them to speak to each other without rancour. He refused to talk to them until they each apologised and forgave the other. Hating her father's disapproval, Ester gave in first. She remembers saying she was sorry, she really was, her words calm and clear as she genuinely tried to resolve the issue. And then April cried — she cried with shame at how badly she'd behaved, at how much she'd hated that this had come between them, at how much she loved Ester, she really did. Maurie cried, too. The house was awash with their tears, and if Ester felt that it was ridiculous, over-dramatic, too much — well, she kept this to herself, because this was how it always was with April.

Standing in the kitchen, she wonders how Maurie would deal with them now if he were still alive.

It is eight o'clock, and Lawrence will be here to get the girls in half an hour. Their bags are packed by the front door.

'Don't think I don't know what you're doing,' Ester says, taking the red hair-tie out of Catherine's hair and swapping it for the blue one in Lara's. She does this for the teachers, to help them distinguish between the two of them, but it is probably useless — they are likely to switch as soon as they are out of her sight.

'What are you going to do while we're at Dad's?' Lara asks.

Ester smiles. 'Sit up late, eat pizza, watch bad television.'

'Or go out with Steven?' There is muffled giggling, nervous glances, kicks under the table, and Ester looks from one to the other, momentarily silenced by their audacity.

They have been at her phone, checking the calendar she keeps separate to her work appointment book. She remembers putting his name in, fear making her fingers clumsy, just as her voice had felt unlike her own when he had called her, and she had answered, aware of who he was the moment she heard him speak, lowering her tone so that she didn't sound herself. She became sensible, serious, dull.

She had met him at a family-mediation course. She had been late on the first day, taking the last seat at the table. He had spent most of the morning session surreptitiously sending and receiving texts. When they were paired for a role-playing exercise, he had no idea what they were meant to be doing.

'You're passive and I'm aggressive,' she told him.

'I'm Steven, actually,' and he held out his hand.

A woman called Heather was their mediator. She asked them both to give her a brief précis of why they were here, the nature of their conflict. She was nervous and shy, her voice almost too soft to hear.

'I don't know,' Steven said.

'We're negotiating a financial settlement,' Ester told him.

'Do we have much?'

She smiled. 'Aside from a house and pitiful savings, there's anger, hurt, and pride.'

His eyes were smoke, clouds, and soft winter sky. He looked embarrassed when his phone chimed again. 'It's work,' he explained. 'I'm so sorry. They're sacking someone I've been working with. It's messy.'

He was a counsellor for executives, brought in by companies when they were concerned that their top-level staff were not performing to the best of their abilities. 'It can be a tricky line. The company pays my bill, but the person is my client.'

'Can we get back to the settlement?' Heather asked, sniffing anxiously as she saw the other groups well into the scenario.

In the break, he offered to make her a cup of tea.

'I don't drink it,' she told him.

'Well, there's a first,' he smiled. 'Someone else who doesn't like tea.'

'I try,' she said. 'But it's the tannin. Makes my tongue curl and my teeth feel like chalk.' She grimaced.

'Clearly, no one has ever made you the perfect cup.'

'They've given it a go,' she told him. 'But it's never changed my mind.'

He asked her where she worked.

'At home,' she told him. 'I'm a counsellor. I specialise in family therapy.'

'Do you like it?'

'Sometimes. On the good days.' She smiled.

'Do you have a family of your own?'

She looked straight at him as she answered. 'Everyone does.'

He laughed, and for the first time she witnessed a flicker of nerves. 'That was a clumsy way of trying to find out if you're on your own.'

She was embarrassed. She remembers and blushes even now. *It is so hard to do this*, she thinks. *To laugh, and be light, and take those first steps.* It is a wonder anyone ever does it — that extraordinary, shimmering fragility so delicate and open. There, high above the city, standing next to an urn, a fake teak box filled with teabags, and, next to the box, carefully stacked white china cups, both of them surrounded by counsellors, she had felt it for an instant — the sparkling brightness of the moment — and it had made her look down at the carpet, his shoes, her boots, the stolid ordinariness of them not quite enough to ground her.

After the course, he suggested they have a drink.

'I only have an hour,' she told him.

The girls were with Hilary, and she called and asked her to feed them. She was running late, she said.

They went to a bar, all warm wood and dark corners, and full of people younger than them. He asked her what she would do if she could start again, 'if money and training were no option and you could do anything, anything at all.'

She considered the question for a moment.

'Maybe a gardener.' But she was lying really, and she confessed as much. 'I wouldn't want to do the actual work; I'd just like to plan it, and then look at it once it was done.'

He asked her about her family.

'My mother is a filmmaker,' she told him, 'and my father was a painter.'

'Siblings?'

'A sister. She was a singer. She is a singer.'

She didn't want to talk about April, and she picked up the coaster, damp beneath her fingers, and then put it down again. 'What about you?'

'I like what I do,' he said. 'But if I could start again, maybe a surgeon. I spent six months in hospital. With a virus that went to my lungs and my kidneys. It was awful, but that whole world, the intensity of it, the drama, the fact that what you do matters,' he smiled. 'It was seductive. I could see why there are so many hospital soaps.'

She liked him. A half hour passed, and then she called Hilary. An hour later, she called again. When she finally left, she was slightly drunk, and the softness of his lips on her cheek as they kissed goodbye had lingered, warm.

It has been a year since she moved to this house, she thinks, two years since Lawrence sat in front of her and confessed. And despite being so tired of the taste of it, she has held his betrayal close.

She looks at the girls now; Lara is uncertain as to whether they have gone too far, Catherine is nervous for her sister.

'I *am* going out,' Ester tells them. She smiles at Lara. 'And what an extraordinary guess. I'm actually having dinner with someone called Steven. Clearly, you're both geniuses or clairvoyant.'

Lara giggles anxiously.

'Will it ever stop raining?' Ester asks them.

Opening the front door so that she can hear Lawrence when he arrives, she looks out across her street, the trees bent low in the downpour, the gutters awash with stormwater, the sky low and sullen overhead. She wonders whether clients will cancel. She wonders if Steven will cancel, and she feels the push and pull of both relief and disappointment at the thought.

And then Lawrence pulls up, his navy-blue station wagon idling out the front, the wipers going backwards and forwards, the headlights on, as he sounds the horn and she calls them — 'Quick, your father's here' — asking Catherine to get Otto on the lead, kissing them and telling them she loves them. She buttons up their raincoats, not letting herself look towards the car until they are out the front door and running through the downpour to where he waits, back door just ajar so that they can get in straightaway.

HILARY OFTEN FORGETS that Maurie has gone. When she wakes, she reaches across the bed, searching for his warmth, feeling the cool of the sheet before she shifts towards his side, stretching a little further out, her fingers certain they will touch him soon.

He died in the middle of the night. She had got up, as she often did, finding her way down the stairs and along the corridor, her night vision never good, hands seeking the walls and then the door frames, not wanting to switch on a light because that would kill all possibility of getting back to sleep. In the kitchen, she had poured herself a glass of water, the plumbing groaning as she turned the tap off.

If she *had* heard anything — and she was never sure later whether or not she had — it would have been difficult to discern above the thump of metal pipes, the heavy clunk as the water ran down towards the drains. Sometimes, she is certain he called out. It was her name, she thinks. Other times, she is not so sure. Perhaps the pain, the massive heart attack he suffered, was just too sudden and swift — all life shut down before he even had a chance to register that this was happening to him.

All she really knows is that when she returned to their room, he was no longer present. He was gone. It was not the shape of him. That had given no indication. It may have been the silence, the complete and utter stillness; no breath, no shift or movement, nothing. But she doesn't think it was quite so prosaic. Maurie —

all that he was and had been and could be and wanted to be, all that she had loved and at times loathed, the great space that he had filled — had left the building.

As the realisation had begun to slowly disperse, cold tendrils unfurling, she wanted only to sit by his side until the first film of day washed across the walls, and the sounds of the street below drifted up: car doors opening and closing, a voice calling out, a dog barking.

Her eyes had slowly adjusted to the light and she saw him then, his face contorted with pain, and she had to look away.

Strangely, it had been April she had called — despite the fact that Ester was calmer and better in a crisis.

'Maurie's died,' she had told her, and April had done what Hilary had known she would do. She had cried, a great outpouring of grief, a wailing, interspersed by questions, her voice still husky from sleep as she had asked how and when, only to sob over Hilary's attempts at answering.

'I'll be over,' April had promised.

Hilary had heard the muttering of a male voice from the bed, and then the flare of a match as April lit a cigarette, the intake of nicotine.

'Don't go anywhere,' she had said.

'Where on earth would I go?' Hilary had asked, only to realise her daughter wasn't actually talking to her but to the man lying next to her.

The bedroom she had shared with Maurie was the only under-furnished room in the house. When the girls had left home, Maurie had knocked two upstairs rooms into one, opening the space up to the northern light. They had painted the walls white, and put their bed in the middle. On the floor was a patchwork kelim. Nothing else. All their clothes were in the back bedroom, along with the spare bed.

It had been Maurie's idea. An empty room to help her sleep. And for two people who had always lived in clutter, it was a strange space, one that surprised her whenever she opened the door. It was like stepping into someone else's room, she thought, and she never quite knew how she felt about that.

She also hadn't slept any better; she still didn't sleep any better, but now that he was gone, she didn't even attempt to for long, often turning on the light to read, or getting up well before it was light to go and work in her studio, only to return to her bed when everyone else was eating breakfast.

This morning, as the rain pours down, April is sleeping inside, the door to the spare room still closed when Hilary went into the house for a coffee. There was something ominous about April's presence, like having a grenade or landmine in the house, or harbouring a criminal; it was enough to send Hilary back to the studio, rather than upstairs for her morning nap.

She closes the doors to the deluge — the sound is disturbing — and pulls the heater close. She has one copy of the film in a postbag, a version uploaded onto Vimeo, and one on her computer ready to show the girls. Like all her work, it is made from fragments — old pictures, images from Maurie's notebooks, archive footage, and film she has shot over the years. She works in collage, layering images on top of each other in order to untangle larger ideas about life. Her work is often called autobiographical, and she resists the term, hating how confining it feels. She prefers to see her work as teasing out complexities that affect others as well as herself, sometimes using her own life as a springboard but never staying there.

This one is called *Keepsake*. She struggled to define it in her notes for the festival. Yes, it is about death, but it is also about living — about what we cling to and what we relinquish — about how we remember, she supposes.

The final footage she shot four years ago, shortly after Maurie died, when it rained like it is raining now. She had gone to their shack on the river, wanting a few days there to help her decide whether it should be kept or sold. She had simply filmed, with no particular project in mind. The swollen river was brown, murky, and ugly, the peak right at the top of the banks. Sitting on the step at the bottom of the path, her raincoat pulled over her head, she had filmed the flow, the swirl and eddy, the relentless rush and then, there, under a knot of tree roots, she had seen a fallen branch, heavy enough to create a small dam — a pool where the flow was stopped, and the leaves and twigs swirled helplessly, with nowhere to go.

Maurie had built the shack when Ester was one and April three. He had gone there every weekend, often with several friends, leaving her at home alone with the babies. When she complained, which she did frequently, he would brush her off, telling her to come with them, oblivious to how impossible it would be to sleep under a tarp with the two girls, let alone to keep them away from nails and tools while he built.

When he took them to see the end result of his labour, he made them all wear blindfolds. Ester in one arm, he led her and April down the track, the smell of eucalypt sharp in the air, the crushed leaves of the lemon-scented gums underfoot, the burn of the sun on her skin, and the tickle of an ant as it trailed its way across her ankle, while overhead there were bees, a soft drone that ebbed and flowed with a hypnotic rhythm.

'The family palace,' he announced.

She wasn't sure what she had expected. She never was with Maurie. Perhaps a one-room dwelling, a caravan attached. He called it a shack, they all called it a shack — then and in the years to come — but it was so much more than that. An Indian pavilion, she thought: the play of the roof, pitched and falling, pitched and falling, the graceful sweep of the old windows that he had salvaged from a demolition site, the delicate turns and curves of the wooden columns, and the generosity of the deep, wide verandah looking out on a row of poplars, their crinkled-paper leaves on slender branches shimmering beneath the sky.

Inside there were two rooms: a huge open living room, and, behind that, a place to sleep, a curtain to divide them from the girls. The floors were old planks, some wide, some thin, the walls a mixture of tin and gyprock, and the ceiling was patched together, painted sky-blue.

'The kitchen,' Maurie showed her proudly, waving in the direction of an outdoor oven and a sink, both sheltered by tin walls and a tarp, and then, beyond that, the bathhouse — an old enamel tub, deep green, under the shade of a cottonwood.

It was one of his finest works.

She had looked at him with tears in her eyes and told him it was beautiful beyond imagining, and, holding the warmth of his face in her hands, she had kissed him, there in the entrance to their shack, while a swallow darted in through the open door and wheeled and turned under that crazy roof — the angles leaning seemingly without method, yet creating a kaleidoscope of pattern that had an order so intricate it made her head reel.

When she told Ester and April that she wanted to sell the shack, it was Ester who begged her not to, although Hilary knows she feels differently about it now, that she now wants the place gone, all memory of it having been tainted. But at the time, Ester had been upset with Hilary's decision, and Hilary had been surprised. Ester was the only one of them who regularly threw out clutter, who sorted old clothes and gave them to the charity shops, who admired the children's art and then surreptitiously slipped it in the recycling bin, who put the lidless Tupperware out with the plastics, and who liked just one work of art on a wide expanse of white wall. Ester let things go — or so Hilary had thought.

April, on the other hand, had told Hilary it was a good idea. She was the one who had gone there as an adult, trying to write her last album in the heat of the summer, only to give up after a week with just one song and mosquito bites covering her long golden limbs. Her voice had trembled slightly as she confessed that she had spent most of the time sitting on the verandah, bored and wanting to come home — a fact she soon forgot when she returned there some time later, only to wreak pain and havoc in all their lives.

April was a hoarder. She would open her handbag to search for cigarettes, and the chaos of her life would spill out: bills scribbled on, broken lipsticks, books she had borrowed, a singlet, a restaurant menu, all spread across the table. Her apartment, bought after the success of her first single, looked out over Rose Bay. The top floor of a grand art deco building, the rooms were magnificent in their sweep, seemingly impossible to fill. She had covered the walls with Maurie's art, selling off paintings as she needed the money, and then replacing them with images that she liked: drawings from the twins, pictures from Hilary's films, even sketches she herself had done. The floors were layered in rugs, her clothes were strewn across the furniture, and the windows were draped in badly hemmed curtains she had made. But when you first walked in, when you first saw the dance of colours and textures, it was alluring, the messiness beneath not evident to the new visitor, only the thrill of such complete disregard for order.

Hilary had thought April would be the one to beg her not to sell the river shack. But she hadn't. Feet up on a chair, coffee cup in one hand, she had barely looked up from the paper. 'Sure. It's up to you.'

And so she had put it on the market, travelling up there to see what needed to be fixed, Lawrence offering to go some months later to do the work.

It had failed to get the price she wanted. In retrospect she was foolish not to take the first two offers, but she hadn't, possibly influenced by her own sadness at letting go of the place. She had taken it off the market, telling the agent to only show people who were genuinely interested, but not to worry about advertising it. No further offers were made until the most recent one — which was a third less than the figure she had initially rejected, but one she would be foolish to let go of, the agent said. Unlike the city, the country was a buyer's market apparently.

She signed the contract three weeks ago, with settlement in ten days.

Looking out the doors towards the house, she watches the rain running down the glass, the light from her desk lamp revealing her own reflection, the face of a seventy-year-old woman surprising her, because she still thinks of herself as so much younger than she is.

Inside the house, April is up. She sits at the kitchen table, wrapped in Maurie's old robe, her beautiful golden hair knotted at the base of her neck. In a rare moment of stillness, she too is watching the rain, raising a hand in greeting as Hilary opens the studio doors, an old newspaper held above her head to protect herself from the downpour.

April had turned up the previous evening, the sweet smell of wine on her breath, cigarette smoke clinging to her wet clothes, her voice loud as she came in, calling out: 'Hello, are you home?'

She'd met a friend for a drink at the pub around the corner, and thought she'd walk down here and crash, rather than try and get a cab. Opening the fridge and pulling out some scraps — cheese, pickles, cold meat, pasta sauce — she'd begun to pile them on a plate, talking, talking, talking.

'I've been thinking about taking myself off to London. Meet up with people that I recorded with, you know?' Her mouth was full of food, and she grinned that beautiful, wide smile as she realised how she looked. 'Sorry,' she laughed. 'Starving. Josie — you remember her? — she's over there doing back-ups, and Simon, he's producing again — and the timing is right. I'm not working at the moment —'

Hilary had to interrupt: 'At the moment?'

April ignored her. 'I could rent out my place, and just go — there's no reason why not. And you're coming to Paris — we could hang out, mother-daughter time, it'd be fun.' She kicked her wet boots off, and ran her finger around the edge of the plate, then licked it, her eyes alive with the energy of a new idea. 'It's what I need,' she said, and then as her phone chimed, she looked down at it, and pushed it away. Moments later, it chimed again.

'Someone wants you,' Hilary said.

April shook her head, eventually picking the phone up and texting back. 'So, what do you think?'

'If it's what you want to do.'

April looked at her. 'But do you think it's a good idea?'

'It doesn't matter what I think,' Hilary told her. 'You're a grown-up, and you seem to be very good at doing whatever you want to do.'

'What does that mean?' April's pale-green eyes were glittering now, glass and razor.

'Nothing,' Hilary told her. 'No hidden agenda.'

April's phone went off again, this time it was a call. She pressed silent. 'If you're referring to Ester —'

'I'm not.' Hilary cut over her, exhausted at the prospect of another argument. 'I've said all I can say. I don't want to say anymore.' And then, wanting calm, she sat down opposite her daughter and took her hand. 'I love you. You're both my daughters and I love you.'

'I've tried,' April told her, eyes welling with tears now. 'You know I have. I fucked up. But I've tried to fix it.'

Hilary helped herself to a slice of cheese. 'Do you want to look at my film?' She wanted to change the subject, but she also wanted April to see it.

'Do we have to go out there?' April nodded in the direction of the doors. The rain poured down the glass, pooling in the courtyard and then forming a river that rushed down the side stairs that led to the street.

'I've used a recording of you in the soundtrack.'

'Which one?'

It was a favourite of Hilary's, one of the first songs April had written as a child: a delicate song that was principally voice and guitar, the husky crack in her daughter's voice almost breaking several times. Listening felt like walking a tightrope — dangerous, too vulnerable.

'I'll show you in the morning.'

'Sure.' April had picked up her phone again, wanting to check the previous message, and then she stepped out into the lounge room to return the call.

Now, as Hilary comes in from outside, she sees how tired April looks. She has no make-up on, and the light from the excitement of the previous evening's plans has gone. Her face is thin, the pale honey of her skin looks washed out in the grey morning light, and there is a smudge of mascara under her eyes, a black thumbprint, like a bruise.

'Coffee?' Hilary asks her.

She holds up her cup, rubbing at her temple with her other hand.

'How are the girls?' she asks, not looking at Hilary as she speaks but at the drawings pinned on the wall. 'Are they okay?'

There is a momentary ease in the rain, a silence, and Hilary glances outside. It hasn't stopped; she can see the surface of the pools of water, pocked by the lightness of the fall.

'They're good,' she tells April. 'They both had a haircut and insisted that it be exactly the same.'

'Do they ever ask after me?'

'Probably,' Hilary tells her.

'I miss them, you know.'

There is so much Hilary could say. She looks around the kitchen, April's dinner plate still left in the sink, along with an empty bottle of wine that she'd stayed up to drink after Hilary had gone to bed, her wet boots by the back door and her coat draped over the end of a chair. She colonised every space within moments of arriving.

She remembers the brief period April and Ester had shared a flat. Ester had moved home after two months.

'I can't bear it,' she'd complained. 'She wears all my clothes, she uses my shampoo, my sheets — and if I say anything, she tells me I'm uptight, ungenerous, that she would happily let me use anything of hers. Which she would. But I don't want to. There's no space between us.'

There was never any space with April.

'Do you think …' and then April shakes her head at the foolishness of the thought.

'What?'

She bites on her bottom lip before continuing. 'Maybe when they are over at your house, you could let me know. I could come over. Just quickly. Just to say hello.'

Hilary sighs. She does not want to be pulled into this discussion again. With her back to April, she rinses the plates. When she turns around, she ignores the question.

'The river shack settles soon,' she says. 'I'm going up there tomorrow. Just to have a last look.'

April glances across at her. 'Do you want me to come?'

Hilary shakes her head. 'I'd like to see it for the last time alone.' She runs her hand down the softness of April's cheek. 'Let's go look at the film. There's footage of the house that you'll like, of Maurie, all of us.'

In the studio, April stands next to the image of the horse, while Hilary finds the files. April hums under her breath, the sweetness both honeyed and rough, and when she comes to sit next to Hilary, the musky smell of her is unwashed but good.

My beautiful child, Hilary thinks, leaning over and kissing her. *My messy, beautiful daughter.*

The voiceover is Hilary's own, and the opening image a close-up of her hands holding a camera.

Like all of her works, it demands trust from the audience, that this seemingly random scatter of images will find a narrative order. From cardboard suitcases carried by children sent to the country during the second world war to Maurie's paints; from her own cluttered studio, and memories of their life together, to footage of a local hoarder's house; from the girls when they were young to herself and her work — the film asks questions of what to keep, what to discard, what clings despite all efforts to dispel it, and what slides away.

On the screen now, Maurie sits on the verandah of the shack. He is eating an apple, chewing slowly, while he stares out across the field of poplars, grey eyes focused on the distance, dirt on his cheek (and Hilary can almost feel the warmth of his skin when she looks at him, the roughness of the stubble, and the lean line of his jaw), his arms stretched out along the back of the bench, long legs crossed. At his feet, April and Ester are fighting — just a slow niggle at first that builds and builds, until Ester hits April and April screams, Maurie oblivious, and as for her, well, she was behind the camera, letting the girls fight because she wanted the footage. And then the camera pans down to the dolls they have been playing with, made by Hilary's mother and posted over from London, still kept, finally dissolving into an image of them as they are now, in the trunk in the hallway.

'I miss him,' April says.

Hilary doesn't reply.

She knows the girls sometimes wondered at how she felt, how calm and practical she had appeared after his death. Ester in particular had urged her to talk more about it, recommending counsellors, giving her books about grief.

She didn't want to.

All that he was and all that their life had been together was pulled inside, a great condensed force, dark and roiling, leavened moments later with a purity and joy that was as sweet and restrained as the crisp clarity of an autumn morning. It was hers, to be savoured and brought out when she needed it, to hold and marvel at, not to be flattened with banal words and sentiments.

As the film comes to an end, Hilary turns to April. Her daughter is sitting in front of the screen, absorbed and still. Hilary takes April's hand in her own and asks her if she is all right with the footage.

'Of course I am,' April tells her.

She had liked the later images of her and Ester going out, wearing Hilary's fifties frocks, the cotton stiff, a twirl of flowers as April spun for the camera, so aware and yet so unaware of the fact that her image was being recorded, while behind her Ester stood, self-conscious and trying to hold her stomach in.

'I still have that dress,' April says. 'Somewhere.' She smiles, standing now, her gaze focused on the rain. 'It's beautiful,' she says to her mother. 'You always capture something — the elusive that you try to hold, and can't. You do it.' She tucks Maurie's dressing gown tighter around her body, and tells Hilary she's going to have a shower and head home.

'But you're not taking that with you,' and Hilary tugs at the sleeve because she knows April's tendency to secret what she likes into the cavernous space of her handbag. A pick-pocketer's bag, Hilary has always called it.

'Can you drive me?' April asks, one arm stretched out to the rain.

When Hilary says no, she asks for money for a cab.

'I have no money,' Hilary tells her. 'Get a bus.'

And she watches as her daughter walks down to the house, not even bothering to shield herself from the steady drizzle, letting it soak into Maurie's gown and ruin the old socks that she stole from Hilary last night, letting it fall on her hair, a mist on the tangle of gold, and she knows that April will stay in the warmth of the shower for ages, before rifling through Hilary's cosmetics to find the moisturiser she likes, perhaps slipping it into her bag, as well as the lipstick that has always been her favourite.

Hilary turns back to the computer screen, the image locked on the credits. This is her last film. She hadn't begun it knowing this, nor has she told Ester or April; she hasn't told anyone. She doesn't want their grief or anxiety, or attempts to fix her with surgery or chemotherapy or radiotherapy, or any of the therapies the doctors have suggested. She is seventy years old and she has been loosening herself, trying to unpick the grip of life from her limbs, aware of how quickly time has been pushing her forward, shoving her now, relentless and sure, into this tiny space — the last moments — where she needs more strength than she has ever needed before.

WHEN LAWRENCE GETS to the school, there's nowhere to park. His windscreen wipers sweep backwards and forwards at a furious pace, and still he can't see. He opens his window slightly, and the rain drives in. Last time he double-parked, he was caught by the camera at the crossing and sent a ticket.

'You're going to have to run,' he tells the girls. 'Really fast.'

'Oh bloody hell.' Catherine looks out and shakes her head, her expression so like Ester's that he's momentarily taken aback.

'It's a shit of a day,' Lara adds, always wanting to take it one step further.

He doesn't bite.

'Quick,' he tells them, leaning behind to open the door.

Catherine is out first, her bag tangled in Lara's. He gives Lara a quick push. 'Just go with her.' He sees them, straps caught, having to run right next to each other, across the playground and into the school.

And then it's just him and Otto, who is panting in the back seat.

Neither he nor Ester had wanted Otto when they separated. It was one of the few things they agreed on. He looks at the dog now — wet, smelling like earth and rotting leaves and old meat — and he knows Ester won't have walked him in this weather, and that he really should take him out before he heads into work.

He drives to the park at the end of the street: a miserable

square of weedy grass, frequently covered by rubbish. It's the flocks of scabby ibises that cause the carnage; they pick out food scraps from the bins, spreading the rest of the garbage in their wake. Lawrence hates them.

He lets Otto out, telling him to 'chase the birds', but Otto just stands there, bedraggled in the downpour, and refuses to participate in the charade that this is some kind of walk.

There is a barbecue shelter about 50 metres away and Lawrence makes a run for it, giving the dog brief joy. He huddles under the tin awning, while Otto sniffs out the food scraps and takes the occasional bored piss against the play equipment. He'll give him ten minutes, Lawrence decides, and then bundle him back into the car, smellier than ever.

An email alert flashes across his phone, and he supposes Edmund has sent through the numbers from the latest poll. It's a standard one on the government's approval rating, which he can guess sits only slightly lower than last time. He hates this government — they appal him — and he knows he will try to spin the results to make them appear even more unpopular, phrasing his press releases to emphasise any bad news.

That's what he always does.

But sometimes he goes a little further.

He feels a strange sense of vertigo, almost nausea, at the thought of adjusting down again, just very slightly, and only for one of the questions. Leadership unpopularity. Just the smallest correction to the figures. Not enough to put him noticeably out of line with the others, and always staying within the three per cent margin of error, but perhaps a little more than he's done in the past. The first time was just a matter of rounding percentage points the wrong way, so small as to be insignificant. More the action of a peeved and bored child, who acts because he can. The second time he was a little more daring, going up a percentage point in a couple of questions. Last time, he'd nudged a question about the Prime Minister further than he had in the past, hoping he might spur one or two different kinds of stories, secretly glad when there was an article about whispers of a leadership challenge again.

He mustn't.

He swore he wouldn't again.

But there is something about knowing he can mess with the figures that he finds hard to resist.

Lawrence used to love doing the polls. They were a sideline, fun, work he did to alleviate the boredom of designing endless questionnaires ranking customer's delight (or lack of delight) with their latest car or fridge or holiday experience. Work he hoped might bring in more interesting research briefs. He ran a couple a year for the paper, before the research company transferred him to Paris. On his return, the editors of the paper wanted him back. The junior who had filled in for him was ambitious, and happy to let the polling go. It didn't bring in much revenue and it didn't look good on his performance review. No one factored in the value of the media coverage — coverage that increased with the return of Lawrence, a man who looked good on camera and knew how to frame a quote.

And so when Lawrence received the call from HR shortly before he and Ester separated, he managed to negotiate taking the polls with him when he left. His job no longer existed, he was told. The latest restructuring had left them without a place for him. HR had put together a package for his approval.

As he was packing up his desk (which didn't require much work — it had been reduced to a 700x500 hot-desk space since his unrequested return from Europe), he received a call from the newspaper. Negotiations were quick, a plan made on the run — if he took this one client with him, it might be enough to tide him over while he tested the waters with music again. He was the face of the polls, the client wanted him, and, as he stressed to the company, the revenue they brought in was miniscule, and a lot less than lawyer's fees for the wrongful dismissal action he was tempted to commence.

At first it wasn't enough work, not nearly enough to survive on, but the media coverage soon brought in other clients, bread-and-butter marketing surveys that he'd always hated and could do in his sleep, research that paid the bills. Polls were reserved for elections, or the occasional divisive policy issue.

The change was gradual. An extra one here and there, increasing as leadership in both parties became more and more unstable, and slowly building into a monthly sport, the results eagerly awaited by journalists across the country.

Otto flops at his feet as he scans for the email attachment from Edmund, a collating of the phone responses. He needs his glasses, but it seems that Edmund has forgotten to send it — which is unlike him.

The dog has found an old chicken carcass, and he cracks the bones noisily as he bites into them. Lawrence tries to kick it away, but Otto lunges for it, displaying no reluctance to go back into the downpour if there is rotting meat to be had.

The rain drums on the awning, fat drops gathering in each dip of the colourbond, swelling and falling, a curtain of silver around him, as he puts his phone back in his pocket.

Otto barks, loud enough to startle Lawrence.

It's an ibis — wanting the carcass. It flaps its wings and honks, and, for one moment, Lawrence thinks it may even try and fight the dog for the scraps, but Otto's snarl sends it beating a retreat.

This time he'd wanted to put in a question about leadership popularity. Who did voters like better — the Prime Minister or his Communications Minister? The editors weren't interested.

'No one wants a leadership challenge story at the moment.' But he'd included it anyway. Perhaps he could play a little with the results of that question, drop it into his media release, make sure to mention it in each interview he does.

He looks down at Otto, who has a piece of alfoil stuck to the corner of his mouth, and tells him it's time to get going.

'I have work to do,' he says.

Not that Otto cares.

'Opinions to report.' He whistles once, and Otto stands.

They could make a run for the shelter of a tree and then a dash for the car, or they could not even bother trying and just get wet. He chooses the first option, Otto the second.

LOUISA HAD THOUGHT she was going to have to bring Jasper with her. She tells Ester this as soon as she arrives, her words tumbling out in a rapid, breathless torrent as they often do at the beginning of a session.

Her mother had called that morning saying the rain was too much. She was anxious driving when it was like this; she didn't think she could come over and mind him after all.

'She helps so little,' Louisa says to Ester, and she glances around the room as though there is someone else there with them, listening to her betrayal and judging her.

'So, what happened?' Ester asks.

'I told her that I really needed to go. That I wasn't coping.' Louisa sniffs loudly, and then bites hard on her lip. 'I mean, I'm not, am I?' Her anger is building now.

This is the usual pattern, and Ester doesn't reply, knowing there is more to come.

'Anyway, she came, but she was pissed, said I needed to call the childcare centre again and demand a place. It was ridiculous how long I'd been waiting.' She tucks a strand of hair behind her ear. 'She has no idea. She thinks it's just me, being hopeless.' She looks out the window, the rain drumming down a hard beat behind their conversation.

Ester moves her chair a little closer. 'It's difficult to hear,' she says, smiling.

'I'm sorry,' Louisa apologises. 'Everyone tells me I speak too softly. Probably because I do. But if I let myself speak louder, it'd be a shout before you knew it.'

It takes a moment or two for Louisa to continue; Ester can see her biting back the harshness lurking behind each word. 'When I thought I was going to have to bring Jasper, I thought I'd just cancel.' Her gaze is challenging. 'You know why I come here? It's just to get a couple of hours to myself.' She has to look away at this point. 'If I could just leave him with mum, go to a café somewhere, buy a pack of ciggies and smoke the lot of them ...' She shrugs. 'Maybe I'd be fine.'

Ester smiles.

'Sometimes I imagine getting in the car and driving to the airport.' Lousia's voice drops. 'I could move to London, New York. Or even bloody New Zealand.' She grimaces slightly. 'I'd send him mysterious birthday presents each year, and then when he was eighteen I'd fly him over to meet me. My son.'

Ester's clients always sit on the two-seater sofa. The room is clean and light, even on days such as this; the large wooden windows face north, overlooking the front garden and the street. There is a single Persian rug on the floor, a beautiful pattern of weeping willows woven into the thick wool, and only one painting on the wall opposite where she sits.

Ester sits back in the armchair that had belonged to Maurie, the one she'd re-covered in deep-green wool. Louisa remains upright, looking ready to leave, while outside the branches of the trees press against the glass; they shiver and shake with each burst of rain.

'It's a cow of a day,' Louisa says.

Ester nods, acknowledging the comment before returning to the issue.

'Last week we talked a bit about your lack of joy.' Ester pauses for a moment. 'In being a mother.'

Louisa stares at the window, not turning to look directly at Ester who watches her, kind, ready to listen. And then, glancing at her feet, Louisa reaches for one of the tissues.

'I keep hoping that will change.' There is a slight tremor in her voice. She has been biting her nails again, and she tries to hide this evidence of her distress by sitting on them.

'How do you think it will change?'

Louisa has her eyes on the floor, like a naughty kid trying to guess the correct answer. 'Time?'

Ester doesn't respond.

There is silence, space for Louisa to continue, which she eventually does. 'Every day I wake up and I think I made the worst mistake of my life. I shouldn't have had a kid. I was insane. Life was so much better before. I spend every waking moment when I'm not caring for him — and there aren't many of those — trying to figure how I can escape.'

She glances across at Ester, and quickly looks away again.

'But you are continuing to care for him,' Ester says gently.

'I picked up my meds last week.'

'And have you started taking them?' This is what Ester has been trying to nudge Louisa towards. Actually getting the prescription filled is a significant step.

Louisa shakes her head.

She tells Ester she had stood in the chemist, feeling like such a failure as she handed the prescription over to the pharmacist. *Another mother who couldn't cope*, and then she looks across at Ester, suddenly still, her pale gaze steady. 'I bought them and then I don't take them.' She reaches for another tissue. 'I mean, I don't know if I'm depressed. I know I might look it.' She blows her nose.

Ester waits for her to continue.

'But who wouldn't feel like this? I don't get any sleep. I spend all my time looking after someone else's needs. I don't see any grown-ups all day. And when Patrick comes home, I put Jasper in his arms and go to my room just to get away. So we never see each other.'

Louisa looks up at the ceiling. 'So of course I feel like shit. I reckon there'd be something wrong with me if I wasn't feeling like this.' She glances across at Ester, who is smiling, just slightly.

'No one wants to spend great chunks of life feeling terrible, unable to cope,' Ester says. 'We need to identify some strategies to help you feel less overwhelmed. Anti-depressants could help with this. There are also practical things you can do.'

'Did you feel like this when you had your children?'

'I don't think there would be many women who haven't felt like this. But it's not how others feel that matters. It's how you feel.'

Louisa stares at the ceiling. 'I can't be the only one who doesn't …' and she stops here, not wanting to utter the words.

Ester waits.

'Love her kid.' Louisa breathes in before continuing. 'I know lots of women talk about how difficult it can be, how hard they found it. But no one comes right out and says: "I made a mistake. I don't love him." I mean, why do you have to love your kid?'

Ester waits until she's sure Louisa has finished. 'I understand you mightn't think your response requires treatment, but what is it that makes you come here? Why did you pick up the antidepressants?'

Louisa doesn't reply, and Ester wonders for a moment whether she has taken a wrong step. 'I suppose what I'm trying to say is that even if you aren't "unwell" as such, you may still want some assistance in coping. The pills could help.'

Still staring up at the ceiling, Louisa shakes her head. 'It's not just that,' she says. 'It's how out-of-control anxious everyone else is around me.'

Her voice a pitch higher now, she begins to tell Ester about the previous evening. She had told Patrick she was going to the movies. She had got into the car, the rain hammering on the metal roof, wet leaves sticking to the windscreen, each window misting up as she sat there, the back of her head resting on the upholstery. She had the keys in the ignition, but she didn't turn them any further. She just stayed where she was, letting the heater warm her feet, the radio on softly, the outside world no more than a general blur. She knew she ran the risk of flattening the battery, but she didn't care.

She could see the light on in the lounge room of her house. Patrick would be watching television, sometimes turning to his phone to play a game, or check out a newsfeed. Jasper would be asleep in his bassinette, probably on his back, arms no longer wrapped tightly by his side, peaceful now. She knew she should be in bed herself, trying to snatch some sleep before she was woken just after midnight and then again before dawn.

Patrick had been glad she was going out, wanting to see this as a sign that she was re-entering the world, that she was happier. 'That's great,' he'd told her. 'We'll be fine.'

He was a gentle man. A kind man, who tried to understand what had happened to her but couldn't.

An hour later, she was still in the car, the rain still falling, steady and cold, the street glittering, slick, and dark. She didn't even notice Patrick coming out to put the bins on the street. She didn't see him realising the car was still there, and heading over because something wasn't quite right, peering into the window to find her slumped against the driver's door, and when he opened it, the cold of the rain hit her like a slap, and she jumped up, screaming because she thought he was an intruder, a rapist, who knows what.

'What are you doing?' she shouted at him.

It took a moment before she saw the shock on his face.

'I thought you'd killed yourself,' he'd told her, his skin blue from the light of the dashboard, his lips pale. 'Come inside,' he'd urged her.

She'd wanted to ask him for just a little longer. Another twenty minutes, but she hadn't. The rain soaking through her coat, she'd followed him, the hall light too bright after the dim quiet of the car, the house cold.

'Why did you just stay out there?' he'd asked.

She'd opened her mouth to speak, and then Jasper had started crying, and she'd taken her wet coat off and gone to him, feeding him in the dim light of their bedroom.

Later, as they'd lain side by side, the sound of Jasper breathing next to them, he'd made her promise that she would start taking the antidepressants.

'I don't think the therapy is enough,' he'd told her.

Louisa looks at Ester now. 'He was shit-scared. He made *me* feel scared.'

Ester meets her gaze. 'Are you concerned for yourself?'

Louisa sits back and shrugs as she closes her eyes. There are tears at the corner of her lids. 'I don't want to be like this. I don't know if I'm sick. But I don't want to be like this.'

Ester watches her.

Louisa leans forward. 'You know what I'd like?' she sniffs back the tears. 'I want to fast-forward. That's all I really want — not drugs or therapy. I want to see me loving him.' And looking straight at Ester, there in the consulting room, the rain steady outside, Louisa waits for words of comfort, a promise that she will soon feel the way she wishes she could. 'But I can't, can I?'

So many of Ester's clients want this at one moment or another in their therapy. Often they reach for her, as though she can haul them out of the abyss they have fallen into and pull them up onto a land of joy, a mythical place they believe they should be able to reach. *I want to be happy again*, they say, looking to her to provide this emotional state.

The words she gives them are careful. Often they don't listen, the need glittering in their eyes, the desire blocking out anything she might say. Occasionally, they hear and they are angry — why can't she give them what they want?

And then sometimes they are like Louisa — bleak and far from home, asking her for a shortcut to the place they long for, all the while realising it doesn't exist.

Ester remembers her own despair after the girls were born. It was intermittent, but when it struck, she would lie in bed and — like Louisa — wonder whether she had made a terrible mistake that she couldn't rectify.

The isolation of living in Paris had made it worse. Lawrence had been offered a two-year contract, and they'd decided to go. There'd been no plans of a baby. She thought she might try to get some English-speaking clients, and, if that failed, she would learn French, cook, discover a new city, read the books she'd always wanted to read.

The flat they were given was on the outskirts of the city, and it was ugly and grim. Two weeks after she arrived, she learnt she was pregnant with twins. She remembers ringing Hilary some weeks after they were born and just crying. There had been no words to describe how she'd felt finding herself alone in an apartment with two babies she felt incapable of caring for.

'That's what it's like,' Hilary had told her in her usual blunt way. 'But it does pass.'

'How quickly?' she'd wanted to know.

Hilary didn't remember. 'Everything feels so momentous at

the time. But when you look back, you realise how brief it was. Insignificant, really.'

She would like to have delivered a long-distance slap.

Ester picks up the tissues Louisa left behind and takes them out to the kitchen. She always keeps the bin in her consulting room empty, clearing up after each client before she runs through the session notes, quickly adding in a few details so that she has all the information she needs to write them up later.

What Louisa really needs is sleep, Ester thinks, *and practical help*. It's what most women with new babies need. That, and time to adjust. But the antidepressants could help shift the state she's now stuck in.

When Ester had the girls, she'd had no family or friends nearby. She remembers the relief of finding a student who came each day for a couple of hours. She'd booked herself into French conversation classes, and although her memory had been severely limited by tiredness, simply going out and talking to an adult had been such a respite. She'd also been glad of the Parisian disregard for small children. In Paris, she was encouraged to bottle feed, to leave the babies to cry, and to hand them over to someone else whenever she needed a break. In Australia, mothers were expected to put all their own needs last.

Still, she'd not been happy there. Neither of them had been. Lawrence had disliked his job, and she'd been bored and lonely. That was where the fighting had begun, the first sowing of a grit that became more and more abrasive.

'I've fallen in love,' she'd told April shortly after meeting Lawrence, barely able to do more than whisper the miraculous words, the sheer glow of them dancing lightly on her tongue.

'Who? Who? Who?' April had asked, pouring them each another drink, the burn of whiskey on ice crackling in the glass, the flare of a match as she'd lit up the joint she'd just rolled, taking a long drag before passing it to Ester, lipstick-stained and soggy to the touch.

As soon as Ester uttered his name, she wished she'd held it back.

'Lawrence!' April had thrown her head back and laughed, raucous, loud, slamming her glass on the table as she'd sat up. 'That sly old dog.' She'd reached across the table for the joint, taking it straight out of Ester's fingers, and shaken her head in disbelief.

He'd played in bands — one of which occasionally appeared on the same bill as April. On the night she'd met him, Ester had been standing at the back of the bar, her beer warm in her hands, wondering if she could leave. It was hot and still, the oppressive air in the room making her feel ill, and she'd edged closer to the door, looking out at the shine of the street, headlights, street lights, the silvery freshness of the evening so enticing.

She'd liked him straight away, the spark in his eyes, the warmth of his smile, as he'd looked at her and said he was sure he knew her. 'It's not a line,' he promised, stepping back slightly. And then his grin had widened. 'Pyschology. I was in your tute for a couple of weeks and then I had to shift. I was more of a stats man — different timetable.'

She didn't remember him. But she liked him even more when he said he was happy to give April's performance a miss, and go somewhere a bit cooler and quieter.

They'd ended up sitting on the beach, the sea a great black heaving beast, sighing and rolling under the white light of the moon. They'd sung all their favourite songs, replacing the word 'baby' with 'monster', and then when he'd suggested that she came back to his flat, he'd confessed. 'I've taken a trip. I might be up talking — for quite a long time.'

'He's a drug pig,' April had told her. 'So unlike you. But he is devastatingly handsome. Also charming when he puts his mind to it.'

And he had talked. For 24 hours. Kissing her in between each roll and lilt of thought. Slow kisses that were like breathing in air. When they both woke, a day and a half later, he'd looked straight at her in the soft light of the room. 'If you survived that, we could survive years together.'

'Everyone thinks they are in love with Lawrence,' April had said.

And Ester had just poured herself another drink, and said he was coming to pick her up soon. She had to get ready.

She had finished her undergraduate studies by then, and was hovering between either really trying to paint as a career, or accepting that she didn't have the fortitude, and continuing her studies to become a practising counsellor. She still had a studio space in Maurie's warehouse, and she would go there in the mornings, sleep-deprived and hungover but languorously happy, her whole body warm and still wrapped in the memory of Lawrence's skin.

Ester has a client who has recently fallen in love. She'd talked about it during her last session, the glow of it suffusing each word and gesture. It's rare that she hears about love in her consulting room. Most of her clients talk of anger, failure, boredom, depression, conflict: the flipside to love. That session had been like opening each of the windows to her room, heaving them up, sashes groaning, and letting in the freshness of an early spring day.

Lawrence, too, had been teetering between a career in music or a full-time job as a researcher. Music was what he wanted, but as April once pointed out, he had the looks but not the talent. He was a 'serviceable guitarist', she said, but he was never going to make a living from it.

And so they had met, both on the brink of letting go of youth. He became a pollster, and, despite the occasional sardonic joke he made about himself, she knew he liked having a media profile. As for her career, he went from quips about her 'Happiness Book' to downright dismissiveness. She pedalled false hopes to a spoilt middle class. She handed out security blankets to children who should just grow up.

And yet, when everything had blown apart, he had begged her to go to therapy with him, and she had refused.

Ester likes to keep half an hour between appointments. It gives her time to empty her head of one client before she begins work with the next. She sits in her room, reading through the previous week's notes for the Harcourts, while outside the rain stops and starts, the sky still resolutely grey. *It might rain forever*, she thinks, staring out at the bleakness of the day.

Across the road, she can see Jenny and Damon have pulled up, ten minutes early. They are sitting side by side in their car, neither of them talking.

She watches them for a moment and then looks down, aware that they can possibly see her. Closing their notes, she puts them back in the file, and then she checks her phone is on silent.

It is, the screen showing a message from Steven. He's booked a place to eat. Is 7.30 okay? Glancing up, she catches sight of her reflection in the window, her fear and excitement illuminated by the desk lamp.

It's been three years since she and Lawrence separated. After a year she had tried to date again, trawling through the various websites, and wishing she were one of those women who could approach the task with a business-like practicality (which is probably how she would advise her clients to tackle dating, she thinks, ashamed at the thought). *If you want to meet someone, you have to put your mind to it. It's much harder when you're older, when everyone has partners and when you don't go out and meet new people.*

Those were the words she'd once uttered to friends who'd found themselves alone, never realising how difficult it was to enter the world of online dating.

She'd gone through the men in her age group, alarmed at how old they all looked, because she still thought of herself as young. She dismissed all the ones who referred to wanting to find a 'lady', along with the many who nominated *The Shawshank Redemption* as their favourite film. It only left a few. There was one she liked, a man whose profile made her smile. He was looking for a woman who agreed that 'there was never any excuse for vertical blinds — ever'. He was probably gay, she thought, and she sent him a 'Kiss', deeply embarrassed by the whole terminology. He never responded.

A week later, she did go on a date. His name was Angus. She had contacted him, and he had emailed her back arranging to meet for a coffee. As soon as she arrived, she knew it was never going to work, dismissing him for surface reasons while battling with herself about how wrong it was to do this. He was seated near the door, legs stretched out in front of him, socks with sandals in full view. (Later, she would laugh about this, turn it into a story, but then it was only part of the sad loneliness of the experience.)

They talked for about half an hour, telling each other what they did. (He was a telecommunications salesperson who was writing a novel in his spare time. He liked going to the movies, eating out, bushwalking, swimming.) (She was a therapist who painted as a hobby, and also liked movies, eating out, bushwalking, and swimming — but she was different, she thought, clinging on to this. Yet surely if she was so much more than this summation, so might he be?)

At the end of the coffee, he asked her what they should do.

'What do you mean?'

'Shall we take this further?'

She looked down at table, breathing in before she met his eyes again. 'I'm sorry,' she told him. 'I just don't think it's going to work.'

'Why not?' he asked.

And she didn't know how to respond. 'I just don't feel a connection,' she eventually said, hating the banality of the words as she uttered them.

He nodded, standing up as he did so.

She stood also, only wanting to leave. 'Thank you for meeting me,' she offered, and as they said farewell at the door, he took her hand in his.

'Could we have a hug?' he asked.

She stood there, frozen, mute, as he hugged her for what seemed an interminably long time but was probably only seconds, before he broke away and said goodbye, leaving her alone on the footpath.

AFTER HE'S DROPPED Otto at home, Lawrence goes to his usual café. It's around the corner from the single-room office he rents at the back of a warehouse. The café owner is guitar obsessed, usually sitting at the table with Lawrence to show him his latest online find.

'Dave in America sent me this,' and he hands over his phone so that Lawrence can scroll through the pictures. 'He wants two grand, but I'm trying to talk him down a couple of hundred.'

Lawrence shakes his head, smiling as he does so. 'And this would be the sixth this year?'

'Seventh,' Joel admits. 'And each a thing of beauty.'

As far as he knows, Joel barely plays, his repertoire limited to average renditions of 'House of the Rising Sun' and the chorus of 'Stairway to Heaven'. Lawrence used to see him at the bars and pubs all those years ago, when they were both younger and leaner.

Lil, the waitress, brings his short black over, and sits with them as well, oblivious to Joel telling her that she's meant to be working, not chatting up the customers.

'Oh please,' she laughs. She takes the phone from Lawrence, and has a look. 'I don't know how you could buy a guitar without playing it first. You have no idea what the action is like.' She sips the coffee she's made for herself.

She's a singer — slow country and western that verges too close to the somnambulistic to ever really thrill him. Fortunately,

46

she's never asked him what he thinks of her songs, and if she did, he'd lie.

'Got the girls this week?' Joel asks him.

Lawrence nods.

Outside, the trees bend and bow, shivering under the weight of another downpour. The sky is dark, the clouds thick and low. A woman comes in with two small kids, all three of them dripping wet, the children demanding a babycino and a biscuit, and Lil takes their order, smiling sweetly as she tells the kids she didn't quite hear that last word they said, 'was it a please?'

'I don't think it's your job to teach my children manners,' the woman tells her, and her eyes are hard, her tone cold.

'Nor do I,' Lil responds, the sweetness of her smile never diminishing.

Lawrence barely glances in Joel's direction, but he catches the shaking of his head and the muttering under his breath as he tamps the coffee, uncertain whether he should be making the order or not. Lil has a way with the rude customers, and they often leave before anything to eat or drink gets to the table.

'I'm paid to serve. Not to be treated like shit,' she mutters as she takes the flat white from him, fending off any possible disapproval he might dare to express.

Lawrence slept with Lil a couple of times in that terrible first year of separation. There was even a night when he convinced himself he was falling in love with her. He'd gone so wrong; marriage, serious jobs, children — none of it was what he'd wanted. Lil was almost twenty years younger than him, but they had a connection. He split the second ecstasy tablet between them, and told her he felt lighter and freer than he had in years.

'I've come back to myself,' he declared. 'This is who I am.' He'd been aware of how ridiculous he sounded as soon as he uttered the words, but he banished the thought, or tried to, until Lil looked at him and smiled, the ecstasy making her a little more tender than she would otherwise have been.

'This is who you'd like to be at the moment. But don't tell me that all the rest wasn't real.' She shook her head, and then pointed at her chest. 'Wisdom from the young,' she grinned. 'Frequently dismissed.' And then, still smiling broadly, she'd told him she didn't want to hurt him. 'Don't you go falling in love with me.'

Wasn't that what he was meant to say to her?

It had been a bad year. One in which he'd disappeared into the terrifying limitless expanse of freedom, a vast terrain that he'd been incapable of controlling, and so he'd roamed untethered, never still, never wanting to rest on the ramifications of what he'd done.

April had told him to pull himself together. 'It's bad,' she'd said. 'I know it. But there's no need to keep making it worse.'

She, too, had been kind to him, although he had been wary about taking her kindness, unsure of what to do each time she came round to see him when he'd had the girls, until Ester had put an end to it, telling him it was wrong. It was too confusing for Lara and Catherine — her not talking to April, him playing house with her.

'I'm not playing house with her.'

'Whatever it is you're doing, I don't want to know about it. I just want her out of our lives.'

And now, here he is, alone.

When there is a pause in the rain, he walks around the corner to his office, the tin door locked, the corrugations streaked iron-grey and rust-red. All the other studios are occupied by artists, most of them young and dreadlocked, who produce fairly average work from found objects and recycled rubbish. The whole building is run by Joachim, who sleeps in his studio and never washes, but he is always cheerful, and often leaves a loaf of bread, scavenged from the bakery around the corner, for Lawrence.

Lawrence took on the space in the terrible year — it was part of reclaiming his youth — and despite knowing it's not really a place to see clients, he's stayed.

The rain is thunderous on the tin walls and tin roof; from inside, it's like a stampede of wild animals overhead, yet when he looks out of the single window, rubbing a hole in the fogged-up glass, he sees that the downpour isn't as heavy as it seems.

He doesn't mind the noise. There's something elemental about its insistence, and he turns on the heater and switches on his computer, calling up a Bonnie Prince Billy playlist before he begins to read through the poll results. The gothic edge to the sweetness of these songs reminds him of April's music. She released her first album when she was only twenty-two. Sometimes he still listens to it, to the throaty crack in her voice, the soar that never quite touches the peak it yearns for, the delicate pick of her guitar, the brush of the snare drums, and the sadness of the piano; they all make him ache. She used to perform in pubs, always managing to still a crowded bar; she would sit out the front, long-limbed, bathed in gold, her gap-toothed smile giving her a cheeky likeability, and that voice, the crack in it always unsettling, the notes never quite where they should be, and yet there was something so relaxed about her performance that each song lifted you with it.

She'd asked him to go on tour with her shortly after he'd started seeing Ester. A guitarist had dropped out, and she'd needed a replacement quick.

'Why you?' Ester had asked. It was still early enough in their relationship that she wouldn't have been disparaging his lack of talent, but he'd wondered the same thing himself.

'I know you,' April had explained, 'it's just so much easier.'

She'd encouraged Ester to join them.

He had too, not wanting to be separated from her for a month.

But in the end she hadn't come — and it had been his last gig as a musician, one in which he'd known he wasn't up to scratch, frequently playing so poorly that he'd been tempted to just quit halfway through if it hadn't been for the fact that he'd left his day job and needed the pay cheque.

While the rain continues, loud and clattering, harsh and hard, Lawrence trawls through his emails, deleting as he goes; junk, an invitation to dinner, a suggestion of a drink from a woman he'd met a week ago, a client wanting a survey on chocolate-buying habits, another wanting one on leisure activities, and then, last, the email from Edmund with the latest poll results.

When he'd glanced at it in the park, he'd opened the attachment without reading the message at the beginning.

Now, as he scans it, he feels acid rise in his gut.

Edmund wants to talk to him. There seem to have been disparities between the data he has been sending through to Lawrence and the resulting reports in the media.

He hovers, wanting to ignore the request, but then he sees the end of the message. Edmund doesn't want to send through the latest report unless they speak.

Lawrence doesn't know Edmund well. He's only met him a few times, always finding him serious, dogged, dull in his laboured determination — all excellent qualities in someone who produces data. He is also a Christian. He has told Lawrence about the church he belongs to in the north-western suburbs — a new one started by a zealot with a passion for linking faith with material success. At twenty-nine, Edmund already owns three investment properties.

Foolishly, Lawrence had assumed the adjustments he had made to the data were so small, Edmund wouldn't notice. Perhaps if he'd only done it once, this would have been the case — a simple mistake he could explain away, perhaps even putting it on the shoulders of the client. The second time might also have slipped through the net. But the last time … He'd been drunk. He'd gone too far.

He answers the email with bluster. They have a contract that specifies a delivery date and time. He has results to get through to the client, with a pressing deadline, and no time for talk. This is work that he has paid for, and Edmund's job is simply to deliver the information, and not to question how it's used. If he wants to continue to have Lawrence as a client, he needs to do just that.

He hovers the cursor over 'send', and then lets his hand fall back into his lap.

He knows that charm is his best offensive. It always has been. And so he leaves the email open on his screen and calls Edmund. It only takes two rings before he answers.

His voice smooth and calm, Lawrence quickly deals with the pleasantries — how is he? It's raining cats and dogs down here, he tells him, a deluge of biblical proportions, and he regrets the reference as soon as he utters it.

And then to business. He's just opened Edmund's email and he doesn't understand.

Edmund clears his throat. 'I do read the results,' he tells Lawrence.

There is a brief silence between them.

'The first time, I just looked at the media reports in passing, and it didn't seem quite right. The second time, I was sure a mistake had been made. The third time, I actually went back and checked.'

Edmund's voice is soft, sibilant. Lawrence has always disliked it, particularly now.

He hovers between loud denial and puny excuses, choosing neither. 'I need to deliver the latest numbers this morning,' he tells Edmund. 'We have a contract. And there is nothing in that agreement that gives you any right to question what I choose to do with those results.'

Edmund takes a moment. But this is what he always does. If Lawrence cracks a slightly distasteful joke, Edmund will even take a few seconds before he clears his throat in dismissal, the silence emphasising his disapproval. *He's a sanctimonious prig*, Lawrence thinks, and he feels ill as the full weight of Edmund's response to his actions sinks in a little deeper.

What he has been doing is tantamount to interfering with the political process, with democracy itself, Edmund tells him, the low hiss on each 's' scraping like nails on a blackboard. Edmund may have a contract with him, but as an independent, free human being who sets great store by choosing the moral path, he no longer wants to work with Lawrence.

The rain beats down.

Lawrence looks out the window. 'What we *do* is an interference with the political process,' he eventually says. 'The questions we ask, when we ask them, how we interpret them — they all shape the debate. You know that. I know that.'

Edmund interrupts him. 'This is different.'

But is it any worse? Lawrence wants to ask him if in all honesty he really thinks it is, but he's already said too much. He can hear another call on his mobile, the beep of the phone harsh in his ear. He is happy to terminate the contract, he tells Edmund, but he does need those last results.

'Which will be published without alteration?'

'Of course,' Lawrence promises.

'And I will receive full payout for the year's work?'

Lawrence has no choice.

Edmund is silent again. 'I will need to think.'

It isn't over. Of course it isn't over.

Lawrence leans back in his chair and puts his hands over his eyes. What was he thinking? He breathes in deeply, and stares up at the ceiling.

As a child, April had hated the bath. She couldn't stay in one place, and she would slip and slide and squirm, splashing great waves of soapy water over the edge before leaping out, running through the house naked and dripping half the bathwater along the way, Maurie and Hilary oblivious to the fact that she was still filthy and that the entire exercise had been a waste of time.

But at the river shack it was different. Maurie would run it hot, the steam rising into the open air, disappearing well before it reached the tracings of branches overhead — fine ghostly gums that cut white-limbed across the sky. She and Ester would take an end each, stretching out luxuriously beneath the trees, the smell of eucalypt sharp as leaves and twigs dropped down into the water, and they would make boats, sailing them forth from April-land to Ester-land and back again.

More beautiful still were the night-time baths, the black-velvet, star-glittered sky, frosty in the winter, warm and soft in the summer evenings, the mournful cry of a bird, or the crackle of dried twigs as a wallaby ventured shyly forth, slipping back into the bush at the sight of two naked sisters lying in a canopy of white steam.

April still isn't fond of baths at home, but this morning, in Hilary's house, she runs one, emptying a bottle of expensive salts into the water, and pinning her hair up on her head before stepping in carefully, the heat gripping her with a pain so tight she has to step straight out again.

She runs the cold, trying to course it through the water with her hand, imagining it as a stream of silver twisting and turning through the fire of molten lava, waiting until she can step in again, one foot at a time, careful now.

She'd lied last night when she'd told Hilary she'd just been having a drink around the corner. She'd been drinking in her apartment alone, the windows wide open to the rain, the great shaking deluge of it shimmering across the distant harbour, sparkling on the streets below, and then, as the wind had shifted and the rain had slanted into her lounge, she'd realised that Sam had no intention of showing up, and the faint chill of having possibly made a fool of herself burnt into her skin, slapped by the brisk breeze.

He was too young for her.

She'd known that.

And so she'd sent him a text. *Can't remember if I asked you over tonight?? Sorry if yes — had to go out.*

She'd caught a taxi to Hilary's so that she wouldn't be waiting any longer.

As she lowers herself into the bath, she feels the disarray of her life in every limb, a jangling switchboard, all wires knotted and unplugged. She does not want to cry. She is thirty-six now, alone, unable to write in the way she used to, and she has fucked up. Badly.

She glances across at herself in the mirror, face pink from the heat, and then she rests her head against the cool of the enamel and closes her eyes.

April has never really known loneliness until now; she has had small tastes of its dregs, like cold milky coffee curdled at the bottom of the cup, but she has always had faith in the fact that it would pass. Now, she is not so sure. And this loneliness is entangled with her failure as a musician, another certainty in her life that seems to have gone.

Most days, she tries to write.

She sits by the window with her guitar and picks idly at notes, strumming chords underneath, humming to herself as she does so. But nothing ever sticks, and she feels as if she is just pretending, playing alone outside a room she can no longer enter.

When she wrote her first album, she didn't even see herself as making a record. She just trimmed and cut and shaped the material she had been working with for years, the songs she had played in pubs and clubs, selected and honed with the help of the producer, until she had it: complete and whole. She had neither chased success nor expected it. To have recorded an album was enough.

But success came. Her songs were played around the world. They are still played. The mark of that first album remains — in fact it has recently restamped itself, with a couple of the songs being covered by younger independent artists, their new versions faint replicas of the original. That collection of songs is who she is. The second album has been forgotten; the third has never eventuated.

April lifts one leg out of the bath. The colour of the bruise is spectacular — mauve, crimson, yellow, and grey. She had been dancing at a party above Bondi three nights ago, the salt of the sea breeze stiff and sharp, everyone young and rich, with careers in film or television. She used to come to the same place in her early twenties when the building had been a run-down boarding house. A friend of hers called Dave had got permission from the owners to build a lean-to on the roof, not dissimilar to the kinds of structures Maurie used to build. Now it was a block of apartments, with a penthouse owned by someone who had only recently turned thirty.

April danced and danced under the polar-white moon, occasionally aware of others around her, often not. When she noticed Lawrence drinking by the railing, she stopped. It had been months since he had told her Ester didn't want her visiting when he had the kids, and she hadn't seen him since.

Handsome Lawrence, she used to call him.

He still was handsome, with his short dark hair, olive skin, prominent cheekbones, and those dazzling white teeth. 'Do you put those strips on them,' she used to tease him, 'or paint them each night before you go to bed?'

'And each morning,' he would reply. 'Lunch time too, if I have time.'

But that was so long ago.

They were shy with each other now, careful, and she came up to him, smiling hesitantly. He introduced her to Sam as his sister-in-law, correcting himself immediately to 'ex-sister-in-law, actually.'

'So I'm an ex, too,' she said, and he ignored her.

Sam was a television-ad director with a short film that had gone to Cannes. 'Are you a dancer?' he asked her, and April laughed.

'I don't know what I am,' she told him, shaking her head.

'You're a singer,' Lawrence said. In the white spill of the moon, she could see the kindness in his eyes, and it had surprised and touched her.

April just shrugged, and then, reaching into her bag, she offered them both a joint. 'I'm also very old-fashioned,' she smiled. 'I still like to get out of it.' She lit the match, shielding its flame against the breeze, and then offered it to Lawrence, who shook his head.

'I've gone modern on you,' he told her.

'No drugs?'

He nodded. 'Well, most of the time.'

She smiled sadly. 'Exercise, too? Organic food? AFDs?'

'That's me, I'm afraid.'

She snorted in disbelief.

Sam took the joint, telling her he was happy to go old-fashioned for the night. He wanted to know about her singing, but she didn't want to talk about it. 'Let's dance,' she suggested, and she turned back to the music, Sam leading the way, Lawrence staying where he was.

'I'll just be a moment.' She had stopped, thinking she would tell Lawrence how lovely it was to see him, perhaps kiss him lightly on the cheek because there was no gesture, really, that could express the layers of loss and sorrow, all attempts frail and sad, but she wanted to at least have tried.

He had walked away.

And Sam had reached back for her hand, pulling her into the throng, apologising as he misdirected her into a table edge.

April dries herself slowly, rubbing Hilary's moisturiser into her legs and arms, and then searches through the bathroom cupboards for some make-up. There is a tan-coloured powder, and a lipstick that is too orange. She rubs a little of each on the back of her hand, and then leaves them next to the sink.

She tries on Hilary's pendant, a great round dish of mother of pearl on a heavy chain, and admires it before wrapping herself once more in Maurie's old dressing gown.

She had planned on heading home. Outside, the rain continues, pouring down the rusted gutters in a great rush, and she watches for a moment before checking her phone messages. There are several from the friends she was meant to meet for drinks with Sam, none from him, of course, and then she checks her email — one from her publisher to let her know that there's interest in one of her songs from a film producer.

This is how she survives: small drips of income from sales of that first album, and regular APRA royalties. She used to get asked if she were interested in writing, but after failing to deliver one time too many, those requests have stopped.

She looks out to the studio. She can just see Hilary through the glass doors, her glasses down on the end of her nose; she is running her fingers through her white-grey hair as she talks to someone on the phone. The conversation finishes and she hangs up, staring out at the rain, oblivious to April watching her from the house.

When April goes in to say goodbye, Hilary is still looking out at the rain.

'You're off then?' Hilary wheels her chair out from her desk and over to the saggy corduroy sofa she'd brought back from the river shack. 'Have a seat for a moment,' she tells April.

Sensing a talk, April begins to fidget. 'There's a bus in ten minutes,' she says.

Hilary laughs. 'You've never checked a bus timetable in your life.'

It's true, and she sits reluctantly, tapping her fingers on her knees as she waits for her mother to speak.

'I don't want to talk about Ester,' Hilary says, and she reaches to still April's hand. 'I've told you I can't say anymore about that. I can only hope time will bring some kind of healing, but I don't know.'

April looks down at the ground.

'I want to talk about you.'

Outside, there is a strange silence, a tentative shift in the day; it's too soon, though, to tell whether the change will last for more than a few moments or whether it will be smothered by a new roll of dark clouds, unable to gather any real force just yet.

'I know you are struggling.'

April bites her lip.

'Creativity is unpredictable. Some people have to make sure

they don't waste a drop, while others have it in great armfuls, so many riches that a lifetime isn't enough. Maurie was like that. Most of the time. But he could struggle, too. There were periods when he couldn't paint, and then he would have to turn to other outlets,' and she waves her arm around the studio. 'That was when he built. You know I also painted before you girls were born?'

April can feel Hilary looking at her, and then her mother cups her chin in her hands and lifts her face so that she is forced to look into her eyes. 'I need you to listen to me,' she says.

'I am,' April replies.

'I gave up. I had years and years before I found filmmaking. And they were hard years. I doubted myself so much. When I made my first film, I was like you — I not only managed to create something special, I was lucky. It was the right work in the right place at the right time, and it had so many blessings showered on it.

'And in some ways, I was even more fortunate than you are. I didn't have to deal with fame. Not in the way you did. And I'm a little tougher. A little more bloody-minded. Perhaps through having kids, perhaps not.' Hilary shrugs.

She looks at April, her grey-green eyes deep and kind, focused and sure. 'I don't know if you'll write another album. You may not. You may start again next week, or in fifty years' time. But you have to let all that go. You have to return to a place where you don't even think about that, you just reconnect with the joy you had in music. You have to forget all this current mess, you have to search for other things that feed you. Get out, read, garden, work, help others, be part of the world.'

And she kisses April, who is crying now, not in the way she usually cries, with none of the drama that April usually gives to tears, but with a sadness and shame that makes her wipe her eyes as soon as she feels the sting.

'I have to go,' she tells her mother.

Hilary tucks a strand of hair behind her ear. 'I love you,' she says. 'I don't want you to ever forget that.' Then she smiles, standing close to April, and holds her palm out. 'Pendant,' she tells her.

April touches the silver around her neck. 'Could I borrow it?' she asks.

Hilary looks at her, the look of someone who wants to soak in the other, drink them up and hold them, precious and close.

'Of course,' she tells her, with a tenderness April had never expected.

ESTER HAS LEFT her desk lamp on, as well as the overhead light, but still the room feels dark and gloomy. She sits with her back to the window, Jenny and Damon opposite her on the couch. She can smell the dampness of wet wool, a soupy smell she has always hated. It is resignation and despair, old men in boarding houses, school jumpers, slippers and dressing gowns.

Jenny is agitated, but this isn't unusual. They have had three sessions so far, and each time she sits on the edge of the sofa, her slender legs crossed, neat dark hair short and boyish, dressed for work, ready to race straight into an appointment with a client. Today, she looks particularly tense, pale and drawn, her eyes darting from Damon to Ester and back again.

She is a solicitor, a partner in a large law firm. 'It was never what I wanted to do,' she'd told Ester. 'It just became too hard to leave.' She'd picked at a small sore on the back of her hand. 'I don't have time to think about an alternative. I thought having children might give me that time. I kept having them, but no solution came.' She'd shrugged. 'I seriously considered having a fourth the other day. But I wouldn't, of course, not with the way things are with Marlo.'

And Marlo is why they are here.

'He has school refusal disorder,' Jenny explained at the first session, doing most of the talking, her sentences clipped, always to the point.

She'd found the term on Google. 'I google everything. I hope that one day I'll phrase my question in just the right way to bring up the answer to every worry I have.' She shifted in her seat. 'Computer gaming addiction, disassociation, lack of empathy, hatred — I've googled it all.'

Ester had turned to Damon, asking him to tell her a little about himself.

He brushed his hair out of his eyes. 'I'm a mathematician.' He smiled shyly. 'And I'm a father and a husband, and a person who loves his work and his students. I'm not sure how to contain myself in a simple description, or what you need to know.'

Ester had smiled back at him. 'And your relationship with each other?'

It was like a funnel. This arms-wide gathering of information, the slow sifting through to the grains and grit that remained stuck.

It was Damon who answered, glancing across at Jenny and then back to Ester: 'We love each other.' He squeezed Jenny's hand. 'I'm the luckiest man alive.'

There was something of the child in him, Ester had thought at the time, and it was an impression that had remained. There was an innocence, a wonder at the world, a dust that faintly glittered.

'I don't understand,' he'd said about Marlo, and he genuinely didn't. 'All that time shut up in his room, playing those games in the darkness by himself — I can't fathom it.'

They had taken Marlo to a specialist, Jenny had explained. 'Greg Mahony.'

Ester had heard of him. His work with addiction and adolescents was world-renowned.

'I pulled favours to get that appointment,' she'd said. 'I didn't think he'd come. I was immensely relieved when we got him in the car without protest.' She'd rubbed at a tic in her eye, all the sharp brightness in her face collapsing into pain as she recalled the moment when Greg Mahony had told them there was no point in seeing Marlo unless he actually wanted to be there. And so he'd asked Marlo directly, and Marlo had looked delighted.

'The smile on his face,' Jenny said, 'when he realised it was up to him. He just got up and walked out.'

Sitting now on the couch, Jenny tells Ester that she and Damon are at odds.

'I don't see the point in us being here,' Jenny says. She has a single gold ring, with a pearl setting, on her middle finger. It is curiously old-fashioned for someone who wears, as Jenny does, well-cut suits and little make-up apart from mascara and a deep-red lipstick. She twists the ring, looking directly at Ester as she speaks. 'Everything we try makes no difference. Last week started well. He was helpful, he even talked with us. He went to school on Monday, and then Tuesday came. I discovered he'd run up a $600 bill on my credit card buying new games. I accused him. He locked himself in his room and didn't come out until the weekend.'

She tries to still her hands, one clasping the other in her lap. 'I'm tired of talking about him. I'm tired of thinking about him, and it never improves. I can come here and tell you how terrible he is, how worried I am, but what will it achieve?' She glances at Damon.

His fringe is in his eyes again, and he brushes it back. 'I'm not so sure that you're expecting the right things from this. I don't want to speak out of turn, or for you, but it feels as though we need to find a different way of living with this situation because we are not doing that well.'

Damon has a hole in the elbow of his jumper, and one in the sole of his shoe. He's taken them off to dry his socks, explaining when he arrived that buying clothes isn't something he's very good at. He sits now, resting an ankle on his knee, only to discover that there's also a rip in his sock. 'That's embarrassing,' he says. 'Two poor items of clothing was more than enough.' He puts his foot down, his smile apologetic.

Ester waits for a moment, unsure whether he has finished speaking.

He hasn't: 'We're not here to find out how to change Marlo, or fix him, but just to try and ...'

She looks at him, expecting him to continue. Jenny, too, is waiting. But when he opens his mouth, there is no sound.

'Not ...' The word he utters breaks down into a sound that is animal, guttural. It is a sob of elemental pain and fear, and in the darkness of the room, it is chilling.

Ester opens her mouth to speak, but Jenny holds up her hand. She leans into her husband, all of her focused on comforting him, Ester a silent witness as the rain falls and Damon cries. He cries as Jenny rubs his back, and Ester hands them her box of tissues.

'I'm sorry,' he says when he finally looks up, his cheeks damp with tears, his Adam's apple working nervously in his throat.

Ester tells him that this is one of the reasons why he is here: to let it out.

'What if ...'

Jenny's eyes are wide, her nostrils flared as she looks across at him.

'I'm so scared he'll ...'

Outside, a black cat slinks quickly across the fence, its fur jewelled with raindrops, its dash to shelter so fast and smooth that it's gone almost as soon as it appears.

Damon watches it, breathing slowly, trying to regain his composure before he turns back to Jenny.

Ester leans forward. 'The situation you're in is very difficult. Unfortunately, it's up to Marlo to change his behaviour; I can't, you can't — no one can but him. Which is why Greg didn't want to see him unless he wanted to be there. And he doesn't at the moment. But I can offer you both coping strategies. And information,' she adds, 'about what you're dealing with.' She has already sent them links to various articles about school refusal and different approaches being trialled by different therapists, as well as a useful article for parents of addicts.

'It's up to you as to whether you want to continue — either together or just one of you by yourself, although I think that dealing with this as a couple would be better. But you need to make that decision.'

Jenny nods. She is picking at a fingernail, and then she takes it up to her mouth and snaps at it, small white teeth cutting through it.

'You've never met Marlo,' she eventually says.

Ester shakes her head.

'He's over six foot. And he's big — broad-shouldered, heavy-set. If he wants to play a computer game, I can't stop him. If he doesn't want to go to school, I can't get him out of bed and into the car. If he won't help with clearing the table, I can't make him. I know I can't force change. I know.' Damon has taken her hand, her pale fingers curled up inside his hold. He strokes her arm gently, and she seems to ease a little, uncrossing her legs, her shoulders slumping slightly as she continues to speak: 'Last week, I took all the keyboards and locked them in the car. He smashed the car window to get in.'

She glances across at Damon. 'Sometimes I hate him.'

Damon pulls her close, his arm around her, rocking her. Even as the cracks in the world around him widen, he has love to give. It is wide and deep, sure flowing and constant, there to carry her moments after he himself has plummeted. Ester sees it; the warmth of its certainty fills the room each time they sit together on the couch opposite her, and it is there now as the rain beats steadily on the cold glass of the windows, running down the panes like sheets of silk.

The clock on the desk shows their time is almost up. She looks at them both.

'You're right,' she says. 'You can't force change for him, but you can change your responses. And you have such a good basis from which to work together. I'd like to talk more about this — boundaries that are possible to draw and ways in which you can enforce them without escalating conflict further. We began to touch on this at the end of our last session, and that's the place I'd like to return to. Sometimes when we are in very difficult situations, it's tempting to keep going over our helplessness rather than focusing our attention on areas in which we do have some power.'

Damon nods earnestly. 'That sounds good,' he says with the enthusiasm of a young child for a project. 'I want to do that, we can do that.' His watch is loose on his wrist, and he pushes it back up again as he reaches for his boots.

Jenny is staring at the floor.

Ester turns to face her.

'Why don't you both talk about this at home?'

Jenny nods.

'I'd like to continue working with you together, but obviously that's up to you.'

When she stands, Jenny only just reaches Ester's shoulders. Her cheeks are flushed as she puts her bag on her shoulder and takes out her phone. 'I've got a meeting,' she says. 'A merger that's gone ugly.' She looks out the window, not really talking to either of them as she composes herself, and then turns back to face Ester, all vulnerability masked. 'We'll be in touch.'

This is what her clients do. They breathe in, leave her house, and re-enter the world, heading back to home or to an office where everyone is answering emails, talking on the phone, seeing clients, making tea. All of them with their own pain — divorce, parents dying, illness, trying to have children and not being able to, daily tragedies like shadows, growing, shrinking, growing again.

A world of ghosts, Ester thinks.

She shakes her head. This is the world she lives in. Here, in this room, it is the shadows that talk. *I am the third miscarriage; the fear each time my ex-husband contacts me; my regret at putting my mother in a nursing home — and my unbelievable sorrow about my son.*

She talks to their shadows, but they never talk to hers.

LAWRENCE SITS ALONE in his room, staring at the computer screen.

Normally, he would have delivered the results by now: summarised data, accompanied by a media release that will form the basis of the next day's front page and a double inside spread. He would be on the phone to Paul, the editor, talking through any queries, trying to nudge the story in a particular direction, usually with little success. He also has interviews tentatively booked in with three radio stations, the evening television news, and a couple of blogs. It is likely that there will be more requests coming through today.

Edmund will be enjoying taking his time deliberating. This is what a man of conscience does. Will he let Lawrence off the hook with a sanctimonious lecture and an end to their relationship, or will he go straight to the paper to inform them that Lawrence has been 'adjusting' the data?

Lawrence contemplates the possibility, a cold stone in his stomach as his mind slips into a habitual weighing of outcomes. On a scale from one to ten, how serious would the impact be on his life, with ten being the most serious?

The answer is as it always is: It depends.

Is he talking about the impact on him as a person, on his identity and sense of self, on his reputation? And if so, would the paper keep quiet, wanting to protect its own reputation? Or would others find out? Is he talking about the financial impact? Again, this would depend on whether his other clients got wind of the scandal. He uses Edmund for other jobs. How far would he go?

One question is inevitably capable of opening so many more. Lawrence shakes his head, and checks his email once again. Still nothing.

And so he stands and stretches, the panic in his gut becoming colder.

His office is sparsely furnished. There is a desk under the small window that looks out over the street, and, next to it, a filing cabinet. A large rug, deep-orange wool, covers the floor, and on the other side of the room is a long, low mid-century couch that he bought for an exorbitant sum when he first separated from Ester. He had thought it was stylish, and it is, but it is uncomfortable as well. There is a coffee table next to it, also far more expensive than he had been able to afford, and, around the walls, speakers, one expense that he does not regret.

He turns the music up a little, but it is hopeless with the drumming of the rain. He cannot hear the slow lilt of Bill Callahan, the tired, sardonic drawl drowned out by the steady rhythm on the tin walls and roof.

He needs to think.

No, more importantly, he needs to buy some time. He should call the newspaper and let them know there has been a problem with the data, that there might be a delay. And then he should alert each of the other interviewers.

He looks at his computer screen.

If he doesn't call them, they will call him.

There is one message on his phone — the number unknown, the time earlier in the day. He remembers now. It was when he was talking to Edmund. It's likely to be another request for an interview, although it's unusual for him not to have the number in his phone. He'll check it in a minute. First, the paper.

Paul answers on the second ring. They are friends of sorts. He and Ester went over for dinner a couple of times, and then, after the divorce, Paul took him out for a drunken night, detailing his own misery at home for most of the evening. Sarah was either haranguing him or cold and dismissive. *I don't love her anymore*, and he'd leant across the table as he'd made this admission, his face flushed and ugly from too much red, his breath stale. Lawrence had recoiled, wondering at how repulsive so many men could be, and then when Paul had asked him what had led to Ester booting him out, he'd shaken his head and lied. *We grew apart*, he said, which, while not untrue, wasn't the whole story.

Paul answers now with his usual clipped work response, a 'gidday' that launches straight into the matter at hand. He hasn't had a minute to look through his emails, he's assuming no major surprises in the poll. And then, before Lawrence has a chance to answer, Paul says he's been wanting to chat to him, to talk about the future. The cost cuts are going to mean big changes, and it's going to affect them.

'But I've got an editorial meeting happening five minutes ago, I'll have to call you back —'

He is about to hang up, and so Lawrence speaks over him. 'No results as yet,' he tells him. 'Which is why I'm calling. There's been a hitch with the data.'

'How serious?'

'Not sure yet,' Lawrence says. 'I'm on the case.' He can hear someone laughing loudly in the background, and that, coupled with the incessant drumming of the rain, means it's difficult to catch Paul's response. Something along the lines of 'get it sorted' and 'talk soon'.

At least he knows Edmund hasn't spoken to them yet.

Jesus Christ, he hates Edmund. Always has, he realises.

Although the intensity of his dislike had crystallised when he had told Edmund that he and Ester had divorced. He doesn't know why he told him — it wasn't like they ever talked about anything personal — but he'd been such a mess at the time he'd frequently found himself blabbing without thinking. Edmund had told him that he didn't believe in divorce. *You make a vow and you keep it.*

Perhaps this is a good thing after all. He'll find someone new. And then he shakes his head again. Who's he kidding? This isn't a good thing. It's a mess, and he doesn't know why he did it. He'd begun when the previous government had hit rock bottom in popularity. He supposes he'd just wanted to make some feeble attempt to counter the relentless flow against them, a flow that his work had helped to create.

But was that all it was?

Ester had once accused him of being in love with the power of lying and cheating. There had been previous girlfriends who'd voiced similar sentiments.

He sits down on his over-priced lounge and looks out at the gloom of the day, his phone still in his hand. The sweat on his palms makes his grip slippery, and he drops it between the cushions, only remembering the missed call as he searches for it by feel, the darkness of the room making it impossible for him to see.

When he finds it, he dials his voicemail, but is unable to hear a word.

He needs somewhere quieter.

He lies down on the couch, pressing his ear on the phone and the phone against the cushion in an attempt to muffle the sound of the rain.

It's Hilary. She needs him to call urgently.

And she leaves her number in case he no longer has it.

AFTER APRIL LEAVES, Hilary goes back to the house. Her daughter's coffee cup is still on the table, the imprint of her lipstick like a fossil on the rim. Her plate is next to it, a half-eaten piece of toast sitting in the centre, now cold.

She leaves them where they are, holding onto the traces of April's presence for just a little longer.

In the hall, Maurie's dressing gown is draped over the bannister, and Hilary leaves that too, breathing it in as she walks past, the faint turpentine from Maurie mingled with April's talcum sweetness. It is almost too much, this increasing bombardment of the senses, each instant passing with a slowness that is pure and painful. It is as though her life has been in fast motion until now, racing forward, a great crush of people, places, moments, anger, joy, love, despair all coming to a sudden stop, colliding into each other at the gate, while she slips through, walking onwards, alone in a quiet land.

Upstairs, she takes two painkillers. The headache is there again, at the edge of her temples, like a dense cloud clotting. She can see it in her eyes and in the tightness with which she holds herself, shoulders and back straight, face staring directly ahead. The doctors have told her that initially the pills should help in dealing with the pain, however they will soon not be strong enough. She hopes that moment hasn't yet come.

The first headache struck on the evening she completed the

rough picture cut. She thought she'd been working too hard, that she might have strained her eyes, although the intensity of the pain had alarmed her.

Something wasn't right.

And then a fortnight later, the world collapsed into a throbbing centre, her entire being at the mercy of its force. Lying in her darkened room, she could do nothing but ride it out, let it wash over and through her, until a day later she emerged, shaken and weak, and booked an appointment with her GP.

There are two tasks to complete before she sees Ester this evening. The first is simple. She has to go to Henry and pick up the drugs. The second is meeting Lawrence. Hilary splashes her face with lukewarm water and then puts on the red enamel ring that Maurie gave her when she turned twenty-seven. She wears it when she particularly needs his presence, the warmth of the copper base against her skin and the weight of the round red disc solid enough to ground her.

She remembers that birthday. They had been living in a studio in Paddington, not far from this house now. It was tiny, surrounded by monstera, the green glossy leaves pressing against each window. She used to call it the 'Triffid room', and although she hated the determined growth of that plant, its thick fleshy stems and pods too alien and alive, she did love the softness of the light filtering through, the coolness of that chlorophyll veil.

They had invited everyone they knew, too many for the flat and the slender concrete balcony that ran along the front, too many for the hall and the driveway, and for the small garden off the street. There had been a moment when she had thought they were going to bring down the long outside landing, everyone tumbling into the monstera, caught in the great spread of its leaves, giant green hands waiting to catch them all.

The record player gave up by midnight, the needle so blunt it couldn't follow a single groove. The alcohol also came to an end early, but no one minded — they rolled fat joints and passed them around, damp Tally-Ho paper pink with lipstick, the sweet smell of grass.

Later, when the crowd had thinned, she found Maurie sitting on the low-lying wall that ran along the footpath. He was staring up at the stars, pinpricks of light in the midnight sky, humming softly to himself. It was unlike him to be alone, and she came up behind him, wrapping her arms around the warmth of his body, burying her face in the softness of his hair.

'We should get married,' he said when he turned around, his voice so hushed she wondered whether she had heard him.

He waited for her to speak.

'Not us,' she eventually told him. 'It's a beautiful night. I love you. But I don't want to marry anyone. Ever.'

He had looked at her and smiled, taking her face in his hands, her cheeks cool beneath his skin, and he had kissed her, once on the mouth, and then the forehead. 'I knew you'd say that,' he whispered. He kissed her again. 'Which is why I asked you.'

Across the road, a drunken couple laughed loudly, and somewhere back in the flats a glass shattered, a sharp, staccato bell as it hit the concrete. Next to her, Maurie had continued staring up at the sky, the warmth of his body close, the smell of alcohol and smoke and paint, and, beneath that, a deep richness that she knew so well.

'We're going to have a good life, you and I,' he told her. 'Years and years and years in front of us, and so much love.'

The roughness of his cheek was fresh against the smoothness of her own skin, the coldness of the night air swallowing her in great gulping gasps as she moved closer to him under the darkness of the sky.

'You're my home,' he had told her.

'And you're mine,' she had replied.

She had been so fortunate, carrying the gift of that love within her, along with an awareness of the keenness to its edge: the possibility of loss glinting just in sight. Perhaps this was why she had always held a certain part of herself in reserve. Or perhaps this was simply who she was. But not Maurie. He saw nothing but the joy, and he wanted to scoop it all up, roll around in it, throw it in the air; a fabulous toy that never ceased to surprise and delight.

'Let's have children,' he'd said on the third night she'd slept with him. 'Hundreds of them.'

Hilary had laughed. 'And will they look after themselves?'

'Absolutely,' he'd insisted. 'They'll grow and flourish and burn bright without us ever having to do a thing.'

He hadn't wanted to stop at Ester. He would have kept going, child after child after child, their entire life reduced to milk and nappies and prams and blankets, heaters drying clothes, the cry of babies like kittens mewling.

'That's it,' she'd insisted, refusing to sleep with him until he had a vasectomy.

And there had been war in their house, silent, pacing war — who could hold out the longest? — a war he never had a chance of winning. It was what she had to do, temper his enthusiasm with a strain of harsh reality, a role she'd sometimes hated him for.

But now, here alone on the other side of their life together, she looks back on those flashes of anger as simply that: no more than jagged cuts of lightning in the sky, so brief against all that stretched before and after.

Out on the street, Hilary drives slowly to Henry's house, the wipers clearing a small arc of vision. She can feel the rain on her skin, sweet and cold, slanting through the window, which is open to clear the fog that persists despite the loud drone of the demister.

It is only a couple of kilometres, a walk if the day had been fine, down the twist of streets to the gully, Henry's home a small flat that looks out on a sandstone cliff, where morning glory tumbles through the cracks, its drooping purple flowers and tissue-thin leaves tangled in the rock.

Once, when Maurie was very drunk, he told a reporter at an opening that Henry was the artist he admired most.

'Henry who?' the reporter had asked.

'Henry Goldstein.'

'Do I know his work?'

Maurie had laughed, his great deep belly laugh rolling through the gathering, making heads turn. 'He's probably produced two finished works. And both have disappeared. So I doubt you've even met his work, let alone know it.'

They had gone to art school together, the three of them; Maurie the loud, confident one, she quieter and more serious, a beauty then, with a tumble of blonde hair and long, slender legs, and Henry, tall, thin, dark-eyed beneath a fall of fringe, softly spoken and alive with ideas.

Henry was in the sculpture department, his work a search for purity, minimalist and austere. He once told her that the only logical conclusion to this desire was to create nothing, which was one of the reasons that he never finished his degree. But then, when she first met him, he was working in marble, making perfect eggs that slid apart, another one inside. Smooth Russian dolls. She had noticed his elegant hands first, and had asked him if she could sketch them.

He had smiled shyly (but with a certain amount of pride) as he held them out towards her. 'How would you like me to pose?'

She thought about it for a moment, the palm of his hand in her own, his beautiful flat almond-shaped nails, smooth olive skin, and the delicate shape of his fingers creating lines and planes of perfection.

'In prayer position,' she told him. 'Here.' And she adjusted the direction just slightly so that the light fell right along the arc of his thumb.

She still has the sketch she did. It is pinned on the wall in her studio, a square of thick creamy art paper with the beauty of Henry's hands almost captured, there in the centre.

(She slept with Henry once — long before Maurie claimed her as his own — and she has never told anyone. She remembers it now as soporific, a blur of limbs, soft and undefined, but they had both taken smack, and the haze of the whole day had wrapped everything, including the sex, into the slow passing of time. In truth, Henry was always asexual, surrounded by friends but never in a physical relationship, nor seemingly interested in one, and her memory of their intimacy is without any sense of his corporeality.)

Over the years, she was the one who stayed in touch with him, not Maurie. Sometimes she would spend the afternoon in his apartment, sipping tea and talking about a film she was making, always grateful for his quiet insights and suggestions. His calm was an antidote to Maurie's ebullience. She knew he had other friends, but he kept people separate, giving her the strange sense that he belonged to her alone.

Outside his block of flats, she stays in the car, watching the rain. There is a sad, seeping slowness to the drizzle now, a blank grey sky and a steady dampness. She can see it rising up the sandstone wall, the gold and pink darker where the rain has soaked into the porous stone. The potholes and cracks in the road form tiny ponds, offering blank reflections to the stillness of the sky above. It is only plants that gain any true beauty in this weather, she thinks. A grevillea is jewelled with rain drops, silver pearls clinging to the trembling tips of the flowers and the fine ends of the spiky fronds; a passionfruit vine gathers clusters of rainwater in the open hold of its leaves, shaking them out in a shower with each whisper of breeze.

The world is a place of wonder.

The gallery opposite Henry's is opening up for the day. Hilary watches as the young woman unbolts the heavy glass doors and steps out under the awning for a moment. She is dressed in red: a crimson wool dress, vermillion fishnet stockings, and rose suede boots, her long black hair styled like a seventies rock star. If it weren't so wet, Hilary would cross the street and tell her that she is her own work of art, no doubt more spectacular than the ordinary paintings lining the high white walls of the front and back rooms.

Next door to the gallery is a small travel agent's. A man hovers in the doorway, smoking a cigarette, cup of coffee clutched in his hand. He glances across to the woman in the gallery, and they nod and smile at each other. He is dressed in grey, a dull foil to her brilliance — charcoal sweater, and jeans that sag at the crotch and run tight along his calves down to his black boots. He blows out smoke, a faint wisp that disappears into the milky sky almost as soon as it appears, and then he drops the last of his cigarette onto the pavement, leaving it to smoulder and sizzle in the damp.

The rest of the street is quiet. This is not a day when people go out unless they have to. It is a day for staying inside.

Hilary told Henry she would get to him by eleven. It is half past. Not that it matters. He isn't concerned by time. She has never noticed a clock in his studio, nor does he have a mobile or a computer.

When she buzzes on his doorbell, he lets her in without a word. The hallway is damp, hard lino floors smeared with crushed leaves, mud, and rain, a row of locked letterboxes along the wall, and a pile of suburban newspapers covering the bottom step, never picked up, just replaced by the new issue each week.

Henry's flat is at the back of the block, his door slightly ajar. He stands awkwardly next to the fold-out couch, thinner than ever, his body like a stretched elastic band, hair still falling over his eyes, silver now, dark pupils an ember of intensity cloaked by a shy hesitancy as he looks at her, uncertain whether to step forward and embrace her in greeting or stay where he is.

Looking across at him, she is overwhelmed, the tightness with which she has bound herself momentarily loosened at being in the proximity of the only person who knows of her decision.

He takes her hand, his skin like cool, crisp paper, the shape of his fingers still beautiful, and he kisses her on the cheek. He hasn't asked her if she is sure, if she knows what she is doing, but she nods all the same.

'I don't quite know how to behave in this situation,' he eventually says.

She smiles slightly.

'Do we have a cup of chai, and just talk as we would always talk?'

She nods again, not trusting herself to speak.

The spices are rich, and their aroma fills the single room as he takes the only two cups he owns out of the cupboard. She sits on the couch, staring out the window at the sandstone. At her feet is a copy of Derek Jarman's *Chroma*, opened at the second last chapter 'Iridescence'.

A beautiful word.

Biting hard on her lip, the salty taste of her own flesh there on her tongue, Hilary looks up at the ceiling, and then, as she takes the cup from him, she tells him she has sent her film off. Work. This is what she could always turn to — safe when all the rest of life was too unbearable to hold; calm, contained, manageable.

'And are you pleased?'

'There was no more I could do,' she says with a smile.

He stretches out his long thin legs, crossing one over the other, and takes her hand again. 'That's the place you want to reach.'

He looks at her now, his eyes resting on hers for a moment, and then he turns his gaze down, focusing on his knees, bony beneath his trousers. 'Do you remember when we were at school together?'

She smiles. 'Of course I do.'

'I was in love with you. And I was in love with Maurie. I was in love with both of you.' He brushes his hair out of his eye, and there is the faintest tremble in those fine fingers. 'But then I found the drugs, and I chose to live my life with them, so there was no sadness, loss, or bitterness where either of you were concerned. Just a faint memory of a love I had. A memory that's still there, on certain mornings when I wake and look back.'

She strokes his hand.

'I once told Maurie I loved him, and do you know what he did?'

Hilary shakes her head.

'He squeezed me so tight my bones rattled, and he laughed.'

It is like Maurie is there with them, the recollection of his hold and that laugh filling the small space.

'After you called I had a brief moment of wondering whether I should be brave and go with you. Living as I do is becoming harder. I'm getting too old. But I'm too much of a coward to do anything other than hope that the decision will be made for me by accident.'

Behind them the refrigerator hums, the motor whirring into life and then dying again, the silence afterwards more pronounced.

Taking his face in her hands, Hilary turns him to look at her, because she wants to say: 'I can't talk about this, please stop.' But she doesn't speak, she just leans forward and kisses him, closing her eyes so that she can feel as if they are young again, his mouth cool on hers, a trace of tears that could be hers, just there, and then gone.

She doesn't want him coming with her.

She looks around his flat, the complete containment of his life within these walls. Even this has a pulsating beauty. Henry once told her he had calculated his life, exactly. The cost of heroin with price fluctuations built in, the other bare necessities he needed to survive, and the money he had from an inheritance. An equation that was occasionally tinkered with, but that had ruled his life with an iron grip for so long, never allowing more than the most minor deviation.

He stands now, the deep softness of his corduroy pants like the ocean, and she picks up the book, the pages opening to 'Into the Blue', and she smiles as she reads the first few paragraphs. This was a film she could have made, an exploration of colour. There were so many films she could have made. She looks up at Henry, watching him as he searches behind one of the piles of books, his body bent down low to reach the package.

Snow white.

Ghost white.

Whitewash. White lies.

'Here it is.' He holds the plastic bag out towards her. 'Jerome was flummoxed when I changed my order. He's been delivering the same amount to me for so long without any need for conversation or question. When I asked him for this extra delivery, he questioned me, several times.' Henry smiles. 'I told him there must be very few dealers who refuse to take a larger order. I was very specific with him about the purity so that our calculations are correct. I've tried it, and I am as certain as I can be that he has told me the truth.'

She puts the heroin in her bag, laughing as she looks at it. 'Imagine if I were arrested on the way home.'

'You remember everything I showed you about how to take it?'

She does. He had been surprisingly businesslike when it came to the logistics.

Outside, there is the sound of a door opening and then closing with a heavy thud, followed by footsteps down the stairs and then the ring of a phone. A woman answers, her voice shrill as she tells the caller to fuck off.

'The tone of the neighbourhood seems to be on the slide again.' Henry raises an eyebrow. 'I've seen it go up and down, and I'm sure it will rise and fall again. The other day I realised I have now been living here for forty years. It's a long time. And I spend most days inside this room, only occasionally going out for a walk or seeing people such as yourself. Some would say I've had a limited life.' He shrugs. 'But it's never really felt that way.'

'Sometimes I wish you'd kept sculpting, or creating in some way,' she tells him.

He looks at her, both of them aware that she has never before commented on his life choices.

'Why?'

'I would like to have seen another one of your works.'

He smiles. 'I couldn't now. I probably couldn't have for quite some time. I made the choice before I really knew what choice I was making. It's the danger of youth. And then there was no turning back. The only blessing is that the choice I made has given me a certain insulation against regret.'

The warmth of the gas burner has diminished now, and the room is cold. Hilary shivers. She puts her bag on her shoulder, the weight of the small package inside it amplified in her consciousness. She doesn't want to say goodbye, and she couldn't bear Henry asking her to stay, or telling her he will miss her. She hopes he knows this.

'The chai was beautiful,' she says.

He replies just as she had hoped, with one hand on the door, opening it to the dullness of the hallway as he leans forward to kiss her on the cheek.

'I'm glad you liked it.'

And he brushes his hair out of his eyes as he steps aside to let her pass.

THREE YEARS EARLIER

APRIL HAD BEEN alone at the shack for ten days when Lawrence arrived.

Each morning, she woke with the first sunlight momentarily soft through the curtain-less windows but soon intensifying, the glare harsh and hard. She hung a blanket, hammering nails into the worn grey corners, but it wasn't enough. There was always a gap at the side, a chink that allowed the daylight, insistent, demanding, to reach across the room and assault her, not as cold as a slap, more a thudding punch in the face.

And so she would lie there, eyes closed, and try to pretend it away. Like when she was a child and she hated Ester, or one of her friends who had come to stay with them for the week and wanted to be with her all the time. She would bend all the force of her will to wiping out their existence, denying every cell of their body with a high-pitched focus like a sonar scream that obliterated all in its path. And so it was now; with eyes tightly closed, fusty bedding pulled over her head, she would grind her teeth and tell herself the day was not yet there, not for her, not at all, trying to summon the denial she had once found so easy to access.

But it was too airless, too unpleasant, to stay there for long. And so she would get up reluctantly, head heavy, and wonder how she was going to fill the slow stretch of daylight until the evening came again, bringing with it the relief of a few hours of unconscious sleep.

She had arrived with a car full of supplies and a heart full of the best intentions. The afternoon had been soft, a pale mauve tinging the gold of the westerly sun when she pulled up outside the shack, the music from the car stereo seeming suddenly loud in the stillness. Here she was. Two bags of clothes, her guitar, a laptop to record herself, and three boxes of food, all healthy, of course: teas and vegetables and fruit, and even brown rice and tofu.

She brought everything inside with a brisk efficiency, play-acting the role of someone else; the creak of her step on the dry boards of the verandah, the thud of the door swinging shut behind her, the rattle of the glass as she opened each of the windows, all too loud, like the sounds an actor in the theatre makes. And that's what she was, April Marcel playing the part of Someone Who Had Come Away To Write.

When she was a child, they had driven here most weekends. She and Ester would sleep in the back seat of the car, surrounded by blankets, pillows, clothes, and food, waking occasionally to the soft glow of the light from the dashboard and the low muttering of Hilary and Maurie talking, sometimes arguing, the radio a hum behind their words.

'Look at the stars,' Maurie would whisper as he carried her in, and she would stare up at the dancing swirl, like a splash of silvery lace under the hem of a twirling skirt, only to close her eyes again straight away, waking hours later, miraculously no longer in the car or his arms, but on one of the divan beds underneath a window.

She had loved that, the transition from one to the other seemingly happening by magic.

She was always the first up, heading down to the river on

her own, oblivious to how damp and dirty her pyjamas became as she sat in the silky sand of the bank and built castles and palaces, singing to herself in the still clarity of the morning light, staying there until Hilary or Maurie's voice rang out from the shack, calling her — breakfast was ready — and she would run up, barefoot, smelling the sugary lemon of the pancakes or the salty fat of the bacon, starving now, the table out on the verandah, Ester setting it as she was told, the birds hopping forward and back, beady eyes alert for any crumbs.

The place had not been used since she was here some months ago. There was the smell of dust, the must of the ash still in the fireplace, and, lingering below it all, smoke from her cigarettes.

As she opened the door to the back bedroom, there was a foulness, the rottenness of death, and she stepped back momentarily, tempted to just close the door and leave it, to sleep in the old divan bed. But once she'd let it out, it was no longer possible to ignore it. It was a bird, only recently dead, ants crawling across the dullness of its once glossy feathers, and she looked, not sure how to deal with it, before regaining some measure of practicality and scooping it up with a plastic bag — the lifeless body a small concentration of weight in her hands — and throwing it some distance away into the bush.

She had nothing to drink.

She had done this on purpose, thinking that purity might help creativity.

How could she have been so stupid?

Outside, the darkness was thickening, soaking into the flat expanse of grass and beyond that the row of poplars, their first spring leaves trembling along the skeletal branches, pale and new.

She would need a drink.

And so, only half an hour after arriving, she got back in the car and headed into town, arriving at the pub just before dark.

The decision was fraught. Should she get one bottle and ration herself to a glass a night until she had to come back for more supplies, or should she be honest with herself and buy half a dozen?

The bottle shop attendant waited.

'Oh God,' April smiled at her. She shifted from foot to foot. 'I have become completely incapable of deciding.' She grimaced, reaching for a bottle and then drawing her hand back.

The woman looked at her, bored.

Shiraz. One.

And then she went back to the shelf.

'You know you can bring them all up at once, love.'

Pathetically, she bought three. Neither here nor there, an each-way bet, a completely useless compromise. Enough to allow herself to slip into the fourth and fifth glass each night, but not enough to save her from having to head back to town sooner than she would like to.

It was completely dark as she drove back, and she was nervous. She remembered Maurie once hitting a kangaroo, the terrible thud of its body, and the shudder of the car as they came to a stop, steam hissing from the radiator. It had been so cold that night, the briskness of the air slapping her cheeks as they walked, each carrying one bag, up the dirt road, abandoning the car to be dealt with in the morning.

'Did the kangaroo die?' she had asked Maurie over and over again. 'Are you sure?'

When he had finally told her that yes, it had died, she had cried and cried, horrified that they had been responsible for its death, and in the end Hilary had stopped, exasperated and exhausted, shaking her as she told her to pull herself together. 'It died. This is what happens. It's terrible. But there is nothing you can do.'

And she had thought her mother was some kind of alien, her

harsh pragmatism so very foreign to all the pain she, April, felt for that poor kangaroo.

She drove slowly now, feeling each pothole and rut, her whole body craned forward as she looked for the dip and bend in the road that she knew so well, but never quite trusted herself to find when it was this dark — and then, there it was, the shack a darker bulk in the distance, one light left on, piercing the night.

She was back. This time with wine. Ready to begin again.

The first few mornings, before she hit upon the idea of putting a blanket over the window, April woke earlier than she had in years.

She slept in an old pair of Maurie's pyjamas, still there, under the pillow. They were flannel, too long and too loose, but they smelt of her father, easing the panic of loneliness and failure that was nipping at her, sharp little bites that threatened to take a chunk of her flesh.

She lay there, listening to the quiet, until she began to discern layers of sound: the call of a bird, the creak of a branch, the slow brush of the breeze, her own breath, rising and falling, and, beneath it all, the pumping of her heart.

She hated sleeping alone, and yet it had been so long since she'd shared a bed with anyone for more than a few weeks. Lex had been the last — ten years younger than her, he'd only just arrived in Sydney from Melbourne. She'd met him at a party, and taken him home for almost three weeks of what she finally had to accept was average sex that rapidly declined to bad.

But there was a sweetness about him, an eagerness, which had at first meant she was happy for him to hang around. He'd just finished a communications course and wanted to work with a film company. He had a hit list, ringing a few producers a day, his voice loud and jocular, his jokes slightly wrong, his laughter too exuberant as he tried to progress the call to a meeting. And then, after those few attempts, he gave up for the day, thumbing through her record collection, putting on his favourites too loud and dancing around her living room, before suggesting they go out to eat. *Like a puppy*, she thought, *clumsy, cute, and irritating*. The same in bed, all over her with a slobbery eagerness that never appealed, and yet when she watched him sleep afterwards, lean and smooth, silky hair ruffled, no hint of a middle-aged snore, she began to see his charms again.

She was happy to let him stay for a while. And then he got work, and she came home to a note and a bunch of daffodils.

She felt no rancour; in fact, she was relieved to have her place back to herself, and even though he promised he'd stay in touch — and they did leave a few messages for each other in a half-hearted attempt at catching up — the wisps that had briefly connected them soon spun away into nothing.

And now she was alone again.

Outside, the days were perfection. Sitting on the verandah, April spoke to the grass, the trees, the flat blue sky, the magpie that watched her, the spider catching flies between the posts and the roof, and the ants that crawled across her toes, tickling the winterwhite of her skin. She told them what she was having for breakfast, the meal she was contemplating for lunch, and then — when she was absolutely convinced they weren't listening — she confessed her fear.

'I am going to leave here having written nothing.'

'Nothing!' She shouted at the magpie, whom she'd come to dislike, frightened it would swoop each time she walked to the stove or bath-house.

It regarded her for an instant and then flew away.

'Do you hear me?' she asked the spider, as it dropped a thread, bouncing, bouncing, bouncing, until finally all was steady enough for it to begin its ascent back to the heart of the matter.

She picked up her guitar and told them she was going to sing them a song, and they'd better be honest when she asked for their opinion. She strummed aimlessly, her voice touching on the possibility of a tune only to dart away immediately.

Inside the house, it was darker. Built to capture the early morning light and then provide shelter from the heat of the summer days, it was always a little gloomy. She made toast with the last of the bread, and yet another cup of insipid herbal tea. She'd buy coffee when she went back into town, and chocolate. This idea of purity was clearly a failure, she told a cockroach as it scurried across the floor.

Sitting on the floor of the bedroom, she opened the old shipping trunk under the window, taking out the clothes that Hilary kept. Heavy cotton summer shifts with huge lurid flowers, caftans, a knitted pantsuit. April used to dress up in them when she was little, and she would have pilfered them years ago if it wasn't for the fact that Hilary was at least six inches shorter than her, and they made her look like she had tried on a doll's outfit rather than her mother's clothes.

At the bottom of the trunk were old notebooks, drawings, and letters. With bright fabric strewn around her, April sat cross-legged on the floor and pulled them all out. She knew the letters between her parents, and she put these aside. Some were in Maurie's dark scrawl, others in her mother's strong slanting pen. She had once started reading them and then felt embarrassed, ashamed, the intimacy too close, and with it the familiarity of both her parents distorted — they became young and in love and passionate, people she did not, and should not, know.

She liked the cards she'd written home when she'd toured Europe. They were tied together with red ribbon, and as she sat and read them, she remembered. It was too simplistic to just say she'd been happy then. She hadn't known how momentous that time was; it had simply happened, and she'd floated along. It was only now that it was gone, she realised how special it had been.

Hilary had also kept drawings they'd done as children, and April took these out as well. Ester's were so much better than hers, which were invariably messy and unfinished. She laid a couple across the floor, remembering the afternoon they'd done them. They'd been on the verandah, and Maurie had given them paper and crayons. 'See that tree?' They'd looked up at it. 'Drink it in,' he'd instructed. 'Now, run inside and draw it.'

She'd scrawled a few branches, and then, bored with the task, had covered them in birds, bright, ridiculous birds with feathery crowns and jewels and fans, and even pipes they were smoking.

It wasn't what they were meant to do, Ester had complained when Maurie had seized April's picture in delight, laughing at the expression on the rooster she'd placed right at the very top.

She looked at Ester's now, and there was a beautiful grace to the lines, an elegance and symmetry. Ester had always drawn well; she was the one destined to become the next artist. And then she'd turned her back on it. Hilary had told her it was a shame. That being a counsellor was dull. Surely she didn't really want to spend day after day listening to dreary people talk about their problems.

Ester had been furious.

At the bottom of the trunk were diaries, the ones they'd kept as little girls. April's rambled from strange fantasy to strange fantasy, tales of animals taking her to live with them, an outpouring of passionate love for a new friend she'd made, a plan to run away and sail around the world (not that she'd ever even been on a boat) — and no mention of Ester.

Her sister's on the other hand, were filled with April's name, anger in every page, as she recounted slights and injustices in fine detail. *How could April have done that? Why hadn't she got into trouble? Surely their parents could see what a liar she was.* April had read it once, completely surprised by the resentment that Ester had carried within her. She hadn't known — and she'd called Ester right then and there, saying they needed to talk. She loved her. She didn't understand how Ester could have misjudged her. It was awful, too awful — and she'd cried into the phone, Ester silent on the other end.

When she finally spoke, her words were dismissive. 'Oh, April. We were children. I don't know why on earth you need to talk about it.'

Like her parents' letters, she didn't read the diaries now. Instead, she took out the drawings that Maurie had done of each of them, rough sketches on scraps of paper that he would have thrown out if Hilary hadn't kept them. April liked these. She'd meant to take them with her last time but had forgotten, instead throwing everything back into the trunk in her clean-up, because she'd faced both Ester and Hilary's anger when she'd left the shack a mess, and it was easier to just put it all back rather than sort through.

But this time, she put the drawings straight into her own bag, and then she wandered back outside to where she'd left her guitar, abandoned on the old daybed.

Under the texta-blue sky decorated with tiny puffy white clouds, she followed a yellow-dirt track. If she drew herself now, she would be a stick figure, she thought, dressed in a red cotton dress, the only person amidst the bold colours of this country. Because it *was* bold today, the sky sharp and bright, the gums stark, the wattle coming out in golden puffs, the green almost iridescent. Nothing but the sound of her boots scrunching on the gravel, and then, as a bird swooped low overhead, the whoosh of its wings.

She should give up and go home.

At the end of the track, there was a truck, engine running, and choking black clouds of diesel rising into the sky. Les, who had an orchard on the river flats, raised his hand in greeting.

'Didn't know you were here.' He squinted into the harshness of the midday sun, closing the gate behind him.

April smiled. 'Been keeping to myself.'

'Hilary still interested in selling?'

April guessed so, although she hadn't spoken to her mother about it recently.

'Nice bit of land your dad bought,' Les told her. 'Just a bad time to be on the market.' He handed April an orange from the front seat, and she held it in her hand, smelling its sweetness for a moment, before she began to break the peel with her thumb, the juice spurting up into her eye.

'Last of the crop,' Les said.

Looking down to the river, April told him she was thinking of going in.

He shook his head. 'You're bloody mad.'

Mouth full of orange, she just grinned.

'Guarantee you'll get no further than your feet.'

She swiped at a fly. 'I'm going to run straight in, fast as fast. Right under.'

Back in the truck, he took his hat off and threw it on top of the oranges next to him. 'Want a lift?'

She smiled. 'Need to walk. Get the heat up.'

And he shook his head again, raising a hand in farewell, as he put his foot on the accelerator, the truck groaning as the engine began to tick over, each panel shuddering as he drove slowly along the corrugated road, leaving a cloud of fumes and dust behind him.

April waited, and then followed in his wake.

The river was still, the banks winding in great curves and loops below the sheer cliffs on the other side and the more gentle incline on this. If she shouted, her voice would hit the grey boulders opposite and bounce back, loud but hollow. Somewhere, a long way upriver, she thought she heard a child, a high-pitched squeal, followed by laughter, and then silence again.

She was alone.

Kicking off her boots and letting her dress drop to her feet, she looked around her once, twice, and then ran naked, straight into the icy chill, the grip of its cold ferocious on her legs, her arms, her chest, until she was completely submerged, all of her encased in ice, expanding, ready to explode.

'I did it,' she shouted at the top of her lungs, perhaps loud enough for Les to hear miles downriver, hopefully loud enough to startle that bitch of a magpie and the cow of a spider. And she shook herself, diamond drops of river water, pure and clean, flying through the air, sparkling in the sunlight, her flesh white and goose-pimpled, before seizing her clothes in her hand and running, as fast as she could, up the bank and across the grass to the bathhouse.

LAWRENCE HAD NEVER found it easy to say no to Hilary. Few people did.

She'd hired the trailer and given him a neatly printed list of everything she wanted brought back.

'I would have asked April to do it, but you know what she's like.'

He didn't really mind. It wasn't as if he were busy at work. And now that the time had come, he was glad to be getting away from home for a few days.

The previous evening, he'd been out until four in the morning. It had been an album launch, a crush of people in a small bar in Redfern. He'd spent the day half-heartedly working on a customer satisfaction survey, followed by discussions around the next poll. He'd intended to just stop by the launch on the way home, or at least that was what he'd told Ester, but he had a restlessness inside, an emptiness at the pit of his stomach, a thirst he knew was dangerous.

The night was chill, and he'd walked to the bar, where everyone had spilled out onto the pavement, the speeches behind them forgotten, the launch itself irrelevant really (he didn't really know any of the band members) and he'd found himself leaning against a brick wall, talking to Jerome and Rebecca, before leaving with them to go to their place.

They lived around the corner, in an apartment above a shop,

the traffic faint below, the rooms spacious and empty. He'd had a brief relationship with Rebecca when they were both young, and when Jerome was out of the room, she said she'd always regretted letting him go.

Which wasn't how he remembered it.

She'd taken too much of something; her whole body was agitated, her eyes darting nervously, her long, fine fingers moving too quickly as she brushed her hair out of her face, scratched at her arm, reached to pour them both another drink and then forgot to complete the action, leaving him to do so.

'I think Jerome might be gay.' She leant close to him as she whispered the words, and then pulled back nervously. 'But I don't know how you tell.'

'Perhaps just ask him.' He raised an eyebrow, bemused by where this was going and how he'd managed to find himself here having this conversation.

'Oh God,' she laughed loudly, unable to meet his eyes. 'As if I could do that.'

He wondered whether she had some kind of mental illness, his memory of her no more than a faint impression; they'd just gone out a lot, drank a lot, taken a lot of drugs, had sex often, and found they had nothing in common on the rare occasions they were together sober.

'You did it all the right way. Stopped all this,' and she picked up the bottle and set it down again, too heavily, on the coffee table between them, 'got a proper job, found a good woman, had a family. Good on you.'

He really should have left then.

But Jerome came back with lines of coke, and, being the drug pig that April had always accused him of being, Lawrence once again failed to say no, the acrid taste cutting through the alcohol fog as he lit another cigarette and grinned.

'Are you gay?' he asked Jerome, who laughed loudly, and then poured himself another drink before looking at Rebecca and telling her she was a stupid fuck. 'Just because I don't love you anymore doesn't mean I'm gay.'

She'd started crying, and then she'd turned to Lawrence and hit him, a rain of angry slaps and punches coming down on him as she'd told him he was spineless, a man with no moral fibre, a fucker, in fact.

He'd tried to stand, the couch so bloody soft it was hard to actually lift himself out of it and get out of there.

He couldn't remember where he'd put his coat, and then he saw it on the other side of the room, but Jerome had stopped him, pulling him back.

'You can't just take my coke and go.'

Unsteady on his feet, Lawrence tried to find a hold on the evening, something to grasp, and he looked directly at Jerome, speaking as though he were talking to the twins when they were naughty, his tone fatherly, sensible — ludicrous in the surreal drift — as he said it no longer seemed appropriate for him to stay, there was clearly something going on between them, and he pointed at Rebecca, who had slumped off to sleep, and then turned back to Jerome, who was laughing.

'There's always something going on,' Jerome replied. 'Oh for fuck's sake. What are you going to do, wander the streets coked up? Or drink with me?'

Neither option was particularly attractive, and Lawrence almost laughed as he weighed the two choices up, wishing he had never got himself to this point in the first place. He'd promised Ester he wouldn't be too late. He should have sent her a text ages ago.

'I've gotta get home,' he told Jerome. 'I really do.' And then he glanced across at Rebecca, who was fast asleep, small body curled up, fists clenched, a slight sweat on the pink of her cheek.

If Jerome didn't love her, he should leave. Or she should leave. One of them should go.

But of course he didn't utter those words out loud. It was no business of his. And she was right — he was a man with no moral fibre, so who was he to pass judgement?

Standing at the door, he didn't look back. He just wanted to be out of there, alone under the crisp coolness of the night air, regaining some sense of sanity in a solitary, and very lengthy, walk home.

The next day, as he drove the trailer through the first of the afternoon peak hour, the seediness of the previous evening still clinging to him, he was glad he'd agreed to go to the shack for Hilary.

He and Ester needed a break.

He'd told her he might stay a couple of nights, and she'd said he could do as he pleased, polite and distant.

She'd been awake when he finally made it home, sitting up in bed and reading, or pretending to read. She'd switched off the light as soon as he opened the door.

'Sorry to wake you,' he'd whispered.

She hadn't replied.

And then, an hour later, when he was finally hovering on the edge of true sleep, her alarm went off.

'I thought you were dead.'

He'd had no idea what she was talking about.

'You said you'd be home early. I sent you texts. An embarrassing number of them. I thought someone had bashed you, or you'd been hit by a car, or fallen over dead drunk somewhere. I should have known.'

They'd had this argument before, but this time it was different. There was just one fierce outburst of anger, her face white and pinched as she'd got up and left, heading off to her consulting room without saying goodbye.

He'd called her at lunch time to say he was leaving for the shack, cowardly in his pretence that the argument was over, even trying to tell her about Jerome and Rebecca but wishing he hadn't as soon as he began. And then he stopped, apologising for failing to look at his phone the previous evening.

'I didn't think you'd worry. You know me. That's what I'm like.'

A sadness had settled into Lawrence's life. It was dank and slow in its creep, damp and stale. He was morose at home, his boredom with work and the stillness of middle age seeping through both of their lives. 'Change it,' Ester used to say when their arguments were still capable of moving into an attempt to understand each other. And do what? They were no longer on the same track, and they both knew it. Hers was the high road, and his — without a doubt — the low.

Outside the car, the city made way for large blocks, huge brick houses with steel roller doors to mark out garage from living, flat dry lawns, and perhaps a sad pony or two. A few miles on, the houses thinned even further and there were turf farms, emerald under the late afternoon sun, great rows of sprinklers tick-tick-ticking over each flat stretch of impossible green. By the roadside, horses slowly chewed grass, ears twitching as a car passed, and then they would bend their long, graceful necks and resume grazing.

He should have brought Catherine and Lara with him. They loved the horses. They loved the river. He imagined pulling over, the gravel crunching beneath the tyres, the chill in the air as the three of them waited still, patient, for one of the mares to slowly lift her head again. They would stroke the warmth of her, her breath grassy and hot as she nuzzled close, the harrumph as she shook herself, one hoof stamping, and the girls wide-eyed in delight.

But the back seat was empty, and he was alone.

When he reached the town, he stopped to have a coffee. The mall was cold and deserted, only one café still open.

'Double shot,' he told the woman behind the counter.

She took a huge mug down from the shelf behind her, and he asked if she had a smaller cup, 'you know, normal coffee size.'

Without a word she reached for another, and he watched with some dismay as the coffee came out of the machine, thin, grey, and disappointing, incapable of lifting the haze of tiredness that had settled upon him.

He was back on the road as soon as he could, following it down to the valley that hugged the river, bitumen slicing through the steep rolling slopes of olive-and-blue scrub, until finally he reached the flats as the sky purpled, great streaks of bruising, slashed with crimson and orange, lurid and beautiful.

When Ester had first taken him here, so many years ago, he had thought it was one of the most special places in the world, a secret valley, so close to the city and yet remote. He had never seen an orange farm before — 'orchard,' she'd laughed, 'not farm,' — or known that water so pure still existed. 'You can drink it,' she'd shown him, scooping up handfuls and gulping them down.

Smiling as he remembered, he drove slowly, aware that this was the time when kangaroos could leap out onto the road. They watched him as he drove past, lifting their heads, their soft eyes unblinking, before bounding away into the dusky dark of the bush.

Pulling over, Lawrence called her, the phone ringing and ringing until Lara picked it up.

'Daddy,' she shrieked across the room. 'It's Daddy.'

Catherine took the phone from her, wanting to tell him that Lara had been in trouble at daycare for hiding her lunch. The story was long and complex, broken by Lara's protests at the untruths of her sister.

'Is Mummy there?' he asked again, his voice thin and hollow in the car, the chill of the night settling around him. He wanted to get to the house before it was too dark to see. 'Can you get her for me?'

Lara called. And then Catherine.

And then Lara told him that Mummy was busy.

'Doing what?' he asked, frustrated.

But Catherine had seized the phone now. When was he coming home? Why hadn't she seen him this morning?

In the background, he could hear Ester saying something.

'In a day or so,' he promised Catherine. 'I'll bring you some oranges.'

The last section of the road petered into a dirt track, the bend down to the shack sharp and sudden. He missed it, driving almost as far as Les' farm before he realised.

Turning back, he slowed right down, stopping at every gap in the trees, until he finally saw what he thought was the gate. He searched for the padlock key, his hangover making him truly hopeless, and then, when he thought he had the right one, he stepped out into the now cold evening, the air tight against his skin, astringent in its briskness, the metal of the lock chill against his fingers, only to discover it was unlocked, the gate ready to swing open as soon as he lifted the latch off the pole.

Of course. April was there.

Lawrence looked down to where the lights were on in the house, glad there would be company, and he drove through, the bumper scraping over the grate, the darkness now surrounding him, all last remnants of the day swallowed by the night.

BACK IN THE CITY, Ester looked at the phone. She had listened to the girls talk to Lawrence, and had waved them away when they had held the phone up, telling her that Daddy wanted to speak to her.

It wasn't because she was still angry about that previous evening. She had reached a point of distance that disturbed her. Seeing him asleep that morning, the rotten smell of alcohol and cigarettes clinging to his skin, his face waxen beneath the darkness of stubble, listening to the low rumble of his breathing, she had seen him as someone she no longer knew.

Their lives had changed. They had children, a house — they were older — and yet, somehow, he was still way back there, dragging his feet, kicking up dust as he trailed behind her, bored, sullen, and then running to catch up, apologising, only to do it all again.

She could have taken the phone and talked to him. He would have told her about the drive, how beautiful it was as the night flooded the valley, still trying to pretend that the argument was behind them and the rift that kept widening didn't exist. She would have heard his words, responding with so little warmth or interest that, in the end, he would have tried for a moment to be angry with her. Shifting the blame, like a dirty piece of laundry. Shoving it back and forth between them.

And so she didn't.

At that point in their lives together, she hadn't liked herself all that much, and no doubt Lawrence had felt the same way about himself.

For the first time since she had arrived, April slept well past dawn.

The light that cut between blanket and window was soft, pearly, and she lay there for a moment, lifting one corner so she could see the sky, smooth and pale, as delicate as cotton wool. Against it, the arc of a scribbly gum traced a sure swoop, graceful and lean, and high up in the branches she thought she saw the magpie. Watching her.

She let the blanket fall.

Next to her the bed was empty, the pillow still slightly dented, the smell of cigarettes and skin (warm, like animal hide) — there was always a distinct smell — and she turned her head not wanting to breathe it in.

She closed her eyes, too.

But she was still there.

He had arrived as night had fallen, the darkness smothering the last of the day, and because there were no clouds until much later, it had been cold. She had lit the fire, using the last of the wood, the tang of eucalyptus as the leaves shot up the chimney in sparks, the twigs catching soon after.

As a child, laying the fire had always been her job. Maurie would take her out into the dusk to gather the right kind of wood. 'Dry, dead — nothing green or rotten.' He would kick aside stumps, soft and crumbly, damp and mouldy, loading her arms up with twigs and leaves, while he brought in the heavier logs.

It was like building, she thought.

'Rip the paper sheets in half,' he would instruct. 'Screw them up into a ball — not too tight, not too loose.'

And she would balance the twigs like a tepee — just the right amount of air — before throwing in the match and squealing in delight at the roar and rush, the shooting flames.

Next the larger logs, and there were lessons in how to put them on — where and when — as well as detailed instructions in how to revive the dying embers. Maurie loved to teach.

Last night, she had made a fire of which he would have been proud.

She had run a hot bath after her swim in the river, soaping herself, and washing her hair, letting out the water and refilling it, steam rising, until it had simply become too cold to stay in any longer. And so she had dried herself by that fire, putting on Maurie's old pyjamas and singing — loudly, happily — without even being aware that this was what she was doing. Because it always took time here, but then, when you weren't looking, the rhythm of the empty days seeped into your blood, and you found yourself living at a pace that was right, and the beauty was that you didn't even know how this had happened.

Her voice was loud and clear, running along the edge of a new melody that had been teasing her all afternoon, still not quite strong enough for her to try and trap it, and she had let herself float around it, oblivious to the door opening behind her until she felt a sudden rush of cold air, and he said her name.

She jumped, shrieking loudly as she turned to face him, brandishing a burning stick without even realising she had seized it from the fireplace, only to find that it was Lawrence. Of course it was Lawrence. She had completely forgotten Hilary mentioning that he might be coming up.

As she lay in bed now, she could hear him, his boots on the verandah, and she kept herself perfectly still. He was bringing in wood. The heavy thud of the logs as he dropped them by the door, and then his footsteps again. She didn't want to move, to get up and have to face it all. And so she kept her eyes closed tightly, the blankets pulled up over her head — *foolish, foolish, foolish girl* — while outside the magpie chirruped and warbled, the throaty pitch of its song cutting through the softness of the morning, broken only by the heavy thud of more logs and the clump of his step as he went to fetch another load.

Last night, he had stood by the doorway with his bag and a couple of bottles of wine, the night descending behind him. Handsome Lawrence, and she had dropped the burning stick into the fire as he had smiled ruefully. He was a little under the weather, he had told her — so much so there'd been a moment when he thought he'd never find the turn-off.

Cocking her head like the magpie, she'd assessed the damage he'd done to himself and told him he had a choice. 'It's either abstinence or the full coat of the dog. Just a hair will do you no good. Trust me, I know.'

If it had been a few days earlier, she would have welcomed his arrival. She'd craved distraction, but, strangely, at that moment she'd only wished him away. The peace she'd found was so fragile and so at odds with the jangling heaviness that cloaked him, a state she'd also been in on arrival.

He'd brought food with him too, and she'd been grateful for that, tending to the fire as he'd heated up soup and bread, his hand shaking slightly as he'd offered her a bowl.

Beautiful Lawrence, with his silvery eyes and coal-soot hair. She remembered how they'd all loved him, every woman and half the men. It was a pity he'd never had the talent. You would have made a fortune from him.

He'd told her about the launch and Jerome and Rebecca, and she'd laughed, snorting slightly as she put the soup bowl down. 'She was mad. But you were always so drug-fucked when you were with her that you never saw it. She set fire to two houses she lived in.'

'Why didn't anyone tell me?'

April had shrugged. 'I guess we just took whatever was dished up as normal. That's what you do when you're young.'

He'd shaken his head, stretching out his legs and staring up at the ceiling. 'Why do some of us grow up more easily than others?' And then he'd corrected himself. 'Or more to the point, why does growing up have to involve letting all that go?'

'Maybe it's just that there are times that shine,' she smiled. 'They have a brightness that's hard to let go of.'

She pointed to the bottle of wine, but he held up his hand. 'I think I'd better take the abstinence approach.'

(And so they hadn't even been drunk, the excuse she'd always had ready should the past have been unearthed.)

She poured herself a glass and then put the bottle away, telling him the river would cure him. 'Tomorrow. At dawn. I'll march you down there myself and throw you in. It's brutal but beautiful.'

'Do you remember the lakes?'

She did. She looked away for a moment.

They had been in England, the first brittle bite of winter in the air, diamond frost across the rolling green fields, crunching beneath the soles of her shoes as they made their way back to the pub after a night in a castle.

He'd been the disinherited son of a Lord.

'Anthony?' she asked Lawrence, who didn't remember.

He'd taken them back there after her show, breaking in through a window, his plan a simple one — he wanted to trash every room before dawn. Because he hated his father. And his mother. And his sisters.

And as he threw the first vase to the floor, April had collapsed in giggles.

'Aren't you glad you didn't fly home?' she'd asked Lawrence. 'When will you ever get another chance to trash a castle?'

They'd slipped out well before he'd finished the first floor, the lake silver in the dawn.

'That was the coldest I have ever been,' April said. 'I remember feeling as though someone had seized my heart and my lungs in an ice grip.' She'd touched her chest. 'And ripped them out. I thought I would never breathe again.'

'Would you do it now?' he asked her.

'Trash a castle? Swim in a freezing lake?'

'Either or.'

She would. 'Which is probably tragic.'

'I don't know if I would,' he confessed. 'Which is even more tragic.' And then he smiled. 'Actually, I would. My tragedy is that I try and pretend I wouldn't, but if the opportunity arose (which is unlikely), I would be in there throwing everything to the ground, or leaping in that lake. And then I would try to lie about it the next day.'

She'd laughed at him then. 'Go on.'

'Point me in the direction of the local castle.'

She'd winked. 'Can't help with that. But I can provide you with a river at the end of winter.'

'Brutal but beautiful, I believe.'

'Precisely. Get your gear off. Run down there. And I guarantee you'll get some of that shimmer back. Or at least shake off whatever it is you're dragging around with you.'

Now as she lay in bed, sheets pulled over her head, she heard him come back inside the house, his footfall tentative. All those years ago, when they were young and at the lakes, he had only been with Ester for a few months; it had been easy to pretend that

111

there'd been no real betrayal, just a drunken loss of direction, a quick career down the wrong path, the mistake never mentioned to anyone or talked about by either of them. It might never have happened.

And then, last night, he had taken them back there.

He had gone out onto the verandah, shedding his clothes in the night air, running across the grass, through the avenue of poplars and down the muddy track that led to the river, while she had sat in front of the fire, clutching her glass of wine, suddenly aware that she was standing at the edge of trouble.

'April,' he called her name softly.

'April,' his voice was a little louder as he put his head around the curtain that separated bedroom from living space, letting the morning light into the room.

She was a coward.

Shifting the sheet slightly, she looked out at him, not knowing what to expect now. Because last night, when he had returned from the river, there had been no shimmer, just a momentary bravado, and then a sadness that had shocked her. Wrapping him in the warmth of a blanket, she had watched as he cried.

'I made a mistake,' he told her.

She hadn't known what he had meant.

'I tried to become someone that I'm not.'

She hadn't said a word.

And then he had shifted, wanting only to brush aside that sadness. 'I don't think the swim was meant to do this,' he smiled. 'I'm just tired, and hungover, and no good at taking drugs anymore.'

But as she stood to leave him, he'd pulled her down again, and they kissed, the softness of his lips, the sweetness of the river water, and it had been so long since she'd had good sex, really good sex, that she didn't care.

Someone had once told her that the beauty of sex was the loss of self.

And perhaps that was all they'd wanted. Perhaps it didn't really matter.

Now, as he came over to the bed, she reached her hand out from under the sheet, her skin pale, a long scratch down her wrist from the walk yesterday, the taste of him still there on her fingers.

He lay down next to her, so close that she could see his pores, each dark lash, the line of his mouth, the curl of his hair still damp from a morning swim, and she kissed him again.

It was only four days. Not long when it's held up, so very contained, against the great rush of life on either side, but long enough for Lawrence to believe — just briefly — that he had fallen in love.

The rain had come, washing over the brilliance of early spring, softening it with a grey mist, shaking out the small buds that had begun to appear and leaving them sodden in the dirt.

That first morning, when he had left April asleep and gone down to the river to swim, he had felt the restorative power she had promised he would find, the shine he had failed to touch the previous evening. Alone, his body heavy from sex and lack of sleep, his heart confused and ashamed, he had stood on the bank and looked across to the steep incline of the other side, the scrub silvery against the deep blue-grey of granite.

At his feet, the river was perfectly still. Dark slate, pocked by small islands of white sand, each fringed by rushes. He swam out, the cold fiercer than the previous evening, and he drank in the water in great gasps and gulps, swallowing it as he stared up at the flat grey sky.

He would pack up and go. Make it work with Ester. He and April would never speak of this. He could trust her silence, he knew that.

But then, as he stood on the bank drying himself, he didn't want to go home. Opening his front door, calling out Ester's name, trying to find equilibrium; he didn't think he could do it anymore. The bracing cold of the river, the softness of the morning; he felt as though his heaviness had been lifted. It was beautiful here. And he was at peace.

Climbing back up the bank, he gathered what dry wood he could find, twigs scratching his arms and legs. He would chop some logs for the evening.

Maurie had once tried to teach him how to use an axe, laughing loudly as splinters of bark flew through the air, Lawrence's fury mounting at what he perceived to be some kind of test that he was failing. Hilary had watched from the verandah, arms folded, a slight smile on her face, until eventually she had spoken, her voice soft but clear: 'You know, you don't have to agree to be his amusement. There's plenty of wood already chopped.'

He had put the axe down, grinning at Maurie, the release so quick and easy he couldn't believe he had failed to see it for himself.

Later that day, as April lit the fire, she asked him whether he was going to go home that evening. Neither of them had touched on what was happening; they had been so careful to not even glance in the direction of what lay before and behind them that her question almost made him jump.

'I wasn't intending to.' He looked at her for affirmation that he was welcome to stay, but she refused to give it.

The twigs and leaves blazed, brightening the dullness of the room, and she stood, stepping back from the heat.

He had to speak.

'I would like to stay for a few days.'

Her eyes widened.

'But it doesn't have to be like it's been,' he hastened to add.

'I just need a bit of time. You can keep trying to write, and I'll do the painting Hilary wanted done, I'll pack up the stuff.' He smiled. 'You can pretend I'm not here.'

'Ha.' Her laugh when it came was loud, and she shook her head, wiping at her eyes, the smoke stinging the corners. 'What's that Oscar Wilde quote about losing your parents?'

He couldn't remember.

'Losing one is misfortune, both is carelessness? Falling for your sister's partner once may be misfortune?' She rolled her eyes. 'I believe we are well and truly in the land of carelessness.'

He watched as she turned her back to him, carefully placing some of the larger logs on the fire before she closed the door, leaving the flue still open. She didn't know where to sit, he could see that, and he shifted over so that there was plenty of space, so she didn't have to be too close.

'Besides,' and she looked out at the soft mist of rain, 'it's hardly painting weather.'

It was unlike April to be direct. In all the years he had known her, she had danced around and at the edge of every matter of substance, a quality that could be both charming and irritating. But she was different now. There was a stillness to her, a calm he had never seen.

'I have a suggestion,' he eventually said.

She reached for her tobacco, the smell of caramel as she began to roll a cigarette, the paper thin and delicate, eyes intent on the task.

'We are so deep in the land of carelessness, let's stay here, just for a few days. There's nothing we can do to make it any worse, so let's allow ourselves to enjoy it. To pretend that nothing else exists, and just be bad, roll around in it, and not even attempt to deal with any of the ramifications. Just be.' Oh god. He looked across at her, still staring at the cigarette paper in her lap, surprising himself with how strong the plea was, the need. Because they were the bad ones. The ones who hadn't grown up. Although he had tried — all that time in Paris, with the job and the twins, and all that time since, pretending that he was a responsible man when, pathetic as it was, he didn't want any of that. Or maybe he just had to turn his back on it briefly, be as bad as he knew how, to be able to willingly become the man he should be. He didn't know. He just wasn't ready to go home. Not yet.

He remembered that night at the lakes, how different it had been. Both of them drunk, all the while knowing that this was not what he wanted. He had woken the next morning and crept out of her bed, his flight leaving from London that afternoon. The note he had left had been curt — a simple 'See you soon, Lx' — and he was gone, every part of him craving the calm of Ester.

But this time, he hadn't been drunk.

This time, he wanted to stay.

After three days, the rain stopped.

They hadn't left the shack. In the morning light, April saw the kicked-back bedsheets, their clothes on the floor, the dishes in the sink, and she covered her eyes with her arm. She smelt of him. His skin, his tongue, the bristles on his chin, the grasp of his palms, his thighs, he was all over her.

She was going for a walk. He should pack up the trailer.

She suddenly felt as though she had been sinking with a drowning man, and she was exhausted.

She took herself upriver, cutting through the scrub to a small bridge to the other side. She wanted to climb out of the valley. The incline was steep and slippery, and she found herself scrambling, hauling herself up with her hands. Above, the sky had cleared, a watery wash of blue, last tufts of clouds speeding south, and the air was rich with mud and mulch and twigs.

Finally, she emerged on the dirt road that looked down over the river that curled below her, silty with days of rain. Beyond that, she could see the shack, the strange pitched roof that Maurie had constructed, a shape that seemed impossible, and yet had a beauty to its rise and fall. She could see the poplars, a delicate line of feathery branches, jewelled with new spring leaves, and, at the end of the grove, Lawrence loading up the trailer.

She looked away.

The shame made her feel ill.

As the day became hotter, she followed the road that led to the valley, a good ten kilometres that would take her downriver from home. There was no sound but the scrunch of her boots on the gravel, a beat that kept time with her breathing, and occasionally, an echo of a call from somewhere far away.

High overhead an eagle followed her, floating on the wind, disappearing and then arcing up into the sky again. She watched its flight, the great breadth of its wingspan a beauty to behold.

Finally, as the sun began to shift further to the south, April reached the end of the road. She was back at Les' orchard.

She could see him in his shed, fixing machinery, and she walked towards him, exhausted now.

'Still here?' he looked up at her, a smear of grease across his chin.

She nodded.

'Hazel made some marmalade she wanted to give your mother. Was going to bring it over this afternoon.'

April looked up to the house. 'Is she there now?'

He nodded.

The house was dim, the wood-fire stove burning, everything quiet. She knocked and called out, until eventually Hazel came around the side. She'd been feeding the chooks.

'Cup of tea?' she offered, and April said that yes, she'd love one.

The walk had been longer than she'd expected. She was buggered.

'You're looking a bit worse for wear,' Hazel agreed, and April felt ashamed. 'Sit yourself down and I'll run you home.'

They talked briefly, mainly about Hilary, and then Hazel asked her how Ester and that handsome husband of hers were.

He was here, April said. Clearing out furniture. She hoped she didn't blush.

'Did he bring the girls?'

April shook her head.

'They're a handful, those two,' Hazel smiled. 'They look the spitting image of you when you were their age. I remember when your dad first bought you here. Hard to believe you were the same age they are now.'

April smiled weakly.

It was darkening on the drive home, the last of the sunlight smeared across the southern ridge. It would be cold tonight, April thought, and she looked out the window, through the fine film of dust, the scrub a soft blur as the ute bounced over the potholes and corrugations in the road.

'I'll jump out here,' April told her, 'no need for you to turn in.'

Hazel reminded her to take the marmalade. 'You need to feed yourself up. You're looking peaky.'

She waved goodbye and walked alone up the track to the house, its lights on, smoke from the chimney, and Lawrence's car with the trailer fully loaded out the front.

'All packed,' he told her. 'I'll leave in the morning.'

That night, as they lay in bed together for the last time, she should have counselled him to keep his silence, to say nothing, to realise this for what it was: a brief escape that they both needed to forget. But she didn't. She thought there was no need.

They didn't have sex.

They just lay side by side, skin on skin, their sleep fitful, the haze between dream and wakefulness thick and smothering, until eventually April got up, the night still heavy outside, the last embers of the fire burnt right down. She opened the flue a little, placing a few of the smaller twigs on top, and watched the flames rise.

She didn't hear Lawrence as he came into the room. He sat next to her, still naked, his skin cold. His face was so familiar and strange, and as she turned to face him, she began to cry, shushing any attempts of his to talk, not wanting soothing words but instead just to let herself cry for what she had done, the terrible mistake of it all, the sheer folly of having laid waste to so much, all of her now out on a limb, miles from safety, alone with her shame.

Lawrence had Hilary's checklist in his hand. The trunk, a cupboard, an easel, a box of crockery, and a crate of books. There wasn't all that much. The rest could just go with the house, she'd told him.

WIWO, April had said.

He'd looked at her quizzically.

'Walk In Walk Out,' she'd explained.

He shook his head.

'I love a real-estate acronym.'

She'd gone for a swim, running down to the river in just a towel, jumping in with a whoop that echoed out across to the cliff and all the way back up to the house. He heard her, the loud throatiness of her scream, and then she was running back across the stretch of lawn and straight under a hot shower in the bathhouse.

He was almost fooled by her spirits, by the way she sassed past him without a stitch of clothing, by the clothes she chose — a short denim pinafore, an old Sherbert T-shirt, and a bright-green cardigan (cute and cheerful to an extreme) — and by the way she told him it was high time he left. She needed to get on with her writing.

'Not that any was happening, but there's plenty of fuel for a tortured love song or two now,' and she'd raised an eyebrow.

He'd kissed her on both cheeks, on the tip of her nose, and on her forehead.

'Well,' she'd said, stepping back from his embrace. 'What can I say? Drive carefully? See you back in town?'

With his hand on her arm, he tried to draw her close, but she pushed him away, shaking her head, and there was something harsh in her smile; it was a little too bright.

Out on the dirt road, the trailer jarred and banged behind him, a loud clanging that accompanied him all the way to where the dirt levelled into flat grey bitumen winding along the river flats, past the first houses in the valley, the horses again, and it was so very strange to be re-entering the world. It had only been four days, but when he caught sight of himself in the rear-vision mirror, still unshaven, eyes hooded from lack of sleep, a nick on his bottom lip from where April had bitten him, it was the face of a man he didn't know. His phone beeped several times, messages coming up on the screen. Two from home, both from the girls, one from Hilary with further instructions just in case she caught him before he was out of range, one from Jim asking him out for a drink, and another from a client wanting research into what women want from a mascara. The crowd of demands depressed him. He pulled over to the side of the road and sent a text to Ester — *On my way, see you soon* — and then turned his phone off.

On the outskirts of town, he considered a coffee, but the memory of his last stop those few days ago made him change his mind. He would just keep driving. He needed to get home.

Home.

The realisation of where he was headed sank in.

He saw other cars, and people shopping, and children and prams, and families squabbling, and he wound the window up, wanting to block it all out. The petrol gauge was low, and he pulled over at a service station.

There, he noticed that his hands were shaking. Trying to still himself, he breathed in deeply, twisting the plain gold ring on his finger before taking the keys out of the ignition.

He and Ester hadn't believed in marriage. Sometimes late at night, in the early days of love, they would propose to each other, elaborate declarations of love and fidelity. He had never lived with anyone before, a fact that made him slightly ashamed. In her, he saw the possibility for stability, calm, maturity — states of being that he felt he should embrace at this stage of life. But it didn't have to entail marriage. Neither of them had ever really wanted that. And then, when he was offered the job in Paris, he was told it would be much easier for her to come if they were husband and wife.

They had made their vows before a marriage celebrant, words they'd chosen from the various options on display in plastic folders, each of them trying to find one that came as close as possible to how they saw themselves and the occasion. Nothing was quite right.

They'd been told they could write their own vows, but in the end they didn't. Nor did they have any photos of the celebration itself. It wasn't that kind of wedding.

Wearing a red wool dress with a plain square neckline, her dark hair tied back in a simple ponytail, Ester had been as she always was — elegant, beautiful, cool, and calm.

'I love you,' he had whispered to her, moments after the ceremony was over.

'I love you, too.'

The few friends who were there hadn't known. It was just a Sunday lunch, or so they'd been told.

'We weren't sure how to do this,' Lawrence had said in his speech. 'Weddings aren't our thing.'

'Well, don't start making them your thing,' someone had called out.

'We could have just left it at the registry, but that seemed strange. And yet we didn't want all the fuss and the presents, and so we decided to just surprise you.'

Their friends had cheered and whooped as they kissed in the clear sweetness of the day, their small garden home to a party that had been better than they'd expected.

Later, as the afternoon became chill, Micky and Louise suggested they all kick on. Micky was drunk and she stood unsteadily, lurching slightly as she clutched at the table before losing her balance. Two months earlier, she'd made a move on Lawrence. He'd been at a party, Ester had gone home, and they'd been dancing. She'd run her hands up and down his sides, leaning in to kiss him. And he had kissed her back, forgetting, as he was so capable of doing, that those days were over. He had almost gone home with her, but then he'd stopped. The music was too loud, her eyes were pinned, and the sweat on her skin had smelt stale.

That afternoon, as she fell, she pulled everything onto the ground. The shattering of glasses and plates and the crash of cutlery rang like bells, and then, on top of it all, a long stained tablecloth, bringing the lunch to a resounding end. Micky looked around dazed, hoisting herself up as everyone began to laugh.

'Well, you sure know how to clear a table,' Lawrence told her. 'Where to next?'

And then, as they began to argue loudly about an array of choices, he suddenly realised he didn't actually want to go anywhere: he wanted to stay home with Ester.

'My wife and I are not going to join you,' he pronounced to the table, and as Micky threw her napkin at him and booed in disgust, declaring that this was what happened to married couples, he folded his arms.

'Everyone!' There was silence. It was Ester shouting now. 'This is a momentous occasion. And I'm not talking marriage.'

Lawrence had shaken his head, grinning as he did so.

'Lawrence is staying home!' She raised the only unbroken glass and gave out a loud wolf whistle to calls of 'shame, shame' from Micky, who was soon shouted down by cheers from others around the table.

'I should've gone,' he told her later. 'We both should've gone.' He looked at her warily, unsure of her response, and she rolled her eyes.

'I don't want to change,' he protested, and then he'd drawn her close and kissed her. 'You knew what you married. Who I am doesn't mean I love you any less.'

But it wasn't the entire truth. Part of him had wanted to change. He had thought that if he wore the clothes, he would become the man. He really had. And yet it was never going to work. The outfit was ill-fitting, the cloth and cut wrong, and he had always known that. Now here he was, the last vestiges of that suit shed with a fierce desperation, leaving him unsure, so very unsure, of the man that remained beneath.

NOW

As the lunch bell buzzes through the silence of the classroom, the teacher looks up. It was only two years ago that they used to send a student out to ring an actual bell, the brassy clang sometimes rhythmic, sometimes jagged and unsure, depending on who was doing the honours. Now it's electric, rung from the admin office, like a loud fire alarm. It still makes her jump, even when she's been watching the clock at the back of the room and longing for its sound.

'Everybody still now,' she calls out, clapping her hands together.

One of the twins is standing, the other pulling her back down to sit.

Outside, it's still raining, wet leaves stuck like scraps of sodden paper to the window, the sky a blank, even grey. The playground is deserted, and pools of muddy water gather in the cracks and dips in the bitumen. C playground is a complete mudbath, and, beyond that, the vegetable garden is bent low from the morning downpour.

Inside, children's raincoats and gumboots are stacked in a riot of bright plastic, tumbling over each other in the corner, and the room smells musty, like wet wool and dirt.

'I don't think anyone's going outside today,' the teacher tells them. Both the twins have their hands up, and are only just managing to stay in their seats.

'Can we get the lunches?' one asks.

Strictly speaking, she hadn't yet given either of them permission to talk, but she relents, knowing she's been tough on them this morning, and not because she doesn't like them, but because they chatter endlessly.

She nods, and it's Catherine, she thinks, who runs to get the washing basket they use to collect the canteen lunches, slowing down as she sees she's being observed.

'Carefully,' the teacher reminds her, the well-worn warning no doubt forgotten as soon as they leave the classroom.

ACROSS TOWN, HILARY sits in her car, hands on the steering wheel.

The key is in the ignition, but she has not yet turned it all the way. Instead, she stares at the pearling drops of rain on the windscreen, each one clinging, poised to slide away, perfectly formed, the entire world held in its translucent beauty. Winding down the window slowly, she reaches out to touch one, chill on the tip of her finger, impossible to hold.

Her head aches. Her vision bends and warps. This is a bad morning.

On the radio, a woman talks about reconciliation and forgiveness, her voice rich and deep, soothing, as she speaks of work she has done with trauma victims, studies with people in countries such as Rwanda.

'But sometimes forgiveness isn't enough.' The announcer speaks in brisk, friendly tones. 'How do you learn to forget?'

'Ah yes,' the woman laughs. 'There is forgetting as well. But the point I am making is that true forgiveness changes even the memory of the event. There is no longer anger attached to the recollection.'

Hilary turns the radio off. Attempts to simplify human behaviour, to rub it smooth, have always irritated her. But she had listened for longer than she normally would have because this is her anxiety, the frayed edge that threatens to unpick her plans. The lack of reconciliation between Ester and April makes her anxious, and it kicks her, hard, on these bad days. It is so easy from the outside, from the edge of a life, to see the mistakes people make and why — to see and understand. But from the midst it is different, and she knows that both her daughters are there, right in the middle, too close still to reflect.

She looks across to the blank face of Henry's apartment building, the bricks washed in the rain, each of the windows the same and yet different: unadorned; grey curtains; crumpled venetians; a torn blind.

She wonders what made Henry turn to heroin — whether it was simply the foolish choice of someone young who wanted to experiment, or whether there was a deeper canker, a grit that had scratched and rubbed and needed to be soothed. She knew very little about him, really. His family were Queensland country people who had no understanding of who he was. 'Maybe I was adopted,' he'd said, a fantasy so many people hold at some stage of their life. 'They probably regret their choice,' he'd added, and then he'd slid away from talking about himself, turning to the music they were listening to, or the shadow of a branch on the window, remaining as private as ever.

Out the front of his building are two frangipani trees. Strange that she has never really noticed them before. The branches are bare; silvery knots streaked with rain arch over the entrance stairway, like a puzzle. Closing her eyes, she tries to recall the fragrant milkiness of a flower, peachy petals in her hands, star-like, scattered over summer pavements, bruised in the shiny sunlight.

LAWRENCE CLOSES HIS EYES. He once did a meditation course with Ester, and, although he made fun of it at every opportunity he got, he still tries to find that moment of absence he had reached. He remembers it. They were all in rows, listening to a young nun in saffron robes. She glowed with happiness. She joked and laughed as she talked to them, and around him, middle-aged women with long blonde hair wrote notes in floral cloth-covered notebooks, their silver bangles jangling as they tried to transcribe each of her words of wisdom. He hated it. But when the time came to meditate, he achieved a total absence of thought that he recalls with longing.

He has never found it since.

He has Hilary to phone back, Edmund to deal with, and then, ultimately, there is Paul, the editor. All three jostle, shove, and lay claim to his mind, a space that refuses to empty, as the rain beats against the tin walls and roof of his room.

And so he gives up, opening his eyes to the gloom as his phone rings again, Paul's number appearing on the screen. He is out of the meeting and needs the polls ASAP.

'This hitch — is it fixed?' he asks.

Lawrence cuts over him, his voice soothing, fast, assured. He is a practiced liar, a man who moulds the world around him into changing shapes to suit his need. The problem doesn't look like it's going to be remedied as soon as he'd like. He realises this throws them out, and he couldn't be more apologetic, but it's out of his control. As Paul would know, nothing like this has ever happened in all their history together, and he'll make sure it doesn't happen again. He's also more than willing to work together in whatever way they can to — and here he is cut off.

'There's been a lot of discussions about the cost of the polls,' Paul tells him. 'I've been behind you as much as I can. I know the value of what you do. But those new robo polls, they're cheap, and the amount of people you can interview is unbelievable. That's the way management wants to go. I was hoping we could hold off for longer but …' Paul sighs. 'We've got a slip-up like this, and it's going to be tough. I can't stem the tide, mate. Not after this.'

'Jesus.' Lawrence stares at the ceiling. 'You know how inaccurate they are. People don't respond to a recording in the same way as they do to a person.'

Paul is silent.

'Let's at least talk about this face to face.'

'Sure,' Paul replies. 'I'm flat out at the moment, but when I surface —'

Lawrence stops him. 'Is my contract being terminated? Officially?' He can hear the silence on the other end of the line.

'That's the way it's looking,' Paul eventually tells him. 'There was only this and one more to go before we renewed — and with the data slip-up, I don't think they're going to be willing to pay you out. I probably shouldn't be telling you this. Joel's putting it all in a letter.'

His voice is hushed now, difficult to hear above the sound of the rain. Lawrence just stares at the wall. This is his livelihood. But he can't say that. To beg, to be needy — he knows it wouldn't help. Normally, he'd have the wherewithal to try to talk Paul out of the decision, to guarantee him that if he gives the robo polls a try he'll soon find that their inaccuracy will only be an embarrassment. He knows, he's seen them in action: the automated calls that ask a series of questions in a robotic voice, directing respondents (or those that don't hang up, at least) to a very limited range of answers.

He shakes his head. 'I thought our years together would at least have given me the opportunity to come in and make my case.' His words trail off. Does he really have any kind of case to make?

And then, as he opens the email from Edmund that has appeared on his computer screen, he realises it is only going to get worse.

At home, Ester has the radio on, a low hum behind her in the kitchen, and she turns it down as she hears the word therapy mentioned, and then searches through the fridge, taking out dinner leftovers for lunch.

The rain is loud in this part of the house. She glances outside, thinking it must be getting heavier again, but it has settled, monotonous in its constancy.

Sitting at the bench, absentmindedly picking through cold pasta, Ester stares out the window, her stillness at odds with her mounting nerves at the thought of this evening's dinner.

'I am too old to be getting date jitters,' she tells herself, speaking out loud because this is what she does on the days she works at home alone. When Otto is here, he gets the benefit of her conversation; when he isn't, it's the walls and doors that have to listen.

She has booked herself a telephone appointment with her own therapist, and she is due to call in ten minutes. Because she likes to be organised, Ester has written down her fears. She glances at the list now, throwing it in the bin moments later.

Sex. That's all it comes down to really.

It's been so bloody long since she's had sex.

And even longer since she's had sex with anyone other than Lawrence.

Biting her lip, Ester stares up at the ceiling.

Gone are the days when she would get rotten drunk before

taking someone home for the first time, the alcohol giving her enough courage to initiate or respond.

'Oh good God,' she says out loud, pushing her plate away, unable to eat any more.

Standing in front of her own reflection, she tries to draw herself a little taller, to look composed, and then she gives up, shaking her head and letting out a shrill scream to banish the nerves, just as the telephone rings.

It's Victoria.

They never waste any time before they get down to business. Therapist to therapist.

'It's sex,' Ester tells her. 'I'm terrified.'

'Of what?' Victoria asks.

Oh God, Ester thinks. 'Everything,' she says. 'Being naked, being a disappointment, that I won't know how to do it anymore, I'll fuck it up — excuse the pun — I'll misread the situation, I'll have to be intimate with someone again. Everything, everything, everything.' And then she laughs. 'I can't believe I'm saying all this. I sound like a sixteen-year-old.'

'It's perfectly understandable to be nervous,' Victoria replies. 'But you also need to realise there's no need to rush into anything that makes you feel uncomfortable. You can take your time with this.'

'But I'm excited, too,' Ester interrupts. 'I feel happy.'

She looks around the room as she says those words — at the school notes on the fridge, the pile of washing in the corner, the clothes on the rack next to the heater, and, outside, the rain, still coming down. The joy she feels, the fizz that dances over the surface of this sheer ordinariness, makes her smile. It's so long since she's felt such a spark.

'It's been so hard,' she says. 'But I feel as though there's a shift. At last. And I don't think it's just linked to this — to meeting someone I might like. I think it was happening anyway. It's good.'

'That's wonderful,' Victoria tells her.

'It is,' Ester smiles.

'Have you thought any further about whether you're ready to make changes in relation to April?'

Ester looks at herself in the window opposite, phone in one hand. She shakes her head slowly, and when she speaks, her voice is soft, her sentiment uncertain.

'I miss her, or I miss the idea of what family was, but when I think about letting her into my life again, I'm terrified.'

'But you still feel this is the place you'd like to reach — a place of reconciliation?'

'I suppose so,' Ester replies. 'But I'm not sure whether this is because I think I should reach that place, or because I genuinely want to.' She looks down at her hand, resting on the kitchen bench: long fingers like her father's, her olive skin pale, her nails always kept short. They have similar hands, she and April, but in the rest of her appearance, April takes after Hilary: fine and delicate, light and wiry, a body that never carries weight, and that sparks and flies and cracks and shimmers. She doesn't want to talk about April today. She doesn't want to think about her.

'You know,' she says to Victoria, 'I'd rather move on. I don't want this session to be about April.'

'Why?' Victoria asks.

'Because I don't want April in my head today. I don't want to go out this evening, to try and trust again, thinking about her.' She is surprised at the anger in her voice as she speaks, and she apologises before asking Victoria if they can talk about Lindsay for a moment.

'The client I told you about last week. The one with panic attacks. I was trying to locate a group session for meditation and relaxation techniques, somewhere local. She's willing to try this.'

Victoria listens, letting Ester jump from the personal to the need for professional assistance, although Ester knows she will want to take her back there soon, if not during this session, then at the next.

As she writes down a couple of names in her book, possible places for Lindsay to go, the phone beeps with another call, and she ignores it, knowing it won't be a patient (they only have her mobile number) or Steven (who also doesn't have her home number). It will probably be a poll, she realises with a grimace. Worse still, one of those new robo ones.

Outside, the rain continues, easing momentarily into a light mist, soft grey against the dull sky, sliding down the glass, the world outside a blur, and Ester listens to Victoria as she tells her about a similar case she had some months earlier, and approaches that helped.

APRIL IS THE ONE who gets the call from the school. Catherine appears to have sprained her ankle. The girls say they are with their father this week, but he's not answering, nor is their mother, and April is named as the second emergency contact.

They are in the sick bay when she arrives. Lara is the one with her foot up; Catherine is sitting by her side, looking suitably concerned.

'Are you all right?' April asks, kissing both girls, and then, holding Lara's chin in one hand, she looks straight at her. Something is up.

'I twisted it,' Lara tells her, pointing to an ankle that looks remarkably unswollen. 'It hurts to walk.'

'I'll take them both with me,' April says. 'It's almost the end of the day.'

The administration woman glances at the clock. Her only response is to pass April a note, which she completes.

As they head out into the hall, it's Catherine who is limping, Lara who is supporting her.

'Have you got your raincoats?' April asks.

'They're in the classroom,' Catherine tells her. 'Do you want me to run and get them?'

April glances from one to the other, shaking her head. 'Are you two scamming?'

'No!' they protest in unison.

She looks out across the deserted playground. Rain drips from the basketball hoops, a halo of silver, and the bitumen shines, wet and slippery smooth, like a sheet of satin. The roots from the Moreton Bay figs lift up great cracks in the surface, elephantine as they snake away from the smooth trunk of those giant trees, the only shelter from the downpour.

'Okay,' April tells them both, 'give me your bags. Catherine, you help Lara, or Lara, you help Catherine. We'll stop at the trees, and then my car is out the front.'

Of course they end up running.

'It's not that bad,' Lara says, pointing to Catherine's ankle.

'Well, that's excellent news,' April replies, winking at them. 'So no need for X-rays?'

Lara considers the offer for a moment. She doesn't mind a trip to hospital.

'Could we go to your house instead?'

April glances in the rear-vision mirror at them. 'Do you know where your dad is?'

They shrug in unison.

She leaves a message for him on his mobile and on his work phone, and then she tells them they are going to her place — 'for a feast'.

'What of?' Catherine wants to know.

'We'll see when we get there.'

It has been so long, and April starts to sing as she drives, silly made-up songs that slip and slide, until both the girls are giggling, and outside the rain drives down, the wipers going back and forth, back and forth, the demister loud, all of their voices rising and falling in unison as they skip from one song to the next with no need to name the tune.

THREE YEARS EARLIER

IT WASN'T LONG BEFORE Lawrence began to wonder whether he had gone temporarily insane.

Sleeping alone in his newly rented office, he couldn't let his mind alight for too long on any of his actions or words over the past week. Like hot coals, everything he had said and done was spread out before him — incendiary, molten, terrifying to witness.

He had a sleeping bag on the couch, the vinyl slippery and sweaty. In the middle of the night, he slid onto the floor, dragging a glass of water down with him and waking with a start from a sleep that had only ever hovered on the edge of any depth. Cold and wet, he sat up, back against the tin wall, which had now come to remind him of a prison cell, and the hollow inside him was vast.

'I want to go home,' he said to no one.

He stood, clutching the vinyl around him, and looked out the single window behind his desk to the emptiness of the street. Across the road, there was a light in the café, and inside he could see Leon, who lived upstairs, reading the paper. He ran the place alone, and lived by himself, his wife long dead. When he heard Lawrence was having 'home problems', he said he could use his shower in the morning.

'No worries by me,' he grunted each time Lawrence came

down the stairs and thanked him. 'You sort out soon.' He nodded when he said this, his eyes on Lawrence, an old man who knew the importance of a resolution.

But when all was burnt to char, there was no rebuilding, no return, no way home. Just waste, waste that Lawrence could never speak of, and shame that gripped his heart and his tongue, clammy and cold.

If it had been insanity — and who knows what insanity looks like or how it speaks — then he had been released from its clutches the moment he told April of his confession to Ester.

'Oh God,' was all she'd said. 'You don't love me. Why would you think that? Why would you say it?'

It was as though she'd pulled out a brick from the bottom of a pile, causing everything to tumble before his eyes. How could he have believed in the structure when it was so very flimsy?

The night before, he'd been bold. He'd put the girls to bed, and come back to the kitchen, where Ester sat, a half-finished bottle of red on the table in front of her, the grey-green of her eyes cool as she appraised him. She was the one who spoke first, her words the careful words of a therapist, all her solicitude useless in the face of the onslaught he was about to deliver, but she didn't know that. How could she?

'I feel we need to talk.'

'We do,' he agreed.

'I haven't been happy.' She looked across at him, about to continue, but he cut over her, his words coming out in a rush.

'I know,' he said. 'This isn't us. Or it's not me. I'm so glad you don't want it either —'

Her hand, which had been resting around the stem of her glass, withdrew. He wasn't observant enough to slow down, to let her take the lead. Exhausted and confused and afflicted by temporary insanity, he kept speaking, the words of a madman tripping over each other as he said he'd come to a realisation when he was at the river. He had loved her, oh how he had loved her, but they weren't right for each other. He knew that, and she knew that. He loved April. He shook his head with the wonder of it. Ester would be so much happier with someone else, someone who was more like her, and he too would be happier. They were alike, he and April. They were of the same spirit. It could work, he had even said. They could build a new structure, a different kind of family. It would be all right.

And there, at the edge of the precipice, he had foolishly failed to realise that the fall was calamitous. In those moments, she had been silent, confused, floundering, and then all the horror of his confession appeared to fill her, and she had pushed back her chair and rushed to the sink, where she had vomited.

Each morning, Lawrence woke wondering where he was. He opened his eyes to the corrugated tin, chalky grey, and the silence of his near-empty room. Sometimes he reached for Ester, certain that if he stretched a little further he would feel the smooth curve of her hip, and he would be able to curl in close to the place he now wanted to return to: one arm draped around her waist, breathing in the sweet lavender of her hair, the richness of her skin.

And if he stayed perfectly still, completely quiet, he might just will their footsteps, Catherine and Lara, both of them running down the hall, one skidding along the rug, followed by the slam of cupboard doors, the scrape of a stool along the ground. One pulling down every cereal packet from the cupboard, the other taking out bowls, glasses, spoons, milk, sometimes closing the fridge door behind her, sometimes not. And then he would shuffle into the kitchen, eyes still bleary from sleep, hoping his pyjama bottoms were tied up properly, telling them it was the weekend, a time for all sane people to 'sleep, sleeeeep little ones, go to sleeeeeeep, tick tock, tick tock' as he swung an imaginary chain in front of them, trying to hypnotise them, until one or the other obliged and pretended to collapse into a deep enchanted slumber, right there on the floor.

April was his only visitor in that first week.

She looked as bad as he felt.

'You fucked up,' she shouted at him, and she hit him, over and over again. 'It was a mistake. You should never have said anything.'

And he had nodded. Because she was right.

She looked around his room. 'How long have you been here?'

He told her.

She had cried. 'It's not just your life that's fucked up. It's mine, too.'

He pulled out a seat for her, letting her speak because it was a relief to hear someone else's troubles, even those so closely linked to his own, and it was a relief to see her, to see anyone. As she rolled them each a cigarette, he offered her a drink, which she refused at first, but then changed her mind about, pouring the whisky into a glass, the fire on the throat nowhere near enough to compensate for the heaviness in the pit of the stomach.

Ester hadn't spoken to either of them since he'd left.

'I need to see the girls,' he told April.

And he did. The ache was visceral.

'Have you called her?'

He shook his head. He had wanted to, lifting the phone to dial so often, but each time he had stopped, scraped bare by the knowledge of what he'd done.

'I'm sure she won't stop you.'

'I just feel so ashamed.'

And April stood up then, and told him she had to go.

It was two weeks before Hilary came to see him.

She was at the door when he returned from his morning coffee, and he almost went back around the corner, wanting to hide away until she was gone.

'Will you come in?' he offered, and she shook her head.

She had known for more than a fortnight. 'When Ester told me, I wanted to come around and set fire to you.' Her eyes were on his, harsh blue. 'I hated you for what you'd done to my girls. Imagine,' she said, 'if it were Catherine and Lara. Imagine.'

He could only look at the ground.

'I was incensed. I have never been so angry,' and she shook her head, wiping at the sting of a tear in the corner of her eye. 'Don't,' she said as he reached for her. 'I've been waking up most nights, imagining telling you how I felt. There were times when I thought I would drive around here at midnight, and pour it all out on you. All my rage. But I have to concentrate on helping my girls. That's what I needed to tell you. That's all I wanted to say.'

She looked straight at him, her fine-boned face fierce and sure, and then she nodded once, and turned and left, her walk brisk and erect, her back to him as he watched her go, alone in his doorway.

That night, he drove back to where he used to live, the place he still thought of as home although he knew he had no hope of ever returning. He sat in the car, two doors down, on the opposite side of the road. Inside the lights were on, but the curtains were drawn.

He could walk down the path now and open the door — he still had his key.

It was all a mistake, he would tell her. A brief loss of his mind. Surely she had to understand and forgive, surely this was what she dealt with daily — the mess we are all capable of, the possibility of an eruption always just beneath the skin? If she were her own client, wouldn't she suggest repair?

He imagined himself standing before her in the hallway,

uttering those words, laying himself bare, the eloquence he was capable of his to use, words unspooling like a ribbon to draw them both together again. And the vision was so strong, he let himself be carried by it, opening the car door without thinking, walking straight to the gate, past the frangipani he had planted when they first moved in, home again, key in his hand.

She had changed the locks.

It took him some moments before he realised this, the metal not slotting into the grooves, nothing fitting, and when the realisation had sunk in, he hammered on the door with his fists, a parody of a broken man, locked out of his own home, calling her name.

It was Catherine who opened the door, Lara right behind her.

'Daddy,' she screamed.

He knelt down low, arms wrapped around them, determined not to cry.

Ester stood in the hall, right behind them, back against the wall, eyes fixed on the ceiling.

'Can I take them with me?' he asked.

She nodded.

'We need to talk,' he said.

She nodded again.

When she eventually spoke it was to tell the girls that they were going to have dinner with their father, 'get your shoes on,' she said, waiting until they had run down the hall before turning to face him. 'Bring them back by nine,' she instructed.

He opened his mouth to speak, but she silenced him.

'Not now.' Her tone was curt. 'I will text you and set up a time. But I don't want to talk to you now.'

IN THE FIRST WEEK, Ester woke each night to find she had been crying in her sleep. She would sit up, the pillow damp, the silence of the house so suffocating that she was afraid of not being able to breathe.

It was just a bad dream, she would tell herself. But it wasn't.

He had fucked April, and he had gone.

She took everything he owned and put it in the garage.

'I'd like to set a match to it all,' she told her friend, Sophia.

Sophia had never really liked Lawrence, which was why Ester sought out her company in those first few weeks. She avoided most of her other friends, particularly those who would try to reason with her, or, worse still, might let her know they had seen Lawrence. Sophia was safe. She had worked with Lawrence briefly when she'd been between jobs, which she frequently was. Sophia was sullen and moody, according to Lawrence. She was rude to clients. He'd told her there wasn't enough work to keep her on, and she'd been furious, coming round to their house one night and declaring that Lawrence was a smooth-talking asshole, a nasty liar. She'd stood in the doorway, her long black hair framing her pale face, her voice loud, her skin and her breath reeking of booze.

'Look at you,' she'd said. 'In your comfortable life, not giving a shit about anyone but yourself. You used to be an artist.'

And so they hadn't seen her for a long time after that, but

when Ester bumped into her outside the local café, she'd asked her if she wanted to have a coffee.

'You were right,' she said. 'He *was* a smooth-talking asshole.'

And all that she'd once found repellent in Sophia — her dark intensity, her simmering anger, her snide remarks about everyone they knew — became attractive.

Sophia had been a dancer and a choreographer who'd never quite made it. She had a teenage son, who spent all his time locked in his room on the computer. She had very few friends. She came to visit frequently, happy to drink Ester's wine and voice her disgust at everyone and everything.

Ester showed her the pile of Lawrence's clothes and books in the garage.

'You should burn them,' Sophia encouraged her. 'Here, I'll help you.' She stepped forward, slightly unsteady in her high-heeled black leather boots, and began to pour the remains of the bottle of white wine she was holding over the lot. She took her cigarette out of her mouth and threw it on top.

Nothing happened.

She was about to bend down with her lighter when Ester stopped her. She scooped the clothes up in her arms, the smell of wine and Lawrence and her own tears pressed close as she told Sophia to just leave her alone. 'This is mine,' she said. 'I'll get rid of it in the way I want to.'

They were both drunk.

Sophia glared at her. 'You were always alike,' she said. 'Both of you thought you were better than everyone else. You deserved each other. And now look at you. All alone and clutching the clothes of a bastard who fucked your sister.'

That night Ester went to April's, barging through the door, sweeping everything onto the floor, trying to pull curtains off the railings, ripping pictures from the walls.

'Why can't I trash your life the way you trash mine?' she shouted.

And then, as April tried to contain her, to hold her, the fury of her anger so pure she could not bear to be touched, she pushed her sister away and told her she never wanted to see her again. Ever.

The next morning, Ester booked an appointment with Victoria.

Each day she called, oscillating between rage and sorrow, see-sawing up and down and up and down until, on the tenth day, Victoria stopped her.

It was enough. You could only burn out of control for so long. *Turn down the oxygen*, Victoria said. *Let's start focusing on the practical.*

The clipped directness of Victoria's tone silenced Ester, her words of fury and self-pity halted before she had a chance to utter them.

'Of course, you've been angry,' Victoria continued, her tone smooth, not dissimilar to the modulation Ester would use when she wanted to offer firm, detached sympathy laced with the implicit instruction that it was time to take those first steps in a different direction. 'But is that anger achieving anything other than very brief momentary relief?'

'No.' Ester sounded like a child. 'But it's bloody good.'

'There were times when you spoke to me about a desire to change your relationship with Lawrence. I'm sure you didn't want it to be changed in this way, but there's no reason why you can't take some control of the situation, instead of letting it control you.'

And so began the many sessions that Ester liked to term her 'lessons in how to talk to her husband'. There were even practice attempts, with Victoria pretending to be Lawrence while delivering techniques Ester could use to stay calm as they tried to negotiate all that needed to be divvied up: bank accounts, the house, time with the girls, means of communicating in the future, even the redrafting of wills. The business of dismantling a marriage was like the business of organising a funeral, a distraction for which she could be grateful.

And so she made lists, pages and pages of them, all saved in a file she labelled 'the end'. What she didn't tell Victoria was that she also saved letters in this file, long missives in which she let her anger off the leash again, sometimes her sorrow as well, correspondence addressed to both Lawrence and April, never to be sent.

She also didn't speak of the dreams she had.

She had loved him once, and it was to this love that she returned in her sleep. There was no conversation, just the deep slate of his eyes on her, his mouth warm and alive, his skin, the sensation of being wrapped in another. It was like she had submerged herself, and the sweetness of it was like a drug, a haze that she did not want to emerge from. But she did. She always did. Waking, gasping for air, the sorrow right there in her ribs, separating the cage that encased her, pulling her apart.

Sometimes she did not know if the heaviness of the loss would ever lighten.

'It will,' Victoria assured her, leading her back to the practicalities.

Finally, Ester was ready to talk with him.

As she dressed herself that morning, she remembered the care with which she would choose her clothes when they'd first started seeing each other, the shiny glitter of knowing he was hers, the desire to just take him home and get him into bed, and afterwards to lie there, the silkiness of his skin, the slow roll of their talk, all of her a-sparkle with him.

So long ago.

And so sullied now.

She brushed her hair, and told herself to be brave.

Courage, Maurie used to tell her when she was in a panic about having to give a speech at school, or present her work for a crit. 'You have far more strength than you ever give yourself credit for.'

It was not that she feared he would argue with her about all they needed to discuss. He was ashamed, and would agree to what she wanted. It was the threat of falling apart again — the fierceness of her anger, the blackness of her sorrow still too present.

And so she walked to the café she had chosen, wanting a public place to meet, somewhere she was less likely to shatter. She had her list in her bag, carefully worked out arrangements that would be unlikely to cause dispute. As she felt for the piece of paper, she wondered whether she would vomit, the nausea so high and dense she realised she might not even be able to open her mouth and speak.

So she stopped, her skin clammy, her throat dry as she tried to utter a simple word, a practice 'hello', her voice, when it eventually came, harsh and grating.

I can't do this, she thought.

She caught sight of herself in the shop window, a stranger she didn't know. A woman about to try and meet up with someone who had once held her safe and loved, only to betray her in a way she could not forgive.

I don't have to do this, she realised.

And she sat on a low brick wall, the realisation that she could just turn her back on this meeting both light and terrifying.

I'm not ready, she told herself.

At the end of the street, she could see Lawrence's car. He was already there. She tried to imagine herself walking in, staying upright, opening her mouth, uttering adult words, looking at him, eyes clear and open — and it was all so impossible to visualise that she knew she had no choice.

Have had to cancel, she wrote, fingers trembling as she tapped on the letters, frequently missing the one she wanted, the predictive text quick to make sense of the jumble she was writing. *Will email this evening with proposed arrangements.*

She pressed 'send', relieved as the message turned green.

It was going to be a long time before she could talk to him.

Perhaps it would never happen again.

And the solid weight of that sorrow pressed down, bruising and ugly, cloaking the shape of her, close.

NOW

THE LAST TIME ESTER saw Steven was a fortnight ago. She had gone into the city to complete the second part of the mediation course — a half-day workshop. She hadn't known whether he would be in this group, or another.

'Ask him,' her friend Marta had encouraged. 'I'm sure you could find him on the internet and email him.'

Of course she could. She'd found him already, googling him the day after their drink together, surprised by his picture on his website. It wasn't how she recalled him. It was a black and white studio photograph, a bit like a magazine shot, showing him in a grey T-shirt and jeans, sitting on a chair and leaning forward, eager to listen. There was something fake about it, and, embarrassed, she closed the page immediately, only to reopen it later that night, a glass of wine by her side.

She read his bio with the same degree of discomfort.

'Steven Lansdowne works closely with clients to help them achieve their full potential. He provides individual coaching sessions for executives and runs highly acclaimed leadership courses.

'Steven began his working life as an actor, appearing in films, commercials, and on stage. In his late twenties, he completed an

MBA, with a major in psychology, and commenced a successful career in change management consultancy, working with companies in the finance industry. During this time, he discovered the importance of tapping into people potential, harnessing the full creative power of the individual to fully realise success.'

Hilary would hate it.

Maurie would have hated it too.

She trawled though old entries under Steven's name, digging up short films, television series, and plays he'd appeared in years earlier. A couple were on YouTube, and she sat back, slightly embarrassed, as she watched — his roles usually those of a pretty boy, a minor love interest at the sideline of the story. He was someone who'd been just a few shades away from becoming a recognised actor at the same time as she'd been letting go of painting. Feeling as though she was spying, she shut down the computer.

Ester remembered the period of giving up painting. Her work was formalistic, strong architectural shapes that repeated themselves with an order that never varied, very different to the seemingly chaotic riot of her father's canvases. Hilary had never been a fan, but she had nonetheless been dismayed by Ester's decision. Maurie had been more sympathetic.

'You can paint,' he'd told her. 'But so can a lot of people.'

She had waited for him to continue.

'You're always going to battle with being my daughter. Sometimes you'll be lauded for it, at other times you'll be pilloried. In order to overcome that, you'll need a certain "fuck you" temperament, and a real desire to be known for your work. I'm not sure that you have either.'

He was right.

She'd glanced across at him. 'I'd like to do something completely different,' she'd confessed. 'Something that's just mine.'

He'd understood.

'It'll mean I'll be a Sunday painter.' She'd smiled at him, knowing that he had little time or patience for weekend artists.

He'd grinned. 'Ah, but you'll be different to all those other Sunday painters,' he'd told her. 'You're my daughter.' He'd folded her close, and told her he'd keep a space for her in his studio, whenever she wanted to use it.

He didn't, of course. The area that she'd occupied was soon filled with his work, and she would laugh when she came to visit him, referring to her ever shrinking corner — a space that he would hastily clean in embarrassment, telling her he was just using it temporarily.

Marta continued to urge her to ring Steven.

She'd been a friend of Ester's and Lawrence's, and, like so many of their friends, she'd chosen to stay with Ester during the split. She looked at Steven's bio on his website but was quick to dismiss Ester's unease. 'A little cheesy, yes,' she'd agreed, pouring herself another wine, 'but he'd have to present himself in a certain way to get work. I mean, look at you —' and she flicked over to Ester's homepage. 'All caring and sharing.'

'Which I am,' Ester insisted.

'I know. But you're more than that.'

Ester tried to articulate her fear a little more clearly. 'What do they call them now? "A player?" That's what he looks like — a player. Smooth and charming.' She shook her head, her words barely audible as she uttered them: 'Like Lawrence.'

Marta looked at her. 'Does this mean you'll dismiss anyone who's handsome?'

'I probably should,' Ester smiled. She remembered the man she'd met on the internet date so long ago, and how quick she'd been to write him off. He was the type she should be considering, she told Marta. Someone safe. She sat on the floor, and looked up at the ceiling. It had been so long, and she was terrified.

Marta slid down the wall and sat next to her. She took Ester's hand in her own and squeezed it. 'Of course you are,' she said gently.

Ester sent him an email in the end — carefully worded, asking him if he was going to the second part of the course on Friday, and if so, did he want to have lunch afterwards?

He never replied.

And so she turned up on the day, hoping he wouldn't be there because she felt so foolish. They took their seats at the round table, the moderator in the middle, and just as she began to speak, he arrived. Seeing her, he raised a hand in greeting, a smile on his face as he tried to squeeze a chair in next to her.

She nodded, hoping she wasn't blushing, and then looked steadily at her notepad as she continued to write. At the end of the session, he asked her if she wanted to have lunch.

'Oh.' Her confusion was obvious.

'You can't?'

She shook her head. 'When I didn't hear from you, I thought you weren't coming today.'

And now *he* looked confused. He'd never received an email from her. He checked his junk mail on his iPad, and there it was — her carefully worded invitation. She couldn't watch him open and read it.

'Love to,' he said.

They talked over a bowl of soup, her nerves soon gone. He asked her if she was religious, or voted Liberal. 'Possibly insurmountable problems if you say yes to either.'

She shook her head. 'What about you? Do you go shooting for a hobby? Maybe we need to give each other a questionnaire.' She smiled, and told him she'd lived with a pollster.

'He came to hate it more and more.' She was about to

continue, to talk about the corrosive effect it had on Lawrence, but she stopped herself, wary of being one of those people who talked too much about their past relationship.

'I've never voted Liberal. I had a teenage flirtation with Jesus that ended when the guy who ran the youth group was outed for kissing just about every girl over thirteen. I thought about Buddhism briefly, but never seriously.' She narrowed her eyes. 'Do I pass?'

He nodded.

'Be careful,' she added. 'I could now do something just as bad as vote Liberal or go to church. I could bring out an iPad covered in a pink fluffy case with "Princess" written on it.'

'Possibly worse,' he agreed. His phone beeped but he ignored it. 'And I've never owned a gun, or used one,' he promised.

She broke herself a piece of bread, and asked him to tell her more about himself, hating her words as soon as she uttered them. She sounded like a therapist. 'Not your problems, of course,' she hastened to add. 'Or at least not the real, real, real ones.'

His eyes were direct, a gaze that she tried to meet. 'Do you want me to start with my childhood, or leap straight to my first marriage?'

She didn't mean to cough into her water, and then it was like a choking sound, embarrassing and foolish. 'Can I ask how many marriages you've had?'

'Are you worried I'm one of those hopeless romantics who gets married on a weekly basis?'

She nodded.

'I've only been married once. And it was to a friend of mine who had a girlfriend in Australia and wanted to be able to stay. What about you?'

She held up a finger, still chewing on her bread.

'Is that an "up yours"? Or a one?'

'One marriage — the pollster. We have two daughters — twins. But you know that.'

'Did it end a long time ago?'

She nodded, not wanting the conversation to veer back to Lawrence.

He asked if she wanted a coffee, and she said yes, relieved at the chance to shift the talk in another direction.

'I didn't know your father was Maurie Marcel.' He looked embarrassed then. 'I did a bit of research,' he confessed. 'I'm sorry. I feel foolish now.'

She smiled, although she didn't confess to her own internet trawling.

'I actually have one of his paintings. I bought it when I got my first paid work as an actor. I've always loved it.' And then he shook his head and smiled again, laughing slightly. 'I almost made a worse fool of myself,' he told her, holding two fingers up, touching. 'This close to saying you'd have to come over and see it sometime.'

'The old etchings line,' she grinned. 'Got used in art school far too often.'

'I can imagine.'

She liked him. Even more than she had the last time she met. Her skin rushed with effervescent sparks of joy and nerves; it was as though each sense had been turned up a notch.

Strange, she thought, *how readily we forget the intensity of attraction, how impossible it becomes to recall.* She'd felt it once before with Lawrence, and years earlier with Matthew, who'd been a sculptor in the year above her at art school. She'd adored Matthew, plotting and planning what she did and where she went in the hope of bumping into him. She took him home several times, back to the share house she'd lived in in Redfern, her bedroom up the top, two French doors opening onto a dust-caked balcony and the constant hum of traffic. They would lie on her bed under the swinging rice-paper lightshade and kiss for hours, his mouth like silk on hers, his pale hair sweeping across her cheek. And then he would fall asleep. Always.

'He's a junkie,' her housemate told her. 'I can't believe you didn't know. Everyone knows.'

She was right. Ester saw the marks on his arms the next time, the tiny black pinpricks of his pupils as he smiled lazily at her before once again drifting away, fast asleep next to her. He'd stolen her rent money twice. She hadn't wanted to admit it to herself, but it was hard to deny. And still she'd loved him, sure that he would change, furious with her housemates when they said they didn't want him round anymore (the kitty had also disappeared).

He didn't even tell her when he checked into Odyssey House; it was a friend of a friend who explained why he was nowhere to be found. He moved to Melbourne soon afterwards, and it wasn't until years later that she learnt of his overdose, the news saddening her more than she would have expected, the memory of her feelings for him enough to take her back there, briefly.

She looked at Steven sitting opposite her, and told him that she'd never had any regrets about giving up art. 'I thought I would have. Which only goes to show I wasn't cut out for it in the first place. I guess Maurie knew that.'

Steven's father had been a used-car salesman.

'Of the worst type,' he confessed. 'He even sold clapped-out pieces of junk to friends of mine, and then refused to give back their money when they wouldn't start. We were always going from boom to bust — living in a mansion one week, fleeing creditors the next. He died of a heart attack two years ago.'

Ester looked at him. 'And your mother?'

'Family life sent her to an early grave.' He grimaced.

It was strange shaping your life for someone else, she thought.

Here they were, both in the business of extracting such stories from clients, spinning tales across the table, tossing them forth to snare each other.

In the days following her lunch with Steven, she resisted the urge to contact him again.

'But what if he's lost my email, or thinks that I wasn't keen?' After four days of waiting, she told Marta she couldn't do it any longer. She felt embarrassed by her eagerness. She'd seen clients ruin new relationships by rushing in, giving too much too soon, and she feared behaving like that because it had been so very long since she'd felt this way.

Marta was the only friend she'd told. She'd come over to help Ester put together an Ikea chest of drawers for the girls' room. She'd worked as an assistant for a sculptor who made public art pieces, and had developed a practical competence that most of Ester's other friends lacked. Lawrence used to call on her too, asking her to help him rehang doors and fix window sashes on their old house, always determined to do it himself, only to find that he didn't have the skills he pretended to have. Marta would take over, dismantling his initial work and teasing him mercilessly as she started from scratch.

She had the instructions laid out on the floor, and was reading through them as Ester spoke.

'Perhaps I should just send him an email?'

'No.' Marta insisted. She tapped the hammer gently on the side of Ester's foot. 'No. No. No. Subliminal messaging from me to you. If you try to send that email you'll feel those hammer blows, and they'll stop you.'

'I don't think so,' Ester told her. 'Although, I will feel foolish and wish I could retract the message as soon as I've pressed send.'

She counted the bolts in her hand. 'Have you got the other one?'

Marta did.

'I had a client once who told me that finding a man was like finding real estate.'

Marta rolled her eyes.

'You have to put in your offer straight away or someone else will come and nab it.' Ester chewed on her bottom lip. 'What if she was right?'

'So what is he?'

Ester didn't understand.

'In real-estate language?'

Ester laughed. 'Harbourside. Off-street parking. Custom joinery. Seamless indoor-outdoor flow.'

'An infinity-edge lap pool?'

'Oh god, I hope not. Far too common.'

She stepped nervously from foot to foot, unable to keep still, her heart too quick, all of her on edge with the potential for disappointment, the potential of not hearing from him again, of finding out he wasn't interested after all. The potential that she had fucked it up. She looked down at the ground and took a deep breath. 'I'm sorry,' she said. 'I will rein it in.' And she picked up the hammer and tapped the back of her hand three times lightly. 'Time to try and let it go.'

'And Lawrence?' Marta smiled at her. 'What was he?'

Ester shook her head. 'One of those new developments that seems so good on the prospectus — and then turns out to be nothing but trouble.'

She bent down to hold the side and the back of the chest together, trying to keep the edge steady while Marta bolted one into the other.

'And what is it you want?' Marta put the drill down and looked at Ester. 'Holiday cottage? Flashy city home? Rustic? Modern?'

'Something where the work's already been done,' Ester

eventually said. 'I really don't want to have to renovate.'

'Can't say I want that for you either. I'd be the one doing most of the work.'

Behind them, Ester's phone beeped. She'd put it on alert so that she could hear emails when they arrived. 'Can I look?'

Marta wagged her finger in admonishment, and then shooed her away. 'Go,' she told her.

And she did, her squeal ringing out from the kitchen to the girl's bedroom, followed by a peal of laughter — loud, embarrassed.

'I am so sorry,' she apologised, leaping up and down, phone in hand. 'I'm behaving like an adolescent. I know I am. I seem to have no control.' She held the phone out to Marta, the message open on the screen.

Lovely having lunch last week — want to have dinner on Friday?

Marta took the phone from her. 'You can reply when I'm gone,' she told her. 'Not until then.' And then she leant forward and kissed her on the cheek. 'I'm glad for you,' she said. 'I really am. Just don't buy without getting all those reports — pest inspection. Building. All of them.'

And Ester had nodded solemnly, eyes wide, as she looked at the phone lying on the floor, all of her a-wonder with the human capacity to fall again and again and again, clutching fast to the sheer beauty of hope in the faith it would somehow stay buoyant.

Today, the rain falls steadily, and she sits in her kitchen, her phone call to Victoria finished, wanting to hold in the incandescence of joy and excitement, to let it burn off the last vestige of the shame and sadness of Lawrence.

It glows.

BEING A CHRISTIAN underpins all of Edmund's actions. It is the foundation for who he is and how he should behave. It obviously takes precedence over any employment contract he may have with Lawrence, including any confidentiality obligations under that contract.

Lawrence reads the email several times.

Edmund does not wish to punish Lawrence — it is neither his role nor his intention. He believes Lawrence should be the one to confess to altering the polls. He has therefore decided to give him 48 hours to come clean to Paul. After this time has passed, Edmund himself intends to write to the editor — regardless of whether Lawrence has confessed or not — to assure him he had no knowledge of the numbers being altered. Needless to say, he no longer wishes to work for Lawrence, and he requests full payout of all moneys owing under their contract. In addition, he encloses the final poll figures.

Lawrence reads the email again.

Edmund is a sanctimonious fuckwit.

But perhaps there is a chance of salvaging other business if Paul can be convinced to stay quiet. After all, they are terminating their agreement with him anyway, and there is no reason why Paul would want to damage his own reputation. No one else need know. He just has to be careful about how he words his confession. He does not want Paul to feel that Lawrence has been making a fool of him. It is delicate.

He sits back in his chair and closes his eyes. Of course he can't confess. It would be professional suicide. He could lie, though. Why not? He does it well. Just pretend that Edmund and he have had a dispute, and Edmund is trying to bury him in a scandal. But what if Edmund sends through evidence? He stands up now, his heart beating like a hard stone in his chest.

He had never envisaged his life here. Middle-aged, divorced, unhappy with his work. It is a cliché of which he is ashamed. And now he is on the brink of being professionally ruined.

What was it he had wanted? He finds it so hard to remember. He opens his eyes to see himself reflected in the rain-streaked window, and flinches. He has fucked up, again and again, and he puts his head in his hands, wishing he could dissolve who he is, go back to who he once was.

He had loved music, but even he was wise enough to know he'd never had much talent. He'd loved drugs — still didn't mind them if the truth be known. Ditto women. He shakes his head. If he is ruined, there really isn't much to draw on in terms of setting up a new life.

Ester used to encourage him to quit. She'd make suggestions — politics, journalism, policy research — all of which he'd dismiss. Eventually, she gave up. What would she tell him to do now, he wonders, and he can see her, horrified at first by the mess he has found himself in, and then not surprised, because this is what Lawrence does: he lies, he cheats, and he fucks up.

As he glances down at his desk, the first thing he sees is Hilary's number scrawled on a piece of paper next to his computer.

He keys in each of the digits, and then hangs up before he presses call. Despite knowing it is unlikely she still wants to berate him (why now after such a long period of silence?), she makes him nervous. She always has.

The first time Ester took him home for lunch, Hilary failed to join them. Maurie cooked, grilling fish with his usual enthusiasm, and making at least four salads — far more than the three of them could possibly eat. He had discovered kingfish, he told them — 'is there any taste more perfect?' — and had decided he was going to eat it every day.

'Who knows, I might even trim down.' He stood, inspecting his girth in the reflection of the window, before turning to Lawrence to tell him that it was only in the last year he'd found himself unable to wear the same pants he had worn since he was in his thirties. 'Soft moleskin. They've never worn out — just become more pleasing with the years. Like your mother.' He winked at Ester, who rolled her eyes before asking where Hilary was.

'She knew we were coming.'

Maurie pointed up at the studio, and then bellowed her name out loudly.

There was no answer.

'She's tetchy,' he eventually explained, his voice loud enough for Hilary — perhaps even the whole neighbourhood — to hear. 'She seems to think I failed to tell her about today. Which of course I didn't.'

'I'll go up.' Ester beckoned Lawrence to follow her, which he did with some trepidation.

Hilary was at her desk, headphones on, unable to hear them until Ester lifted them from her head and asked her if she was going to join them.

'This is Lawrence,' she'd said, slightly shy as she introduced him.

Hilary had turned to look at him. Her blue eyes were sharp, her pale hair escaping a tangled knot at the back; she wore no make-up, and little jewellery, just a startlingly large silver ring, heavy in his hand as she reached out to greet him.

'I'm too busy,' she told them both. 'He knew I was planning on working all weekend, so I'm afraid you'll just have to eat without me.'

'Just for half an hour?' Ester asked.

But Hilary had already put her headphones on and turned back to the screen.

Ester sighed. 'I'm sorry,' she told Lawrence loudly, 'my parents seem to be locked in some childish fight.'

The headphones came off again, and Hilary turned to face Ester. 'I have a film to finish by Wednesday. I'm sorry I can't eat with you — but if he stays around,' she nodded briefly in Lawrence's direction, 'which remains to be seen, there'll be plenty of other opportunities for lunch.'

On the way home, Ester apologised for Hilary's rudeness. 'It was nothing to do with you. It's part of a long, ongoing war she's been having with Maurie about the lack of respect he gives to her work. Which isn't entirely true. Although if he'd had an exhibition to finish, he wouldn't have been there — and no one would have questioned it.'

Lawrence had grown used to Hilary over the years, although he was never entirely sure of how she felt about him.

Shortly after he and Ester had returned home from Paris with the girls, she'd taken him aside and told him he needed to 'change your act — pronto'.

She was worried about Ester not getting enough time to work.

'You earn enough to pay for extra childcare,' she told him.

Ester was quite happy working part-time, he replied. There was no need for her to go back full-time.

Hilary narrowed her eyes. 'Is that you saying this, or her?'

He lost his temper then, asking Hilary a similar question. If Ester was unhappy with the arrangement, she hadn't expressed it to him. And if it was simply Hilary who was unhappy with how they were living, then it was none of her business, and he had no interest in listening to her complaints.

She hadn't flinched. 'Fair enough,' she agreed.

He'd shaken his head. 'You're incredible,' he'd muttered.

She smiled then. 'She's my daughter. And I don't want to see her, years down the track, with regrets.'

'We all have regrets,' he countered.

She looked at him, surprised by his response. 'I don't,' she'd said, and she had seemed completely genuine.

She doesn't, Ester had agreed when he'd relayed the conversation to her later that night. 'She loves Maurie, her work, us — she doesn't hanker after anything or wish she'd lived a different life. She's genuinely happy with where she's at.'

'She's possibly one of the only people in the western world who could lay claim to that,' he'd replied. And he'd raised his glass. 'To Hilary.'

He dials her number again, knowing he should have called back straight away. What if something is wrong with Ester? It has been so long since they have spoken. If she was sick, she might even not tell him, he thinks — although surely she would for the sake of the girls? He is suddenly overwhelmed by a desire to see her, to have her centre him, right him, and then he shakes his head. Ester wouldn't want to know about putting him back on track. Not anymore.

Outside, the sky is low, darkening as another downpour builds. He glances across and sees Leon closing up, pulling the blind down on the front door of the café. He struggles for business most days of the week — the neighbourhood is now home to four or five fashionable new cafés — and today is hopeless. Lawrence wonders how he survives.

And then, after four rings, just when he is about lose his nerve, Hilary finally answers. Her voice is less certain than usual, the faintness heightening his anxiety so that he speaks without waiting for her to say any more than his name — 'Is Ester all right?' — his words cutting through any awkwardness.

'She's fine,' Hilary assures him. 'Unless there's something she's been keeping from me?'

And now it's Lawrence's turn to reassure, telling Hilary that if there were, he wouldn't know. She, Hilary, is far more likely to have heard. 'You called me,' he says. 'Asking me to ring you. I'm sorry I took so long. It's been one of those days. Terrible.'

She doesn't feign interest in what's been happening for him. Even if they had been on friendly terms she may not have asked him, assuming he would tell her if it mattered.

'I need you to help me,' she says. 'I don't want to discuss this on the phone. I need to see you.'

The next downpour has begun. Everything heaving with the weight of it, slanting sheets of rain, and across the road, a man tries to shelter under the awning over Leon's front door, but it is hopeless. The rain drenches him, his jeans darkening, his coat sodden. The drumming against the tin is so loud, Lawrence isn't sure if he has heard her correctly. He doesn't know how to respond.

'This is important,' she tells him.

Of course it is. She has never been one for just calling him to have a chat, and he laughs nervously as he tells her he gathered as much.

She cuts over him. 'I'm dying,' she says.

And he is appalled as he wonders why she needs to tell him — what does this have to do with him? He stands now, trying to move somewhere where he can hear more clearly, but also because he cannot sit still, he is feeling ill, and he doesn't know why.

He begins to utter a response, words of 'how awful', or something similarly pathetic, when once again she stops him from continuing.

'If you could come to my house and we could talk?'

He is shaking his head, mouthing the word 'no' and pressing the phone to his ear, when she utters the word that surprises him most of all.

'Please,' she says, and in that instant, the rain stops, as suddenly as it began, the clarity of her plea sharp and sudden, the only word he has truly heard.

'Of course,' he tells her, his panic dissipating as quickly as the downpour. And in the silence that follows, he looks out at the sky, still again, and asks her if she is at the same address.

She is.

'Do you want me to come now?'

She does.

And he is not to tell Ester or April. Not yet.

He stands alone at his window, his face reflected back at him, older than he ever expects — lines across his skin, greying hair, mouth drawn — and he watches himself as he tells her he will be there soon.

APRIL HAS PLAYED the record six times now, but they want to hear it again: 'I Can't Stand The Rain', louder each time, all three of them singing with the chorus, Catherine abandoning herself to the performance, wailing with the sadness of the refrain.

'Again,' Lara demands.

But this time, April shakes her head.

'I think we need something a little happier,' she tells them, searching through her old vinyl, the record covers a smear of colour across the floor. *It's on an old hits album, later than 'Ripper',* she thinks, and then there it is — an eighties disco collection she used to love.

'Now this is a good one,' she tells the girls.

The needle crackles, sliding round and round the edge. She lifts it and places it right in the groove this time, the music building and building until those first words take it to its crescendo —

Hi, Hi — We're your weather girls and have we got nooooos for you!

They love it — and of course they want it again and again, each of them familiar with all the words by the third hearing, Lara throwing her head back and singing to the sky, Catherine taking her pretend microphone and working the room.

When it ends for the fifth time, Lara wants to know what it means.

'Who'd want it to rain men?' she asks.

April shrugs. 'Sex-starved women?'

'That's gross,' Lara tells her. 'Really gross.' She looks out the window, a huge arched pane of glass looking over grey rooftops, the heavy sky low over the charcoal sliver of harbour, a strip of metal shimmering dully. 'Imagine if they were coming out of the clouds,' Lara says. 'They'd squash everything.'

April can only agree. 'But some of them might survive. And they might be fun.' She sniffs the air. 'I believe a cake may be cooked.' There's a warm sweetness, the scent of molten chocolate, and it's good.

'Perfect,' she says — and it is.

Her capacity to cook is something that always surprises people. She used to make the meals with Maurie, neither of them afraid to experiment, both of them with a nose for balance — 'when it comes to food,' April would add ruefully, 'but nothing else.'

Lara hovers, ready to stick her finger right in the centre, but April slaps her away, tickling her under the arm as she does so. 'Let it cool,' she says. 'Just a bit.'

It's 3 o'clock. She needs to call Lawrence again, but her phone is nowhere to be found.

'Here it is,' Catherine tells her, pointing to the landline long since disconnected.

'Doesn't work,' April replies.

'Then why do you keep it?'

She shrugs.

'Okay,' she tells them. 'Our mission is simple. Locate the communication device. If you find it, you win an extra piece for yourself and your sister.'

'What happens if *you* find it?' Catherine asks.

'I'll have to cut an extra piece for Ester.'

Lara rolls her eyes. 'What would be the point? It's not like you could give it to her.'

This is true. 'Maybe one day,' April tells her. 'I could put it in the freezer until then.' She looks around the room, hands on her hips, practiced in quickly scanning the chaos as a means of finding what she's lost. Sometimes it works immediately.

'Ah ha.' She had left it in a sensible spot. Hall table, next to her keys.

Lawrence answers on the third ring. He is in the car, he tells her, static making it difficult to hear as she asks him whether he got her message. 'I have the girls,' she tries to explain. 'It's complicated, but they are totally fine. I can bring them to you when you get home.'

He is heading in her direction, he replies. He can pick them up — if she doesn't mind keeping them for a little longer.

Of course she doesn't. 'It's lovely to see them again,' she says, but the call has disconnected, or at least this is what she'd like to presume, and not that he's hung up on her.

'There's no need for you to avoid me,' she'd once said to him, and she'd meant it, once her horror over his confession had subsided, and the cold chill of shame passed. 'We may as well try and be friends.'

The sadness of knowing they might have loved each other was always present, and even now there were times when she would wake from a dream of him, surprised by the intensity of her longing. But she was always quick to push it aside, to give it no air, trying for a more pragmatic assessment of their relationship. If there had been no obstacle — and when they first met, there had been none — would they have chosen each other? And would they have lasted? Of course not, she would tell herself. They would have enjoyed a period of drug-and-alcohol-fuelled days together, only to eventually sicken of the excess towards which they both tended to drift.

She'd had brief affairs with men like him. She knew what

happened. They were often drawn to her, sure that she would let them be who they wanted to be, that she wouldn't try and constrain them. But after an intense period of wild unadulterated fun, there was no net holding them together, no substance to anchor any connection between them, and it was over.

April stands in the doorway to her kitchen, where the girls are leaning together, both tall and slender, long limbs in school tracksuits smeared with flour and cocoa from the baking, tangled hair escaping pigtails. They concentrate as they serve up the cake, carefully cutting even slices — one for each of them, two for April, and an extra plate also with two slices.

April used to have them to stay when they were little. Ester would drop them off, each with a carefully packed bag containing neatly folded pyjamas, clean underpants, and toiletries. Her instructions were lengthy — bed times, number of stories, toilet routines, tooth brushing, hair brushing, sugar rationing. After the first time, April simply pretended to listen.

'And I'm trying to get them to sleep on their own,' Ester told her as she'd left. 'So if they get into bed with you, it'd be great if you could take them back to their own room.'

April had nodded earnestly, failing to tell Ester that she didn't actually have another bed for them to go to. The one in the spare room was covered with old guitars and clothes she'd been intending to donate to someone whenever she could figure out who might want them.

She always slept with both the girls. One on each side. Lavender shampoo and sweet milky skin, warm arms and legs tangled around her own. She would wake to them chattering, sometimes to each other, sometimes to her, and she wanted to drink them up, all of them — their little white teeth, clear eyes, and their breath, as fresh as water.

No longer seeing them had hurt.

She clears the records to one side of the lounge room floor and spreads a deep red blanket across the ground, scattering cushions around the edge so that they can have a picnic.

Ester had once asked her if she wanted to have children of her own. April had told her how much she loved them, that looking after them was never a chore — and she had meant it. It had been a rare moment when they had sat and talked, the girls still having their mid-morning nap when Ester had come to pick them up.

April said she found it hard to imagine herself as a mother. It had never been a vision for herself.

'But you'd be good at it,' Ester had replied with what seemed to be genuine enthusiasm.

'Really?'

'Yes,' Ester had continued, and she had looked around April's apartment — last night's dinner dishes still in front of the television, papers scattering in the breeze through the window, brilliant yellow daffodils stuffed into a vase with half-dead roses, a pile of clothes by the front door. 'You're so good with chaos.'

April shakes her head as she remembers.

Now, as Lara carries in two plates, one for herself and one for April — with two slices on it — she asks April if they should put Ester's pieces straight in the freezer. She has milk around her mouth, a slender line of white fur across the pale pink of her upper lip, and chocolate crumbs along her fingers. Behind her, Catherine also waits for April's answer.

'Or we could just take it home with us and give it to her?' she suggests.

April smiles at them both. 'It might be a bit silly to freeze it,' she eventually says. 'Besides, I'm not sure if your mother even likes my chocolate cake. And as it was me who lost the phone, I probably shouldn't win a prize for finding it.'

'So can we eat her pieces now?' Catherine asks.

April nods, her mouth full of cake.

'Is Daddy going to pick us up?' Lara wants to know.

He is, April tells them.

'So we can't stay the night?'

She shakes her head, knowing the questions are heading in a direction that should be avoided. And so she reaches behind her for a record and tells them that they are going to play a game. 'It's called disco queen,' she says.

They wait for her to continue.

'Follow me,' she tells them, standing and beckoning towards the open door of her bedroom. 'Your wardrobe and make-up await you.'

ESTER HAS BEEN seeing Sarah and Daniel for almost six weeks now, and yet she has surprisingly few pages of notes. Reading over the little she's written just confirms what she knows. They're stuck — the three of them, really — wheels grinding round and round, mud splattering on all of them. If she is truthful, she dreads these sessions. She doesn't particularly like Sarah. In fact, to be more honest, she actively dislikes her.

It was Sarah who contacted her first, booking a session for herself and Daniel. Ester chatted to her on the telephone for some time, trying to get an indication of what it was they were wanting from counselling. Sarah talked a lot, breathlessly skipping from topic to topic, leaping from Medicare details to the intimacy of her sex life with no pause between the two, her words rapid, the link between each sentence so tangled that Ester felt like someone had upended a basket of toys in front of her.

'We met in India. At an ashram,' Sarah told her, turning up alone for the first session. 'The attraction was like, how can I describe it? Red-hot? I mean, he was gorgeous, and we were both young, free spirits. You don't have a herbal tea, do you? Love a tea when I chat.'

He was a recovering alcoholic learning to become a yoga teacher. She was a student. 'A lot slimmer then.' She laughed, adjusting her skirt in the chair, the cotton crushed up against the side of her legs to reveal the paleness of her thigh, white and dimpled.

She was nothing like the person Ester had pictured, imagining someone small, too light to settle anywhere, the rapid speed of her endless talk burning up whatever physical substance she might have had. But Sarah was large, dressed in bright, fun clothes, her hair hennaed scarlet, jewellery covering her neck, her fingers, her wrists, all clanking loudly each time she moved.

She was pregnant, she declared in the first session. 'My fourth. I'm one of those women. Fertile as. You just have to look at me and I'm knocked up.'

Daniel wanted her to have a termination.

'We live off a yoga teacher's salary.' She brushed a curl out of her eyes. 'Doesn't leave much after feeding all those hungry mouths. But I'm a mother. That's what I am. This is what makes me sing. It's what I love.' She ran her hands through the air, following the shape of her own breasts, her belly, eyes widening as she leant forward. 'He knows that. Telling me he wants to kill it,' and she leant forward here, her words almost a hiss, 'it's like he's striking at the very heart of my being.' Her breath smelt of peppermint, her skin of musk.

Ester had to control herself from recoiling. She actively leant a little closer to counter all in her that wanted to pull away.

'Do you feel you need my help in talking this decision through?'

Sarah laughed loudly. God no, it had to be her choice. It was her body.

By the end of the first session, Ester still found it difficult to determine whether Sarah wanted counselling with Daniel or to see a therapist on her own. Were there issues in their relationship that she wanted to address? There are always issues. That's love. Was there a reason why Daniel hadn't come?

Sarah began then to talk about a rebirthing therapy Daniel had been doing. It was through an American who ran courses in the States and set up online support groups. Daniel had been three times. He spent a couple of nights a week talking to his group. He was very into it.

Was it causing tension?

It was why he didn't feel he could come to see Ester. They weren't meant to do two types of therapy at the same time.

Why did she want him to come with her?

Sarah paused for a moment then, her intake of air audible.

'He has anger issues.' She shook her head sadly. 'And he needs to take responsibility for them.'

As she stood to leave, she paused, putting her hand on Ester's arm, her voice hushed as she spoke. She had been abused as a child. A family friend had let himself into her room while her parents were downstairs having a party. She was fifteen, and he was forty. It had gone on for a year.

'I thought I loved him and he loved me. But I was young, vulnerable, foolish.'

Ester hated it when patients did this at the end of a session. It forced her to dismiss the issue, to tell the client that this was something they could discuss at the next appointment.

She used to tell Lawrence that she had to find the 'self of calm curiosity' to do the work she did. A client would come in, and Ester would always feel that moment when an array of selves, each responding differently, would jostle for position. There could be compassion, anger, judgement, fear, boredom, frustration, very rarely indifference — though occasionally even that was there — and they were all possible.

'I'm like a pack of cards,' she said. 'And with each client there's an immediate response. I have to take a deep breath, push that response to the back, and draw the same card every time.'

'Calm curiosity?'

She nodded.

If Sarah was without bounds, Daniel was tightly contained.

He came to the next session, sitting on the other end of the couch to Sarah, silent as she talked.

She had lost the baby, she declared. A miscarriage after she came home from the session with Ester. She'd reached for Daniel's hand to take it in her own, having to shift her entire body to get to where he sat. Her eyes were glassy as she looked at him; he remained staring at the ground.

Ester outlined her rules for working with both of them, one of which was a session with each of them on their own.

As soon as they were by themselves, Daniel told her Sarah had been lying. She was never pregnant; she made up stories all the time.

What made him think that?

They hadn't had sex for months. He looked straight at Ester, his grey-green eyes cold, his pale skin dusted with freckles. *He looks like a young boy*, she thought for a moment, like a Daniel you might see in the playground. He shifted nervously on the seat.

'She believes it completely,' he said.

Ester asked him why he was here — what did he see as the key issues in his relationship with Sarah?

He shrugged.

Could he talk a little more about the lack of sexual intimacy in their relationship? Did he feel this was a problem?

He no longer loved her. He hadn't loved her for years.

Then why did he stay?

He met Ester's gaze for a long time before he spoke. 'I don't know how to leave,' he eventually said. 'I mean I do. But she won't let me. It's like she's some kind of sinkhole, and I'm stuck.' He almost sneered as he uttered the words, his loathing for himself, Sarah, and the situation they were in naked on his face.

Another time, Ester told Lawrence that she felt she spent most of her days talking to frogs in boiling water. 'They come in, and I can see they are boiling,' she said. 'The water is bubbling. But they have been immersed for so long, and the temperature has been going up and up and up — it's only when it reaches critical that they try and leap out. And I have to help them do that.'

'Well, they're idiots,' he'd replied, putting his headphones back in so he could continue listening to music.

She'd remembered that conversation a month later, when he'd come home and told her he was in love with April.

She sits in her consulting room now with Sarah and Daniel, trying to banish all selves other than the calm and curious Ester. Sarah is crying, alone at her end of the couch, while Daniel remains impassive, looking only at the ceiling. He has been inching further away from her, his whole body pressed into his side of the couch, as she accuses him of not really trying, of not participating in these sessions.

'What do you want from me?' He glares across at Sarah.

The silence in the room builds, all the more pronounced with the steady hum of the rain outside. Eventually, Sarah tells him she doesn't deserve his anger. 'Jesus, darl, I love you. I do everything for you.'

'You don't fucking listen,' he mutters.

She seems relieved he has finally spoken, her words coming out in a torrent. 'Of course I listen to you, darl, but I've got a lot of people to listen to, what with the kids demanding attention all day. If you want to be heard, you've got to speak up,' she turns and smiles at Ester. 'It's chaos in our house. No one could be heard, really. Even I have a hard time being heard above the din, and that's saying something.'

Daniel's skin is even paler than usual, the tension in his jaw revealing the sharp line of the bone. Ester knows she should intervene, but Sarah keeps on talking.

'We need to make more time for each other. Get a babysitter, go out one night a week, talk about what's happening in our lives. I know I could try and arrange a swap with some of the other mothers at kindy. Give you a chance to be heard?' She turns to Daniel, reaching for him and smiling as she does so.

He presses further into the side of the couch.

'Do you feel that would help?' Ester looks at him. His hands are clenched in his lap, his top lip pressing down hard on his lower lips, the flesh white.

'No. It wouldn't help.'

Sarah shakes her head, mouth pursed. 'You see? This is the problem,' she says. 'Every time I try and come up with a solution — and it's always me doing that — you just reject it outright. Like the time I told you to go and have a holiday. When you were so depressed and miserable, which you probably don't remember because you're depressed and miserable most of the time. It's hard to be around. Honest. But I told you to take a week off, get away, I'd take care of the kids, I even found you somewhere to stay, but no. You just told me that a holiday wasn't the answer. Fine. But how am I meant to help if I don't even know what the problem is?' She crosses her arms across her chest and shakes her head.

Ester wonders whether Daniel will shout; she can feel it, the great bulk of all those unsaid words right there, the danger of them being dumped all at once in a truckload. She turns to him, breaking the silence before it builds any further.

'How do you feel about Sarah's response?' She keeps her voice low, even, and she focuses her gaze straight on him, willing him to lift his head and look her in the eyes.

'I don't want a holiday. I don't want a night out. I don't want to be here.' He stands, shaking.

Sarah tries to pull him down, her hands reaching up, her bangles jangling as he shoves her away.

'I don't love you. I don't fucking love you.'

Sarah's eyes widen, and the whole world flickers across them: disbelief, anger, denial, blink, blink, blink, grief, horror, fury, each so fast, and then, last, there is the need — bottomless in its depth, rapacious as it swallows all else.

He doesn't love her.

I don't love you.

The love has gone.

Every time those words are said, there is so much pain, Ester thinks. She has seen it before in this room — the utterance ripping through lives like a gunshot, a bomb, hollowing out the centre and leaving an all-consuming ache. You go to sleep to it, you dream of it, you wake to it; food is dry and tasteless, air is difficult to breathe, colour bleeds away. She knows this.

But there is also relief and the possibility of change, waiting just off centre-stage, hovering and ready to be allowed to tiptoe in. Not straight away, never straight away — in fact, those emotions cannot even be acknowledged for quite some time. But they are there.

Daniel is still standing, leaning against the wall now, and Ester talks, knowing she needs to bring this moment to some kind of resolution so that they can step out of her room and face each other alone.

She offers the box of tissues, but Sarah doesn't even see them. She puts her head in her hands, and her whole body heaves. *This is what's been at the edge of all of Sarah's talk*, Ester thinks. Sarah has known that it was there. It is always there. The layers and layers of words, even the fantasies, if that is what they are, had done little more than cover the knowledge that love would soon be ripped away.

Ester turns to Daniel, who has one single tear, perfect in its form, building slowly. He wipes it away.

'What you've just said is very difficult to say,' Ester tells him.

She looks at Sarah. 'And what you've just heard was very difficult to hear.'

She talks to them calmly about the impact of this moment, and the need for them both to navigate through this with an awareness of their children.

As soon as she mentions the kids, Sarah loses the last semblance of control. She sobs loudly, she says she can't bear it — *we're their parents* — her plea is to Daniel, and it's terrible in its despair.

'We're still their parents,' he says.

'No, we're not,' she replies, and she begins to hit him, beating him across the shoulders with her fists, shouting that he is a liar, he has always been a liar, they are a family, he has to love her, and as Ester tries to reach for her, to get her to stop, Daniel stands.

'Fuck this,' he tells them, and he is gone, the sound of the door slamming behind him followed moments later by his boots on the gravel as he walks off through the rain and around the corner.

ALONE IN HER HOUSE, Hilary knows that once she speaks to Lawrence, she will have begun to put into place a plan that grips too tight each time she lets her mind alight on it. The call to Henry, or perhaps the visit, could also be seen as first steps, but articulating her decision to Lawrence will be harder. She's scared he will lose his nerve and talk to the girls; April, most probably. And then they will beg her, and that's something she could not bear.

She has to stay calm. She has had to break it down. Step by step. Moment by moment. And if she falters, she only has to contemplate the alternative — the failure to act — and she finds she can lift her feet again and move that little bit closer.

She opens her bag, wanting to see the packet of heroin one more time: fine white powder in plastic. She holds it for a moment, surprised by its lack of weight. And then she puts it away.

She sits on the lounge, a faded forties couch covered in deep-red cotton, and sinks into its softness. She has never appreciated the comfort, she thinks, the joy of just sitting here. This is a beautiful room. The kauri boards are a deep honey, scratched and worn in places, covered in rugs that she and Maurie had bought over the years. There are bookshelves on either side of the fireplace, with paperbacks jammed up against each other, some in small piles on top of others, many of their covers now yellowing, the cardboard dog-eared or torn.

She has always been the reader — no one else in the family is that interested. She had carted her books from house to house as a student, the boxes growing in number each time, keeping them because she could not imagine doing otherwise, and because she thought that there was something permanent in a book, that it lasted forever. But now, when she takes an older paperback out to reread or loan, she is surprised at how fragile it has become, the paper threatening to tear in her hands if she turns the page, tiny black specks embedded in its tissue pages; bugs, probably. She should have cleared them out, she thinks. Packed them up in boxes for recycling. No one would want them when she was gone.

She comes from an era that has passed. Books, films, theatre, the art world — all are in an extraordinary shakedown. The films she makes no longer have any place in the currency of culture; they are meditations on fragments that take hold of her, often rambling, looping round and round and round an idea, using images, words, and sounds to play with notions that surface and sink, surface and sink. They would never show on television, they would never get a cinema release, they would not be watched by anyone on YouTube. They screen in festivals, mainly overseas, where she is often invited to talk, and where the few devoted followers of such work know and admire her.

She has never been sad about this, or bitter. She regards herself as exceptionally fortunate, actually. She found her niche at the tail end of this particular incarnation of cinema, and she was able to keep making work. She didn't want fame, although some notoriety ensured her work was screened and she received the occasional funding to produce another film. She also didn't want money. Maurie's success meant they had enough to live well.

He had more ego invested in his work than she ever did. He pretended it wasn't the case — he always said he painted for himself, and to an extent, he did. But the truth was — and she shakes her head at the memory of the tirades he would go into (or worse still, the slumps) whenever he was passed over for a prize or didn't receive a prominent enough review — he wanted mass adoration.

His paintings cover the walls of this house. Many of them are now quite valuable. She looks around her, letting her gaze settle on each of the ones in this room, trying to assess them without his presence. His work never changed. In all the years of painting, he stuck to one style: strong, thick brushstrokes, harsh lines of colour criss-crossing each other, almost as though they had been smeared on with the back of his fist, the effect striking, energetic but — and she smiles again — also perplexing.

She has never understood his paintings.

Once when they were very stoned, she admitted as much to him.

'I mean, are you thinking anything at all, when you do this?' She had begun to giggle as she waved her hand over a canvas. 'You call it "Terrain", but you could call it anything, couldn't you?'

Maurie, who had always had a sense of humour, had laughed, the great sonorous delight of his amusement filling the studio. 'I'm changing its name,' he pronounced, 'to "Hilary".'

'Oh no,' she protested. 'I'm not that one.' She looked around the room, her eyes finally alighting on a larger, more dramatic canvas, one that threatened to spill over onto the walls. 'That's me.'

She presumes he too had been exploring ideas, within his own language, although that was not a language she spoke with any eloquence. She responded on an aesthetic level only — the nature of the colours and shapes either arresting, or pleasing, or too ugly for her to want in the house. She was the one who selected which of his works they kept, aside from the few paintings he gave her, which she had to like.

She had contemplated sorting through the collection, calling the State and National Galleries to talk about keeping them together, and then she hadn't. *The girls can deal with it*, she had thought. She looks up at the ceiling and bites her lip. This is her sadness. Leaving them and knowing they aren't speaking to each other. Not that her being here has brought them closer to mending the rift.

Fuck Lawrence.

She rubs her temples slowly, wanting to ease the pain that is beginning to creep through the pills she took this morning, its sharp nails scratching at her brain. She is not meant to take any more medication until this evening — but what does it really matter? And she looks through her bag for the canister, her hand shaking slightly as she opens it, the smooth capsule falling onto the floor.

She is alone.

She takes slow, deep breaths, steady, steady, steady, picking the pill up and swallowing it without water. She has to bring everything down to the moment, to stay right in the present. She must imagine she is in a bubble of the immediate, able only to see, hear, taste, smell, and contemplate the world that is right next to her. Nothing beyond the boundaries.

She takes her shoes off and lets her toes rub through the carpet, the silky softness of the wool soothing against her skin. She runs her hands along the worn patch on the arm of the sofa, feeling each frayed edge of cotton, fine and delicate. The curtains are open to the courtyard, and she looks at the moss growing in the brick, jewelled green, luminous, velvety, so beautiful as it creeps, determined life in its growth, along the cracks and across the surface of the stone.

The rain is pouring over the gutters in a translucent sheet, bringing with it the occasional leaf or twig. *They need clearing*, she thinks. Another task to be completed — or not — by someone else. Because, conceivably, she could go, and all of this — her house, the remnants of her life — could remain, left to slowly rot away, back to nothing. The couch, the paintings, the books, the rug, the walls, roof, and floors — all disintegrating.

There is a slight break in the clouds, a piercing of light through the sombre darkness, and she stands to see if the day is clearing, but the vision is gone almost as soon as it has appeared, and a new sheet of grey covers the gap, bringing only more rain. What a day. She opens the door and steps out, wanting to feel the moss underfoot and the sweetness of the rain as it falls, cold and constant, soaking into her hair, beading on the surface of her skin, saturating her clothes. It is extraordinary that it can keep doing this, raining and raining and raining. And she stays where she is until she is too cold to bear it any longer, bringing a trail of damp mud and twigs into the house as she heads up the stairs to dry herself and change before Lawrence arrives.

When Maurie died, she took all his clothes to the Salvation Army, packing them up the day after his funeral.

'You don't need to rush,' Ester told her.

It was the smell of him each time she opened the wardrobe. It made her tremble.

He'd had a ridiculous amount of clothes. Jackets, pants, shirts, belts, all no longer worn, but kept in the certainty that there would come a time when he would be as trim as he'd been as a student, and he would put them on and look as handsome as he had in his youth. Some she remembered as she packed them. A beautiful worn green leather coat, soft to touch; an op-shop suit of heavy navy wool, double-breasted and stylish; a steel-grey sweater that his mother had knitted him. He hoarded.

'You might want to keep something,' Esther had suggested. She'd looked at one of the boxes, taking out a fat buttercup-yellow silk tie. 'Lawrence might like this,' she'd said.

And Hilary had told her to take it, to take anything she wanted, but to do it now because the boxes were going down to the car as soon as they were packed.

When she'd finished with the clothes, she went to his studio. That was easier. She took the paintings, and the rest she left, calling friends of theirs and asking them to clear it out. 'And please keep whatever you like,' she'd urged.

When she saw the 'For Sale' sign, Ester had said she needed to slow down. 'Maybe you'll want to convert it into a museum? You don't know.'

It was sold to a developer who remodelled it into a warehouse apartment, realising more than three times the purchase price. She never went to the open inspection, but Ester did, showing her the brochure afterwards. She'd been angry.

'How could they just wipe him out like that? Don't they know what that space was?'

Hilary had told her it was good. 'He's gone,' she said.

Because that wasn't him. Not the studio, not the paintings, not the clothes. They were all nothing without the flesh and blood of him, the warmth and bristle and laughter, the curve of his hip, the beautiful line of his back, the sharp focus of his gaze, his hand warm on her skin. That was her ache and her pain, even now, and she closes her eyes to the memory of him, the physical sense of his presence enveloping her.

He's gone.

She doesn't know what she believes, but she certainly has no faith in being reunited with Maurie in any kind of afterlife. That is not what this is about. If she expects anything at all — and she cannot let her mind rest for too long on any consequences flowing from her decision — she supposes it is the peace of absence, the calm of non-existence, that awaits her. Which isn't to say that she would regard herself as atheist. To deny the possibility of mystery is abhorrent to her, although to claim any knowledge of that mystery is equally repellent.

She dries her hair slowly, the steely white of her curls coarse in her hands. In the mirror, the age of her skin, the droop in her eyes is, as always, a shock to her. The towel is soft beneath her fingers, and she breathes it in deeply. She can smell April, and she presumes that this is the towel she used this morning. There is a milky sweetness to April; beneath the alcohol and cigarettes, the fear and the sadness, there is the hint of frangipani, and she holds it close.

When April had told her what had happened with Lawrence (and she hadn't done so until Hilary had gone over to her house, furious and sad and unable to comprehend how she could have been so stupid), the anger she had felt had been knotted, a squall as dense and dark as any she had known, but it had quickly dispersed.

She had so often seen April's tears, her drama and her capacity to hijack the emotions of others. But on that morning, she had been different. Hollowed out, unable to speak, she hadn't responded to Hilary's anger — and in the face of that silence, Hilary had stopped as suddenly as she had begun. Shaking her head, she had simply held April and told her that this was a mistake that they would all need time to recover from, aware as she uttered those words that the time required could extend beyond what they had.

She changes into dry clothes: a dark-grey cotton top and loose black trousers. The few clothes she owns are all similar; they always have been. She is a practical person, someone who finds a style that suits her and is easy to live in, and then stays with it. If she wears colour, it is usually a discrete flash — a bright scarf or her enamelled ring. And she puts this on now, the red like a crimson petal, concentrated in its beauty.

Sitting on the edge of the bed, she looks out the window to the last magnolia blooms, the first pale leaves of spring unfurling cellophane-fine along the branches, soon to crowd out every petal with a luridly healthy display of green.

Hilary loves this tree. She planted it when they moved to this house shortly after Ester was born, and it grew strong and beautiful, so perfectly sure of its place. In winter, when the leaves are gone, the sun shines through the window, and she delights in the beauty of each flower. Port-wine petals, smooth and waxy, cupped open to the sky. And then, as the summer sun increases in intensity, the foliage provides a cool green shade against the heat of the day.

She won't see it bloom again.

She bundles her damp clothes into her arms to put in the laundry. Conceivably, she could just leave them where they are, on the floor outside her room. Or she could throw them out. They should go to a charity shop, where they will be put on racks with the rows and rows and rows of other pants and tops without an owner — a decision that may just be a delay of the inevitability of contributing to landfill, but one that she likes to think is less wasteful than going straight to the bin. However, this is not the only reason why she takes them downstairs. She is committed to the choice she has made. That much she knows. But it doesn't mean she can bear to take steps that prematurely signal the finality of all she must do. Not yet. And so she holds them under one arm as she walks through to the laundry where the rain drums, ratatatatatat, on the tin roof, on and on and on, while she hangs them on the rack as though she will need them again.

But she won't need them again.

Enough. It is so hard trying to keep this voice at bay.

In the kitchen, she takes a pear from the fruit bowl, and holds it in the palm of her hand. It is firm and round, the brown skin rough, furry enough to send slight shivers up her spine. She slices into it, not because she is hungry, but because she needs to calm herself, absorb herself in a close examination of something, anything. (*It was so much easier when she was finishing off her film.*) The flesh is creamy-yellow, crisp, the sweetness of the pear almost almond-like, a sugary granulation to the juice along the edge of the knife.

There. And as she sits and takes a bite, disliking the sensation of the skin against her tongue, she focuses her mind on the experience only, her sense of calm returning, cautiously, like a whipped dog creeping back to its master.

LAWRENCE DRIVES IN the rain, the windscreen wipers clicking back and forth, back and forth. He has the demister on high, and it cuts a hole through the fog, but the noise is too loud. He turns it off and opens the window, the cold and the wet forcing him to close it again moments later.

He's glad April has the kids (even though he knows she shouldn't). In this weather, he wouldn't get back across town to collect them from afterschool care until much later than usual, and they would complain — no doubt telling Ester as soon as they could, painting him as the neglectful parent.

He takes a wrong turn and swears loudly. *This is not a day to be out*, he thinks, and he cranks the demister up again, the rattle loud as it clears the windscreen to show him what he already knows: it is raining heavily.

Pulling over to the side of the road, he stops. The corrosive acid of worry is making his gut ache, and the truth is, it's his own predicament that's the principal cause of this. He glances at himself in the rear-vision mirror. Hilary's news is terrible. Terrible. But deep inside, he is glad for a diversion from his own trouble, and he is ashamed of how appallingly pervasive his own self-absorption is.

He will be a national scandal.

No, he won't.

He shakes his head. The paper isn't going to want his confession

to go public. They won't want to look like fools. He will be fired
— which is happening anyway. But he will get no good word for
the work he has done. He will spend the next years of his working
life scrabbling for dull jobs measuring customer satisfaction, brand
recognition, product loyalty — all the while getting less and less
work as his name sinks into oblivion.

Perhaps it won't even be that bad. Paul won't want anyone
to know. And it is not as though he needs any kind of reference
from the paper. His name has been out there for long enough. He
will tender for other political jobs — internal party polling —
something that doesn't have a public profile, so Edmund won't be
tempted to salvage Lawrence's conscience with another confession.

Perhaps everything will continue as it has been?

He winces slightly.

On a scale of one to five, where five is extremely satisfied and
one is extremely dissatisfied, how do you feel about your life?

He used to do the odd bit of direct phone polling, just to
keep his hand in as to which questions worked and which were
problematic. It was years ago, when he still had days in which he
could fool himself that he liked his job, that it even mattered.

Sometimes the respondent would argue.

'Are you talking about how I feel right this instant? As I'm
wasting my time answering your questions on the phone? Or
are you talking about five minutes ago, when I was enjoying a
peaceful drink at the end of a hard day?'

Fair enough.

Every question had so many potential nuances, and for each
there were so many responses that could be given at any moment,
influenced by something as simple as having just heard a song that
irritated the shit out of the person, or having eaten a delicious
meal.

It was the horrifying conclusion of democracy, an attempt

to capture and measure the extraordinarily infinite range of our desires, beliefs, thoughts, dreams, and hopes. Everyone had the chance to speak. Worse still, the dross of it was actually being listened to; extracts of sludge were being drawn out, held up as truth, and it pained him more than he could bear. Was that why he had done it? Perhaps that was part of the reason. And because he *could*. That was the strange thrill of it — knowing he could tweak a little here, tuck a little there, kid himself that he was making the voice of humanity sound just that bit better.

Sometimes, late at night, Lawrence would go out. He would walk the streets on his own, thinking he was going to find a bar and have a drink, thinking he might even take someone home and lose himself momentarily in sex.

He would open the back gate onto the laneway, the smell of the jasmine that grew over the rotting wooden palings sickly sweet, the air dark and soft against his skin, the sounds of laughter in other houses, sometimes shouting or arguing, the lights in the rooms framing all the lives within — lonely, messy, hopeful — television screens glowing, dishes being done, heads bent over desks, a young girl dancing on her own in her bedroom, a child asleep on a couch, a dog barking relentlessly. And he would know he was not going to stop at a bar; he was just going to walk and walk, letting it wash over him, the great chaos of it all, impossible to contain.

And so, at the end of the laneway he followed the maze of streets until he was out on the oval — empty except for the occasional midnight walker like himself — and he would sit on a bench and look out across the expanse of green, floodlit by the lights that bordered the path in the distance, a spill of brightness under the sky.

He felt at peace then. Tired and empty, but at peace. Yet sadness was inevitable. As soon as he realised that he was content, it would dissipate, the awareness breaking up any stillness of his soul, stirring it into a thousand particles that floated away, only to be replaced with a gnawing dissatisfaction, a sorrow that this was not his usual state.

This was the way it had always been.

As soon as he finally held what he wanted in his hands, he lost it.

Across town, Ester has her next client for the day.

She had had no break after Sarah and Daniel. Sarah had sat and wept in the waiting room for ten minutes after the session had ended, and then Ester had told her she would have to leave, another client was due to arrive.

'How am I meant to cope?' Sarah had asked as Ester had shown her the door. 'What am I meant to do?'

'Do you have a friend you can call?' Ester had suggested. 'Someone you might go and sit with until you feel a little calmer?'

Outside, the rain slanted down towards the house, and with the door open, they were getting wet. She asked Sarah if she'd brought an umbrella with her, a raincoat? Sarah didn't respond.

'I have to get home to the kids,' she said. 'I have to face the kids after that.'

'Perhaps you could see if someone could come over?'

But Sarah wasn't listening. She was buried deep in the darkness of rejection. She looked blankly at Ester and shook her head, and then she walked out across the street and into the rain, letting it soak into her, darkening the purple of her top, bleeding into the crimson of her skirt, her hair dripping as she headed towards the main road, where she would wait for the bus, oblivious to anything that lay outside the circle of her misery.

Ester looked across the street to see if Chris had arrived, relieved his car wasn't there yet. She had a few moments to clear out her bin (there were a lot of tissues), to plump up the cushions on her sofa, and to jot down one or two key points she wanted to remember so that she could write up her notes in the few hours left at the end of the day.

The room felt dank. It was the gloom and the perpetual rain of course, but — and she didn't like to admit this to herself — it was also Sarah. It always felt this way after she left. Gardenias and sweat. She wished she could open the window wide and let the air in, but the rain was too heavy. She smiled as she stood in the corner and waved a wad of paper around — a useless attempt that was more for herself than for any practical purpose.

It was strange, this blank slate you presented to each client. You existed only for them. Nothing else happened in this room, before or after. They came, they went, and then the next one arrived. None would know how much sorrow and shame and grief and fear this room had seen, from small ordinary madnesses to great howling despair. When the day was finished, she didn't like to open the door. She locked it behind her, grateful for the warm evenings when she could leave the windows open to the night air, letting the outside world in to cleanse, so that, in the morning, the space felt a little better for having breathed. But on nights like this, she had to leave it closed up, hoping that somehow the misery would disperse, seeping under the cracks and out the front door.

There — the room felt better.

Across the road, Chris had pulled up. He was turning off his phone, and she watched as he walked across the street. He too was oblivious to the rain.

His daughter had died 18 months ago.

He had told her the story during their first session, sitting upright, chin lifted, voice level. Her name was Zoe, and she had been eight years old. Completely healthy, happy, ordinary — not a child that either he or his wife, Marina, worried about.

At first, she had simply complained about a pain in her shoulder. It was just one of those things. Marina wanted to take her to the doctor. He thought she was being overly anxious. The GP, who was new and young, couldn't see anything wrong with her. She'd probably just slept in a strange way. It would fix itself.

Three days later, she went back to school, determined to run in the cross-country.

She dropped dead 400 metres in.

These were the hard stories. As he uttered the words, Ester had to steel herself.

Zoe had a blood clot. It had gone to her brain.

'It's unusual for a young girl,' he explained. 'It's not the kind of condition that a doctor would normally look for.'

He was silent, staring out the window, breathing slowly before he continued.

Marina had wanted to sue the doctors. He hadn't. Marina had raged and ranted, and called lawyers, and screamed at him and everyone — *how could he have told her she was over-anxious, how could he have made her doubt herself? How could the doctors have missed something so obvious? They should have given her an ultrasound.* She had downloaded article after article about the condition, underlining the symptoms, showing him how simple it should have been to detect. Next, she took to parking outside the GP's rooms for days on end, waiting for any doctor to come out, wanting to shake each of them, to tell them of her anguish, but never doing it. Sometimes she was there well into the evening. He knew when he called her, the sound of the traffic behind her as she lied and told him she was somewhere else.

And then she had become silent.

The house had been quiet. The pair of them barely talking, barely eating, slowly being swallowed by the emptiness that followed her rage.

He should have tried to reach her. He knew that now. But he'd been lost in his own pain, unaware of her pulling away until it was too late.

'I can't stay here.' Her voice was flat, stripped bare, as she told him she had applied for a job in London. She needed to go. She had arranged everything without his knowing, and he had done nothing to stop her.

The next day she was gone, and Chris had looked at the emptiness of their house and known how perilously close he had come to losing all hold on his desire to live.

His GP had prescribed antidepressants and anti-anxiety medication, both of which he took.

'But I need to talk,' he had told Ester during their first appointment. And he had put his head in his hands and wept. 'I need to talk.'

Ester knows that this is often the case with people in grief. She has seen this in her practice, and she reads about it in the literature debating the effectiveness of bereavement counselling. There are many articles about whether talking is of any assistance in the healing process. She doesn't know, but her instinct with Chris was strong. He needed to speak.

For the first few sessions, he wanted only to talk of Zoe, alternating between remembering her as she'd been and the despair he felt at her death. The stories he related were like snapshots, an album of a life he had loved beyond compare. He would open a certain page and tell Ester small stories. When she was about two, Zoe had loved dandelions, the ones you could blow into the breeze. She called them blowflowers. *I hope so the blowflowers*, she would say each time she went anywhere. She didn't like girls called Maya. There had been cruel Mayas at daycare and at school. She was shy, but she pushed herself, entering the public speaking competition at her school. *She got to the State finals*, Chris told

Ester. *I have never seen anyone so nervous.* She woke up in the morning convinced she couldn't speak, and he and Marina had to get her to sing her favourite song, trying to show her that she hadn't lost her voice.

She shouldn't have died.

He should have been more alert.

He should have known it was serious.

She read voraciously. When she was little she had favourite books for months on end: *Madeline, Where the Wild Things Are,* and a fairy tale she loved about a young girl who wanted a man to marry her, but he ignored her. He and Marina had to read those tales, no others, over and over again.

She had a trampoline and she bounced on it, morning and night, every day, making up stories in her head. If he went out to the garden, he could sometimes hear her, her whisper slightly louder as she came to a dramatic place in the tale. Chris thought it was the rhythm that she liked; it helped her to create the narrative.

As he spoke of her, his eyes became brighter, he sat up straighter. It was as though he were bringing her back to life with his tales.

He wished they'd had another. He was the one who'd put a halt to the idea when Zoe was young. Marina was keen, but he wasn't. It was money, he'd told Ester, staring up at the ceiling. He hadn't wanted them to be managing on one income again. But if they'd had another child, they would need to go on. They would be forced to continue.

She'd died at school.

Away from them.

No one had listened to her when she complained of pain.

They had failed her.

Sometimes he woke up, anxious that his own heart was stopping. He couldn't breathe, he told Ester. It was as though he had forgotten how. He had to concentrate, to think about taking air in and letting it out, because if he didn't, it wouldn't work. And at other times, he would think that maybe he shouldn't try; maybe he should just let himself die. Maybe that was what he deserved. But that too became a question of effort, of trying to stop, his body forcing him to inhale each time he came close to the edge.

He is always polite and gentle, apologising when he talks for too long without pausing, rarely crying since that first session, reasonable when she suggests ways in which he might begin to allow himself to move through the pain of what has happened, appearing to listen to her when she speaks. His surface rarely ripples, only occasionally revealing a tremor across the smooth darkness, a moment in which there is a glimpse of the eternal lack of light below.

She has talked to him about there being no 'correct' way to grieve, no 'normal' coping strategies. They have discussed letting go (an idea that he found abhorrent), and choosing to keep the relationship alive. They have talked about ritual, ways in which he can continue to honour Zoe's life. And in the last session, they began to discuss ideas for how he could learn to be more gentle towards himself, more forgiving, allowing himself to provide some comfort to his grieving self. She had suggested that he write a letter to himself. As though he were a friend who had suffered a similar loss many years ago — words that he wished he'd heard at the time.

He sits opposite her, on the couch, hands neatly folded in his lap, shoulders slightly hunched forward.

When she asks him whether the exercise had helped, he becomes agitated. He tried, he says.

Ester waits for him to continue.

'But each time I sat down to write, it felt so false.' He scratches at his wrist, pushing his sleeves up and then pulling them down again. 'I'm not that person.'

'Which person?' she asks.

'The comforter, years down the track. If I knew his words, I'd be all right.'

'We can know the words we need to hear. We can know how we would like to lead our lives. And we can know what we would like to say to others, how we would like to be in this world, yet it doesn't mean we are able to live that. But sometimes attempting to articulate those words can help bring them closer. Make them a little more real.'

He takes a single sheet of paper out of his coat pocket, clutching it tightly.

'You did write something?' she asks. Her smile is gentle.

He nods.

He has his shoes off, a habit he has had from the first session, preferring not to wear them inside. He had asked her if she minded, and she told him it was fine. His toes inside his socks are scrunched tight, digging into the softness of the carpet beneath his feet.

'I wrote to the man I was, before — ' He cannot continue.

She looks at him holding the letter, the paper damp from the sweat on his fingers. 'What did you want to say to him?'

'Not much,' he tells her.

She waits for him to speak again, but there is silence for a moment and then, to her slight surprise, he clears his throat, an awkward cough, and begins to read.

Dear Chris.

He isn't looking at her. His eyes are fixed on the letter, his voice steadying as he continues.

You were such an ignorant idiot. And then you lost everything. I can't bear to look back on you.

'That's all?' she asks.

He nods.

She is curious as to why he is angry with his former self.

'Because he had everything. He was blessed with an ordinary life. And he didn't even know.'

Outside, a delivery van has pulled up, beeping as it reverses into the neighbour's driveway; it is almost the only sound, that mechanical beep, and then the rain starts up again, pouring down on all the blessed, and Ester waits until she feels she has her composure, until she can open her mouth to speak, while opposite her, Chris folds the paper in his hands, carefully pressing down on the creases. He puts the letter back in his pocket, one white corner still showing.

And then he looks up at her.

She meets his gaze. 'It's how most of us live, paying so little attention to the good fortune we enjoy. Perhaps we have to stay ignorant of our blessings. Perhaps we can only carry our good fortune with us if we don't know that we are doing it — otherwise we would be overwhelmed by anxiety at the possibility of its loss.'

She waits for him to speak.

'Will I ever come back?'

She leans her head to the side slightly, unsure of what he's asking.

'To the world. To ordinary, everyday, shitty stuff that makes you forget just how lucky you are. All of that.' He lifts his arms half-heartedly, as if to embrace life, and then he lets them fall again. 'I don't even know if I want to. I don't want to be that stupid.'

He turns to the window, hands once more clasped in his lap, unadorned apart from his wedding ring, which he still wears.

Ester would like to reach for him, but she can't, and so her own hands are also clasped, her wedding ring long discarded, and she listens, aware of the truth and beauty in his words, and that here in this room, she too is blessed — an awareness she doesn't have enough, she realises, as the rain continues to fall, sweet against the soft grey of the sky.

It's been a long time since Lawrence has seen Hilary, even longer since he has been to this house.

He brushes against damp new leaves unfurling on the giant magnolia, the last of the flowers dropping their petals to the ground, where they lie bruised and bedraggled. He tries to shut the iron gate, but one of the hinges is rusted, and he gives up, bending low beneath an overhanging branch, the drops shaking loose and running down the back of his neck, cold, as he hurries to the shelter of the front verandah.

Hilary is there at the door moments after he knocks — the same, and not the same. She stands, shorter than he remembered, her face like April's but stronger, her gaze more focused. And yet there is a frailty in her eyes that he hasn't seen before, a slight twitch at the corner. But perhaps he just imagines this.

They are awkward in their initial greeting. In the past, he would always have kissed her on the cheek, but now they each lean hesitantly towards the other, unsure of how to say hello. Then she takes charge. Taking his hand in her own, only for a moment, she tells him to come in, out of the wet.

With the front door shut behind him, there is quiet. No birds, no hiss of distant traffic, just the faint tapping of the rain. The house seems empty, but then he has only ever experienced it at family gatherings, with Ester, the girls, sometimes April, and, in the more distant past, Maurie as well. There would be noise, disagreements, family frustrations, and joy as well. He had usually witnessed more than participated — this is how it is, he presumes, when you are not blood. Part of the family, but not. Definitely not now.

Ester used to worry about Hilary being lonely after Maurie died, but she had always seemed so busy to him, so capable, so self-contained that he'd found it difficult to imagine her experiencing anything as aimless and frail as loneliness. Yet now, as he follows her past the living room — hushed, neat, too large for one person — and down the hall, he recognises the emptiness he experiences in his own place when the girls go back to Ester; everything packed up, cleaned up, waiting, waiting for people to make each room exist again. Because that is how it feels sometimes — as though both he and the house in which he lives are not real when he is by himself. Who is to say they exist, other than himself? — and he smiles at the thought, the ludicrous existential spiral his mind is following because he is nervous about this meeting.

The kitchen has floor-to-ceiling glass windows on two sides — one looking out at an ivy-covered wall, the other across a courtyard. He remembers this room well; April and Maurie making salads, terrines, casseroles, marinading meat, all to be brought to the outside table. Which is still there, the wood sagging, damp and rotten in places, its surface covered in leaves, the legs laced with spider webs, glittering with perfect raindrops. What was the French phrase for a web? The star of the spider? Something like that.

There is a dining room as well, just behind them, but they rarely used it. He glances through there now, and it is like the rest of the house: empty, waiting, the large Victorian table pale with dust, one of Maurie's earlier paintings hanging on the wall behind it. He and Ester had once had sex in that room — and he blushes at the memory.

Opposite him, Hilary pours them both a glass of water. Her

hand is trembling. He opens his mouth to speak, to say something foolish like *how are you* when she has already told him she is dying, but she cuts over him, fortunately, taking charge once more.

'You look older,' she tells him.

He laughs. 'It's been a bad day.' He speaks without thinking, aware of how puny his complaints are in comparison to hers as soon as he utters the words, and he grimaces. 'Although not so bad — in comparison.'

There is almost a smile on her face. She clasps her hands around her glass, and asks him if he would like a coffee, a tea, or perhaps even a stiff drink.

'I'm tempted by the last one,' he says. 'But I have to pick up the girls and get them home.'

'I'd have one myself, but I'd probably pass out with the pills I've been taking.' She meets his gaze, and there is, in that instant, so much sadness in her eyes. 'I need your help,' she tells him. 'And I figure if there is anyone in the world who owes a debt to me and my daughters, it's you.'

Lawrence bristles. He shifts in his seat. He is pushing the chair back now, suddenly aware that he is quite ready to leave if she begins to berate him for the past, but she stops him.

'I haven't asked you here for us to argue. I've asked you here because I'm hoping that you will hear me out, understand, and ultimately help me.'

She tells him she has cancer.

He is sorry, he says, but she waves his condolences away with her hand. 'It's life. And I genuinely mean that. I would like to go on living, but it seems I can't.'

How long has she known?

'I will tell you everything,' she says. 'And I'm sorry if I'm a little slow or I repeat myself, but it's becoming harder to focus. My head hurts and I get terribly tired.'

He nods, waiting for her to continue.

'I went to the doctor about three months ago. I was getting blurred vision and aches,' she touches her temples. 'I've never suffered from anything like that so I was anxious. They sent me for scans and various tests — it seems I have a brain tumour, the most aggressive kind.'

He is silent as she breathes in.

'There is only one other person that I have told this to — apart from various doctors, of course. His name is Henry, and he is an old friend. He is helping me too, but more about that later. What I'm trying to say is that I'm not accustomed to speaking about this. It's far more difficult to voice than I expected.' She shakes her head slightly, bemused by her failure to rise to the occasion with as much strength as she normally displays. 'We all know we are going to die. It's all we know with complete certainty, but it's still an extraordinary shock when you find that your time has come. Even for me — and by that I mean, it's not as though this has come to me when I am still young. I'm not very old,' she smiles, 'but I'm at an age where death is less of a shock.

'I had to sit with the news for a while. It's the kind of person I am. I don't really want to discuss things — although if Maurie were here, I would have talked to him. In fact, I might even have asked him what I am going to ask of you. Although I'm not sure. He was always so optimistic, it is likely he would have fought me, convinced there was hope.

'The doctors have told me that there's not much they can do. It's inoperable. There's a new drug that they are trialling, and I could have taken part in the tests. But it was of so little benefit. If you are given it — and you might just be given a placebo — it can make you very ill — vomiting, diarrhoea, there's even the possibility of internal bleeding — and at best you will get another six months. I simply couldn't see the point.

'The time that they've given me isn't long, and I would say that I'm right at the end of the best of it. The headaches will become unbearable. I'll lose control of my bodily functions, and I'll be delusional. I'll go into palliative care, and I will die.'

Lawrence is silent. He does not know what to say in the face of this news, and she's made it clear that she doesn't want sympathy.

'I don't want to put myself through that kind of misery, and I don't want to put others through it either.' She stands now and looks out the window at the rain.

He can see the reflection of her face, fogged in the glass, and for a moment he thinks she is crying, but it's just raindrops, sliding down the pane. He waits for her to turn to face him, but she doesn't.

'I decided early on that I was going to take my own life.'

This is what he has been expecting, and he dreads her telling him the role she wants him to play in this. He coughs awkwardly, and he is aware of sweat on the back of his neck, clammy against his skin.

'I looked into finding a doctor that could assist me. I even spoke to my own GP about it — sounding her out, I suppose. But it's so difficult. I don't want her or any other doctor to have to carry the consequences of my decision. I really don't.'

Or me, Lawrence wants to add. *I don't want to have to bear the consequences either*. To go to court or, worse still, to jail for this.

She has turned around now.

'Don't worry.' She smiles. 'I'm not going to ask you to kill me.'

Lawrence laughs nervously, and he is too loud in the quiet of the kitchen. 'I wasn't thinking you were,' he lies.

She shakes her head, amused. 'I might have disliked you a lot over the last few years, but not that much.'

She can't resist, he thinks. One more go at him. And it won't be the last. But this time, he says nothing. It doesn't really matter, not in the face of this news.

Hilary picks up her bag from the floor and comes to sit at the table again. 'I find it difficult to stay still,' she apologises. 'It makes me more aware of the pain.'

She reaches into the zippered central compartment and brings out a bag of white powder, placing it in front of him.

He looks at it and then up at her.

'It's heroin,' she tells him matter-of-factly.

Lifting it in his hands, Lawrence turns the bag over. 'You know I've never tried it,' he says. 'In fact, I'm not sure I've ever seen heroin. And I know that may seem hard to believe, given my reputation, but it wasn't a drug I sought out, and it never seemed to come my way.'

She reaches across for the bag. 'Well, it's not for you.' There is a spark, flinty humour, in her eyes. 'It's mine.'

He hands the powder over to her.

'I did my research,' she continues. 'And it seems that an overdose is the least painful way to go. But obviously it's a matter of making sure you have the right dose. That's where my friend, Henry, came in. He's had a controlled habit for decades. He bought this for me, he's shown me what I have to do, and —'

She is silent then, swallowing, the ripple down her throat revealing the difficulty she has in uttering her next words. 'Now it's up to me.'

'Are you sure?' he eventually asks.

She nods. 'It's not like I haven't thought about this. I've thought about little else. The alternative terrifies me to such an extent that —'

She glances out to the studio. 'I wanted to finish my last film. And I've done that. I now have nothing left to distract me. And it is so hard to remain resolute, to hold onto my nerve. It is so hard.'

He takes her hand in his and says nothing. He knows her well enough to recognise that she does not want to cry. Her skin is cool against his, her touch loose, but it is almost as though he can feel her pulse, the determined, desperate life beat, there in the palm of her hand, and he is momentarily overwhelmed by the vastness of what awaits her. But he knows this is not the time or the place. His role is to listen and to find out what she wants. Whether he will be able to do as she asks is another matter.

'So,' she removes her hand from his and stands again. He watches as she fills a glass with water from the tap and sips it slowly. 'Why have I asked you here?'

'I don't know,' he smiles. 'I would think I'd be one of the last people you'd want around.' And then he starts to tell her how sorry he is. 'I shouldn't have made such a mess. I really shouldn't. And I wish I'd never caused such hurt. It was terrible. I can only apologise, so deeply and truly.'

She shushes him. 'I know,' she says.

The softness in her response almost brings him undone.

'I need you to deal with finding me.' She looks straight at him. 'I don't want a stranger to find me. I don't want the girls to find me. I hoped you would be able to do this for me.'

He can't say anything.

'And I want you to try and help the girls understand my decision.'

'You won't tell them yourself?'

She shakes her head vigorously. 'There's a lot I can do. But not that. Not that. If they begged me not to go ahead, I would cave in, completely. But it's not what I want. I mean, I don't want any of this at all — of course I don't — but I want to at least spare myself and others the indignity of what's to come. I want to choose how I'm going to go. And I know there is considerable arrogance in that — it's something I've grappled with, I still grapple with — but surely I can take some control?'

He looks down at the table, at the backs of his hands, hairier now in his middle age, liver-coloured spots appearing on his skin. He does not know if he's up to this.

'Perhaps it would be easier if I just told you my plan?'

He nods.

'I am going to go to the river shack tomorrow. I have written letters to Ester and April, explaining what has happened and why. I will have them with me. When I get there, I want to go for a walk and a last swim.' She looks out the window and grimaces. 'Although it's hardly swimming weather. But things can't be just how we want them, can they? And then I plan to text you and take the overdose. I would like you to come up. I don't want a stranger to find me. I don't want the people who have bought the place to find me. Just come up and call the ambulance.'

He has never seen a dead body before. He does not know if he can do this.

'Why can't I just call the ambulance from here?'

'You could,' she tells him, and he realises she has thought all this through. 'I suppose I just wanted to know that there would be someone there to check that everything went as it should. I wanted someone who knew and understood what I was doing. I hoped that you could tell the girls that you saw me and that I was peaceful, and that this was what needed to happen. I hoped you could watch over my body until the ambulance came.' Her gaze is direct and clear.

'And what happens if you don't take enough? If I arrive and it hasn't worked?' He can hear a slightly shrill panic in his voice, probably audible only to himself.

'It's up to you, really. I don't want to you to put yourself at risk, but if I seem close to gone —'

'Oh, I can't kill you,' he tells her, suddenly struck by how surreal this conversation has become.

'No, but you could take your time in calling for help. If I

seemed peaceful. If it seemed close. But I have to leave that up to you. And I have to assume that Henry is right. The amount is correct. And if you can't do this, if you can only call the ambulance for me from here, I understand.'

Lawrence rubs at his cheek, the palm of his hand against his skin. He pushes his chair back slightly, also finding it difficult to sit still. He goes to the tap and pours himself a glass of water. He tries to swallow.

'Why me?'

She is sitting again now, and she turns to where he still stands, at the sink.

'There's enough distance and enough closeness. And as I said, I feel that you owe me. But I don't mean that in an angry, vindictive way. I suppose I saw this as a way of making amends all round.'

'And you think April and Ester won't be angry that I didn't alert them to this, that I didn't try and change your mind?'

'They probably will be initially. But then they'll be glad that you helped me do what I needed to do.'

'You haven't given me long to think about this,' he protests.

'I couldn't. I was afraid you'd tell the girls if there was too much time, that after a few days, your doubts would grow and maybe ebb again, only to grow once more, and then, eventually, you would just cave in and tell them everything. I really don't want them to know. You must promise me that much at least.'

He is silent. The tap drips, and he tightens it. Maurie would have fixed this in the past.

When he eventually speaks, it is to ask a question, his voice feeble at the shame of confessing his potential cowardliness: 'And what if I can't do this?'

She looks at him. 'Then I suppose I just go there and don't return. When they notice, they will call the police, or maybe someone will find me before then.' She scratches at the kitchen table, her nails tightly clipped, her fingers fine and square-tipped. 'I'll be gone.'

'And they'll find your letter, explaining why you did this?'

'I hope so,' she tells him.

'Does it mention me?'

She doesn't understand what he is asking.

'Am I woven into this scenario, even if I don't want to participate?'

She nods. 'I tell them that I explained my decision to you, and that is why you found me.'

'And then I have to explain to them that I chose not to help you? That I wasn't there. And that I didn't warn them of what you were going to do?' Lawrence shakes his head, the full ramifications slowly seeping in. 'And when you don't come back from the river, I'll either have to tell them that I know what happened to you, or I'll have to lie.'

She is standing again, looking out the window at the courtyard; the pattern of wet leaves across the bricks is a patchwork of brown, gold, silver, green, and russet. 'If you don't want to do this, I can change my letters. But you need to let me know your decision.' She looks tired. 'I can't talk a lot more about this. It's up to you, really.'

No matter what he chooses, she has told him of her plans. Even if he says he can't be part of this, even if she changes her letter, he will see their anxiety when she fails to return from the river, when she doesn't answer their calls. How can he remain silent then? He sits at the table, hands clasped in front of him and looks up at her, still standing by the window.

If only she hadn't asked this of him.

'I wish I could see them grow a little older,' Hilary says.

Looking out at the rain, he thinks for a moment she is referring to a plant, something she is growing in the courtyard, before he realises that she is, of course, talking of Catherine and Lara.

'They'll miss you,' he says.

'For a while.' She smiles. 'And then life goes on, and I will be someone that they remember occasionally, with fondness, but with no real substance to the recollection. And that's the way it should be,' she says. 'You get a brief time, and it's so vivid and wonderful and not to be wasted, but of course you only know that when it's about to be snatched away. And then there's a fainter imprint left behind, a period in which you are remembered. After that you are gone.'

The rain stops and the silence is sudden, broken by the fall of drops from the gutter. He looks out the window. They are hitting the edge of a metal pail, the sound loud in the new quiet. He is exhausted. For an instant, his mind returns to the mundane, the practicalities of picking up the girls, the weariness he feels at the thought of cooking dinner. They will get takeaway, he thinks. And then, as quickly as he had veered off on a tangent, he is back again, here in the silence of this room, unable to grasp what Hilary has asked of him. He thinks he might cry. And he is appalled. He stands then and walks to the door, opening it so he can smell the sweetness that follows each shower.

'I'll help you,' Lawrence tells her.

'I knew you would.' She looks at him. 'You're not all bad, you know.'

He unclasps his hands, eyes still fixed on her. 'If you weren't dying, I'd tell you that you could thank me.' He laughs, a strange sound, tugging between tears and anger and frustration and sadness, and then he just shakes his head.

'Thank you,' she says to him, and she holds her hand out.

He takes it.

As he holds her in the silence of the kitchen, he is emptied completely, the frailness of her, the impossibility of imagining the line she is preparing to cross so much bigger than his own self, his worries and anxieties.

And then she pulls away, telling him he'd best get going. She is tired now and she needs to be alone.

ESTER'S LAST CLIENT for the day has never had a sexual relationship.

'Which you think might mean she's never had any issues either,' Ester once joked. 'I was tempted to congratulate her on her wisdom.'

The friend she was with raised an eyebrow, and Ester smiled. 'Well — imagine how simple life would be.' She shook her head. 'It's probably something I don't even need to imagine — it may be the life I live from now on.'

She never used names, but there were times when she talked about her clients. How could she not? She was immersed in their lives all day, the intensity sometimes blanching her own of any colour or substance.

Hannah was forty years old. Tiny, dark-haired, pale, she wore all black, her make-up equally dramatic: white powder, dark mascara, and a deep-plum lipstick. Her clothes were expensive, Belgian designer, deconstructed to make them look they hadn't been stitched properly, with tiny signifiers to let those in the know see that they were the real deal: a white cross on the back of the neck, or a small square near the hem. Ester used to try clothes on like this in Paris. She even bought a coat once, and then felt ashamed at never wearing it. But the truth was, she found the look ugly, hard; or perhaps she just didn't get the language of high-end designer fashion. What were they trying to say by making them look like they had been roughly made?

She had tried on a few identities during that time, unsure as to who she was, alone in an apartment with the twins while Lawrence went off to an office job each day — both of them unhappy. On the good days, he would assess her with amusement on his return, or when they met for lunch, eyes narrowed as he tried to pinpoint her latest look — 'It's *Breakfast at Tiffany's*?' 'A lesbian golfer?' 'An uptight academic?'

She'd feign innocence, shrugging his comments off and denying this loss of self — until he came home late one night, drunk and dishevelled, to find her sitting on the floor, crying. She was lonely. She didn't know who she was anymore. She wanted to go home.

He'd held her, kissing her softly, sweet and boozy, as he'd told her he would quit, he hated it as well, they would go home, the four of them would live in sharp white light so harsh it hurt; they would wake to salty skies and the lazy drone of insects, perhaps they would buy an inner-city house that would seem spacious and bright and almost bucolic, he laughed. And she might get back to just being Ester.

Whoever she *was*, Ester thought, but she didn't utter the words out loud.

Hannah, too, has lived in Paris, and New York, and London, and even Brussels, briefly. She is a corporate counsel for a major international brand, but she wishes she were an architect.

'I'm good at my job,' she told Ester. 'But I don't enjoy it.' She reconsidered her statement. 'That's probably not entirely true. I get satisfaction from doing it well, and there are times when it's intellectually challenging. But if I tried to explain what I did most days, you'd stop listening.'

Ester smiled. 'I'd try not to.'

Hannah's laugh was tight. 'You're paid to, regardless of how dull. Essentially, it's work that benefits wealthy shareholders by putting more money in their pockets. I don't create anything, or make anything. I don't help people. I don't have any belief in the necessity of what I do.'

'And do you want to change this?' Ester asked.

Hannah contemplated the question for a moment. 'There was a time when I wanted to. Very much. But I'm pragmatic. I'm used to earning well. And I wouldn't cope with being at the bottom of the pile. Not at this stage of my life.'

Work is not the reason she came to see Ester.

She was frank from the outset about her failure to have a relationship, her words clipped and direct, almost daring Ester to look startled as she uttered the words: 'I've never had sex. I haven't even kissed anyone since I was in primary school.' On her wrist she wore a leather cuff, and she turned it, too loose on the white skin. 'It's not that I don't want to have a relationship, although I probably am fussy.' She pressed the cuff tighter. 'And if I met someone, how do I explain who I am? That I'm this age and I've no …' she paused, 'experience?'

Ester asked her to tell her a little more about herself.

Hannah was adopted. She hadn't been told this. She had discovered it when she was 17, after her mother died, the papers in a neat folder at the bottom of her underwear drawer. She'd tried to find her birth mother, lodging a request for contact with various agencies, but she never received a response.

'How did that make you feel?'

Hannah shrugged. 'Disappointed?' She glanced at the fireplace. 'That's a beautiful painting. Is it a Maurie Marcel?'

It is, Ester said.

'Are you related?' Hannah asked.

Ester said they were.

She had to be quick; she learnt that within the first hour. Hannah would talk in a seemingly open and frank manner, and then stymie any attempt to analyse or investigate a little deeper. The third time she did it, Ester smiled, gently pointing the habit out to her.

'I don't think there's anything further to say about the matter,' Hannah replied, and she looked genuinely bemused.

Her childhood was neither happy nor unhappy, she said. 'Colourless.'

They lived in an outer-northern suburb, and Hannah went to an ordinary suburban public school. She studied hard, she had few friends, and in her final year, she became ill. 'Glandular fever. I had to work from home. I took the exams and did well enough to get into law — not as well as I would have done otherwise, but well enough. And then my mother died. I was on my own.'

'And was that hard?'

'Not particularly,' Hannah said. 'We were never close. I was self-sufficient.'

Hannah just doesn't know how to meet someone. Doesn't know how to fall in love, to have sex, to be normal, and she asks these questions during most sessions with the persistence Ester has come to know during their time together, wanting this to be just another problem that can be solved with a logical and determined approach.

Today, she wears slim-fitting black pants, boots with a strange lacing system that makes them look a little like orthopaedic shoes, a loose black knit, and several silver discs around her neck. Her hair is damp from the rain, and she musses it with her fingers to dry it, beginning the session with her usual barrage of talk. She is late — as she often is — and she has excuses banked up: meetings that went over time; the need to get something off layby on the way here (she is a compulsive shopper who puts everything on layby, stretching the terms of the agreement to breaking point); taxis that didn't come.

Ester has told her that failing to be on time only sabotages the session for herself. 'It's very hard to do effective work in under an hour.' She has also made rules with Hannah. More than ten minutes late, and the session will be cancelled. Hannah usually arrives moments after the ten-minute cut-off. Late twice in a row, and the therapy will come to an end. They have come perilously close to this point several times.

Over the last month, Hannah has commenced internet dating.

'Browsing actually,' she always says.

She finds it demeaning and demoralising. 'I don't think this is something we should shop for. You reach a certain level of income and you can buy most things — cooked meals, a clean apartment, someone to do your chores — but I'm not sure you should purchase a relationship.'

'What makes you think of it as purchasing?' Ester asks.

Hannah considers the question. 'I realise there's no exchange of money, but it's still like a display of goods, an advertising of the wares.' She rolls her eyes. 'And most of the wares aren't that enticing. I knew there were a lot of dull men out there but to be reminded of this — en masse —'

Ester smiles, remembering her own experiences of internet trawling.

'But I've decided this is a mountain that needs to be climbed.' Hannah leans forward, her words becoming more rapid as she confesses her decision. 'I need to have sex. I've picked one of them — the least offensive I could find — and I'm meeting him tonight, for a "date",' she puts inverted commas around the words with her fingers and raises her eyebrows, 'so I can go to bed with him. I can't put it off any longer.'

Then, sitting back in her chair, Hannah asks whether Ester has changed the room around. 'I like it,' she says, appraising the space, which hasn't altered since Ester moved here, let alone in the fortnight that's passed since Hannah's last session.

Ester tells her no, following up with her own question before Hannah gets another chance to divert her, aware that these sessions are sometimes like a sprinting competition. She has to be on her toes.

'So you see the problem as being simply one of not having had sex? That this has held you back from having a relationship?'

Hannah nods earnestly, and there is something childlike in her desire to believe that such a simple solution is possible. 'Once I've had sex, I won't feel so anxious. Will I?'

Ester tells her it's one approach. 'But perhaps it's worth also looking at why you haven't had a physically intimate relationship — or encounter — until now. There are fixes and there are fixes,' she says. 'It's a little like the difference between a quick surface clean of a room, or a thorough clean. The band-aid or the operation.'

Hannah nods. 'The surface clean shouldn't be dismissed. It can make a difference.'

Ester crosses her legs and smiles. 'If you decide to take this approach,' she says, 'will you promise me one thing? Look after yourself. Don't be afraid to back away if you feel uncomfortable.'

Hannah nods, and then laughs. 'Actually, I can't promise you that. It's inevitable I'm going to feel uncomfortable.'

Ester smiles. 'Fair enough. But don't push yourself into a place that feels completely wrong. And, perhaps more importantly, be prepared to accept that this may not provide the miracle cure you're looking for.'

Hannah looks down at her hands. She has delicate, slender fingers, the first signs of age on the paleness of her skin, the back of her hands dry and papery, livery age-spots freckling the blue of her veins. She scratches at one of her nails, shaping it. The silence is rare.

When she looks up again, her eyes glitter. She turns to stare at the rain on the window, the film over the darkness of her pupils gone as soon as she glances back to Ester.

'All my life, I have been lonely.'

Ester remains silent.

'I knew it, but I didn't know it. When something is constant, you're often not aware of it. The house was quiet with just my mother and me. She went to bed by nine, and I spent most nights in my room, studying. I listened to the radio while I worked. People rang the late-night show. Love songs and dedications, it was called. They would talk about their husband who'd left, their first love, their partner that cheated on them. *And what would you like to say to him?* the announcer would ask. *I forgive you*, they would say. Or: *Come home, I miss you.* And then they would play a song for them.

'One night, a woman rang. She had no one to make a dedication to. And so she was making it to a man she was yet to meet, a man who would love and cherish her. *I'm sure he's out there for you*, the announcer said in his smooth, deep voice. *I know you will cross paths one day soon.*' Hannah stares at Ester. 'Who was he to make that assurance?'

Ester smiles.

'I've become so used to being alone. I find it hard to imagine this will ever change.'

Ester nods. 'You have learnt to be extraordinarily self-reliant, and to do without people. This was probably very necessary as a child. It helped you survive. But the survival skills we develop as a child often don't work so well for us when we are older. And breaking down patterns, habits, ways of being that are entrenched, can be a slow process.'

The rain drums down, down and down and down. Ester looks at Hannah sitting opposite her — intelligent, original, fierce, determined — and she is seized by a foolish desire to give her something more than this careful response.

They all come in here, day after day, session after session. Loneliness, heartache, despair, anger. Most of her clients are there at the uncomfortable edge of one of the darker facets of life. She could stand up now in her room and open the window, let the rain pour in, across her desk, onto the beautiful carpet, her papers curling up, ink smudging, the sound of the downpour uncomfortably loud and close, and she could look at Hannah and tell her to just go for it — have sex, have it often, throw herself into life with no reserve.

But she does not utter those words to Hannah. Of course she doesn't.

This temptation often creeps in at the end of the day. And she always resists.

Opposite her, Hannah is picking up her bag, a large, soft, leather pouch.

'I understand how you could feel that having sex will break down the barriers quickly.'

Hannah grimaces.

Ester smiles: 'Apologies for the unfortunate choice of words.'

'I know what you're saying,' Hannah interjects. 'You're telling me to be careful. To not expect too much.' And she stands, tiny, delicate in her black, bag swung onto her shoulder. 'I like your skirt by the way. Is it a Paul Smith?'

At the end of day in her room, Ester sits for a moment. She would like to do a little talking herself. This is how she feels at the end of most days, actually.

On the afternoons she picks the girls up from school, she tests out her voice when she is alone in the car, sometimes venting her frustrations with particular clients out loud, sometimes reminding herself of tasks she is meant to do, or even expressing her own feelings to the dashboard. The sound of her words is strange after sitting in a room alone with other voices washing over her — woes, joys, and grievances layered and twisted and knotted, and dumped, one after the other.

She used to ring Lawrence for this purpose, and the beauty of it was that she didn't even care that he was — as he so often was towards the end — non-responsive. She would simply talk, chatting about what she would make for dinner or her plans for the weekend, or about a movie she wanted to see, an issue in the news, or her own anxieties about Hilary, or how difficult she found April.

Often she could hear the music he was listening to in the background: the low hum of a guitar, or the steady beat of drums. Sometimes, he was in a café, and there would be other voices around him, a clatter of plates. He would grunt in response, only occasionally asking questions or contributing himself. She didn't care. She just wanted to talk and talk and talk.

It must have been irritating, she thinks now, smiling as she does so, because her thoughts towards him are not unkind, and this surprises her. It's happening more frequently, her mind resting on Lawrence momentarily, alighting with a well-accustomed wariness, only to find that the landing is softer each time.

'Perhaps we *will* speak again,' she says to herself, because this is one of those days when she is at home alone and the easiest solution to that immediate need to talk is to bore herself with her own words, which she does.

Opposite, she can see her reflection in the window. The desk lamp is still on, a pool of light in the glass, revealing the pale lines of her face, her dark eyes, brown hair pulled back, the lipstick on her mouth faded now. She imagines facing this woman in this room and talking to her.

'My husband cheated on me with my sister, and, for over three years, I have been unable to forgive either of them.'

The words are bald when she utters them, and she glances up at the Ester in the window, eyes a little too wide for the calm and curious self who usually listens in this room.

'Almost three years. And I have not uttered a word to either of them.'

And now that other Ester responds. 'What are you afraid of?' she asks, leaping several steps ahead because they know each other well, this client and this therapist, and there is no need for the cautious steps she would normally take.

'What am I afraid of?' Ester repeats the question.

Letting go of that anger and hatred. She tries to imagine it, while knowing that the remnants she hangs onto now are tattered scraps, frayed and symbolic only. What would she have left without it?

Ester closes her eyes. It is April she sees. They are in their early twenties, and they are at a party. April is dancing, oblivious to everyone around her. Men and women drift in and out of her orbit as she moves under a hazy night-time sky, the few stars obscured by the sea-spray fog, the air warm and humid, so salty she can almost taste it. It's 'Sign of the Times' by Prince that she's dancing to, and she's lost in it.

Ester's boyfriend of the time is off trying to buy some ecstasy. The plan is for the three of them to go and take it before the night gets any later. But the truth is that Ester doesn't really want to. She never likes taking drugs when she is with April. Ester knows what will happen. She will sit removed, watching the evening from a distance, judging April, judging her own boyfriend, telling herself that it's just the drugs making them have such a good time, as though they are cheating. As though, somehow, this is a game with results, and they are cheating. And she doesn't want it to be like this. She wishes they had never decided to buy any.

She stands, slightly unsteady in her new heels, and weaves her way through the bodies. She has drunk too much, and, in the heat, she feels vaguely ill. These are April's friends — she doesn't know many of them — and she takes her sister by the hand and tells her she needs to go home.

April runs her fingers down Ester's arm, her touch surprisingly cool despite the warmth. 'Dance with me,' she says. Ester shakes her head, but before she knows it, she is moving with her sister, as they used to do when they were young, the music loud in their bedroom, dressed up in a strange array of clothes they had stolen from Hilary and Maurie's wardrobe, and she feels all her self-conscious anxiety slide away, tumbling like silk to the dance floor where she kicks it off to the side, out of their orbit, both of them aware of nothing more than the music and each other.

She is having fun; beautiful, bright, fizzy fun, and April is right there with her, the pair of them sparkling in the joy of it.

Opening her eyes again, Ester is surprised to find herself crying.

'I miss her,' she says out loud to the other self, who is a terrible therapist because she is crying too. They smile at each other.

'The truth is really very simple,' Ester the client says to Ester the therapist. 'And also very complicated.' They laugh.

Lawrence should have been with someone like April, but all the time he would have wanted to love someone like Ester. He'd known that. And so he'd fallen for Ester because that was what he'd wanted to be — a man who fell for a woman like Ester. And yet, wanting is not enough.

She'd loved him. But sometimes she wondered whether part of her love came from being so amazed that someone like him had chosen someone like her.

'He picked me over my sister.'

'And then he didn't,' the therapist says. Or is it the client?

She leans forward and switches off the lamp, the darkness of the day seeping in now. She stacks her papers neatly on the desk and powers down the computer. Lifting each of the cushions off the two-seater couch, she shakes them, the feathers fluffing up; they are full again, as though no one has sat here all day.

Last is the bin. Still empty after Chris. Hannah doesn't cry. Ester remembers this as soon as she looks at it, and she pushes it back under the desk, ready for next week's tissues.

Closing the door behind her, she steps out into the house, the corridor dark, the silence heavy. She needs to work out what she is going to wear, and she flinches from the prospect of trying to decide, because it is not something she is good at. Lawrence had an eye for clothes. He would often advise her if she couldn't choose, knowing what would suit her and what wouldn't. She shakes her head at the thought of ringing him now.

'Help me,' she would say. 'I need an outfit for my first proper date.'

And he would tell her to avoid black, and the librarian look or the lesbian golfer, unless, of course, this date was a man who went for a more uptight get-up.

'Which you do well,' he would say, one eyebrow raised, the old Lawrence again, the one from their early days, teasing her as he used to, such a long time ago.

HALFWAY TO APRIL'S HOUSE, thc nausea that Lawrence feels gets the better of him. He has the heater on too high, and he winds down the window, the chill slap of the rain on his skin a relief. Sticking his head out, he breathes in deeply, only to quickly recoil as a truck passes, the fumes and oil and rush of wind sudden and fierce.

He doesn't know how he will act as though everything is normal. He doesn't know if he should. He wishes he could ring Ester and ask her advice. She was good at listening and guiding him to a decision. But eventually he began to recoil from that, wary of the therapist in her, and feeling that she was turning their relationship into client and counsellor, which made him behave badly.

'Red rag to a bull,' he would say when she accused him of drinking too much, and he would pour another wine without flinching from her gaze.

He turns the news on, the results of a rival poll making headlines. The issue is climate change and whether the government should do more to combat the effects. He switches to music, not wanting to hear the tedium of the analysis, knowing that if he does, he will pick holes in the questions. Besides, what does it matter what people think? What does it fucking matter? The world is dying, and we are still asking the opinions of every person on the street while failing to listen to what our experts are telling us. He finds he is crying, his eyes as blurred as the windscreen, everything awash, wiping the tears with the back of his hands as the blades go back and forth across the glass.

By the side of the road, he winds the window right down and puts his head out to vomit. The hazard lights tick, a steady rhythm over the hiss of other cars as they rush past. The music is off. When he closes the window again, there is only silence, and he sobs, the salt of his tears diluted by the rain, everything fogged up so there is just him and his terrible sadness.

'Okay,' he says to himself in the rear-vision mirror. 'Enough.'

He puts the key in the ignition and turns back onto the road, wipers flicking back and forth, back and forth, breathing slowly to calm himself before he gets to April's.

Catherine has always been the artist. She lies on the floor, sheets of newspaper spread out in front of her, crayons and textas to choose from, her legs swinging behind her in rhythm to the music as she contemplates which colour to use next.

Lara is on the couch reading, although her boredom is evident; half her body has slipped down toward the ground, and he can see she is ready to start causing trouble.

'Daddy,' she calls out, and she jumps up, Catherine right behind her.

He hugs them both tight.

'So who hurt herself?' he asks, and they look momentarily confused — the whole accident at school forgotten — and then they point at each other, while he shakes his head in mock disapproval. 'Have you been good for your Auntie April?' He grins at them.

'Angelic,' April says, and she sits back on the old leather couch, feet up on the coffee table as she asks him whether he wants a cup of tea.

'And a piece of cake,' Lara adds.

'Or something stronger?' April glances at the clock. 'It's getting to that time. Besides, it's so bloody dark and miserable outside it might as well be night.'

Why not, he thinks, and he tells her a whiskey and cake is just what he needs.

'Lara, you be the barmaid,' April points to the cupboard where the bottle is. 'And Catherine, you serve the cake. I'm shagged.'

Lawrence shakes his head. 'I don't think you're meant to ask young children to serve alcohol,' he says, aware that in the absence of Ester, he becomes very like her.

April smiles. 'I'm not asking her to drink it. Just to make it. Ice and a dash,' she adds to Lara. 'Pouring a drink is a useful skill.'

'For an alcoholic.'

April raises an eyebrow. 'Shitty day at the office?'

He smiles at her, aware of how like a parody of a married couple they are, and then he looks down at his jeans, still damp from the dash across the street, and steadies himself because he remains perilously close to tears. 'Thank you for getting them.'

Catherine has two plates of cake on a tray. She curtsies and giggles. 'May I serve you, oh lord and lady?'

Behind her, Lara waits with two very large glasses of whiskey in her hands. She inhales deeply and then curls her lip. 'Disgusting.'

'This lady is going to renounce her cake and give it to the serving girls,' April says. 'Why don't you take it through to my bedroom and watch some television?'

'I'll come and get you soon,' Lawrence adds. 'We need to get home for dinner.' He knows he is saying this to April really, to let her know he won't be staying, and he takes a long gulp of the whiskey, ice cold, burning in his throat.

'What's up?' April's pale eyes are focused on him.

He shrugs, lying badly. 'Just tired.'

She doesn't buy it. 'I've known you for a while. In some very trying circumstances. Is it the girls being here?'

He shakes his head. 'They shouldn't be here, but I appreciate what you did.' He takes another slug of the whiskey and then puts the glass down. 'I've got to drive.'

In the soft light from the lamp next to the window, April's long, fine arms are golden, her fingers delicate, two heavy silver rings on each hand. The glass is sweating in her grasp, and she too puts her drink down, running her damp palms through the curls in her hair before standing slowly and coming over to where he sits. 'I'm not going to bite you,' she says, and she leans down and kisses him gently on the cheek, her touch warm and kind. 'Nor am I going to try and make you stay. You just look sad.'

He shifts in his chair, wanting to pull her towards him and hold her close, to cry and tell her everything; he doesn't know what he wants, really. It's been so long since he's had any idea; he can't even remember when he knew, or what it was he desired. It's all shifting, and he is seasick with the motion, so he closes his eyes, letting in the sound of the rain, the low hum of the television from the other room, the softness of the couch. There is a velvet smell — roses — heavy and funereal above the richness of the cake and whiskey, and, last, the touch of April's hand resting warm on his arm.

'Has something happened?' she asks. 'Are you ill?'

He shakes his head.

'Ester? Is Ester ill? Is no one telling me?'

No, no, no.

And then he tells her — not about Hilary, not that — he tells her about Edmund and being caught out, and he probably does it to avoid relaying the news of her mother, and because it's all too much now. He says it all — how he fiddled with the last three polls, just slightly, why, he didn't know. He hated the government? He was bored witless with what he did? Did it make any difference? No. It was a puny misdemeanour, really. There were many legitimate ways he could, and did, meddle — the questions he chose, the timing, the slant on his interpretation of the responses. As he talks, he finds it hard to understand his actions. He finds it hard to understand anything.

'Fuck me.' April looks at him and grins.

He doesn't know whether to laugh or cry.

He doesn't mean to kiss her, but he does; it is like a default mechanism, kicking in as a response to desperate floundering; her mouth is soft, whiskey-warm on his, and it is like hovering above the edge of a deep pool, only to be stopped by her hand on his shoulder, pushing him away as Catherine asks what they are doing, her voice clear above the rain and television.

'Nothing,' he says too quickly and loudly.

'Why are you kissing April?'

'I wasn't,' he lies.

'Well, you were, actually,' April responds, the only one keeping her head, and she is laughing now. 'Which was stupid of your father, but sometimes too much rain and whiskey makes idiots of us all.'

Catherine just stares at them.

'Come over here,' Lawrence says, and he pats the arm of the chair.

She turns and runs out of the room.

In April's bedroom, he tries to sit Catherine on his lap, but she continues to resist him.

'It's all right,' he tells her. 'There's nothing happening with April. It was a mistake,' he says. 'I had some bad news today, and I'm not behaving how I should.'

'I don't want to talk,' Catherine says, fingers blocking her ears.

Lara is transfixed by the television.

'Okay.' Lawrence sighs. 'We'll head home in a few minutes.'

In the lounge room, April looks up at him. 'She'll be fine,' she says. 'Just don't make too big a deal of it.' And then she picks up her glass and shakes her head. 'You need to grow up,' she tells him. 'And stop falling onto whoever is closest when the shit hits the fan.'

That's rich, he thinks. *Coming from her.*

'So what are you going to do?'

'Confess,' he eventually says. 'I don't have any choice.'

'I would have thought you'd have dreamed up something more interesting than that. Tell them Edmund has lost his mind. Or that you've fired him and he's seeking revenge.' She pours herself another glass. 'Or go brave. Tell them the polls create their own truth.' She smiles. 'Become a political rebel.'

He's had enough.

'I'm not a kid anymore. This is my work.'

The clock chimes behind him. She doesn't shift. 'You hate it. You're miserable. You have been for years. If you're going to fiddle the results, at least have some guts about it, shout it out loud. You've got nothing to lose.'

She doesn't get it.

'And live off what?'

Her eyes remain fixed on him. 'What else is going on?'

He ignores her, standing to leave, calling out the girls' names as he does so.

'So I presume I won't see you again for a while,' April says. She begins gathering the twins' bags, putting them next to their raincoats by the door, and then she scans the chaos of the room one last time to see if there's anything she's forgotten.

He, too, surveys the mess. Records and newspaper spread out across the floor, cake plates on the carpet. The rain is soft against the windows.

'Do you think we could have been happy together?'

The question is without rancour or sadness. Her voice is soft so the girls won't hear, but still he looks quickly to the closed bedroom door.

He doesn't know the answer.

'Maybe,' he says.

'I'd like us to be friends. I'd like to see the girls. But more than anything, I want to have Ester in my life again.'

He can see the need in her eyes, and he looks away.

'I'm going to call her tomorrow. And if she won't answer, I'm going to go to her.'

He doesn't reply. But in that instant, he wants, more than anything, for her desire to be realised.

He calls the girls, loudly now: 'Come on, you two,' his voice too harsh, startling enough to make them both obey, Catherine still refusing to look at him as she picks up her school bag and waits for him in the hall.

HILARY DOES NOT know why she has always felt a greater vulnerability around Ester. She is afraid for her, and slightly afraid of her. And yet, by all measures, she's the more sensible of her daughters, the one who considers before she acts, who listens and usually responds with reason. She doesn't fall into great drama over an event of little incident, nor display a lack of interest in an important moment.

Perhaps it is Hilary's sense that this calm simply covers all that Ester hides, a shield to cloak her frailty, just as Hilary hides behind a stern facade. They are alike, and that is what makes her more afraid for her younger daughter.

Ester sits at the table now, the smooth sheen of her dark hair rich in the softness of the lamplight, her skin pale. She looks beautiful this evening, dressed in a silvery-grey sweater and black jeans; she is also wearing make-up, which for her is unusual, the dark around her eyes and the red on her lips bringing out the delicacy of her features. Like Hilary, she wears little jewellery — just a fine gold bracelet and a beaten-gold ring that has a dull shine.

She is translating the program notes, reading them aloud, head bent in concentration, one finger running along each line of text, but Hilary is not listening. All she can hear is the stillness of the evening — the rain has eased — and, floating above the silence, the gentleness of Ester's voice darting over and around the steady beat of a drip drip drip, the last of the previous downpour earthbound from gutter to ground.

Ester looks up, waiting for Hilary to comment, to demand certain changes — which is what she usually does — or to signify her approval.

'It's fine,' Hilary tells her.

'Even being called "elderly"?'

Hilary just nods. She no longer cares about the film or the program. She just wants to drink in Ester, take her fill. 'Where are you off to this evening?'

Ester hesitates before answering, and then a smile escapes the corners of her mouth, and she folds up the translation. 'I think I've met someone,' she says. 'We're going out to dinner.'

Hilary holds her daughter's hands in her own and lifts them slowly, kissing the smooth skin, and squeezing them a little before she lets them go.

'He's a lucky man,' she eventually says. 'You are a beautiful young woman, and so easy to love.'

Ester blinks and stares up at the ceiling.

'Don't doubt it for a minute,' Hilary leans closer, about to continue, but Ester shifts back. She never wants to talk about this.

'Listen to me,' Hilary continues. 'I'm elderly so I do know some things. I forget others, but what I remember has some value. You've been hurt, I know that. And your anger was understandable. But now it's time to let it go and enjoy your life. It's so short. Don't waste it.' She stands because the throbbing pain is too much. Her hands shake as she pours herself a glass of water. 'Shall we have a wine to celebrate?' She shouldn't drink on the painkillers, but what does it matter? She could down the whole bottle if she chose. She could do anything tonight — and with that realisation comes a strange vertigo that makes her clutch the fridge door a little tighter to steady herself.

Ester notices. 'Are you all right?'

She is tired of lying. 'I haven't been feeling well,' she says.

'You should see a doctor.'

And there she is, balanced on the point — *I have*, she could say. *And I don't have long to live.* But as she opens her mouth, her throat dries up, and fortunately Ester is too distracted by the evening ahead to press the point.

'Just one glass,' she tells Hilary.

'Are you nervous?'

Ester always avoids discussing herself. And so she too stands and looks out the window at the courtyard, glistening under the light from the kitchen. 'Didn't you want to show me your film?'

Hilary no longer cares. But if it means she can keep Ester here for a little longer, she will.

She has tidied the studio, cataloguing all her stills and working drafts into neatly labelled boxes. April hadn't noticed this morning, but Ester does. 'God, you've been busy. Why the big clean-up?' She walks around, reading the notes on top of several boxes, and then she turns to Maurie's drawing of the horse. 'I think that's my favourite work of his.'

Hilary looks at it. She smiles. 'Mine, too.' It is the arch of the neck that she has always liked best. 'No one will be able to keep it when I'm gone.'

In the silence that follows, she can feel Ester watching her for a moment, hesitating, and so she turns quickly to the computer and loads the film. 'Here,' she pulls out a seat for her daughter and dims the lights.

She had been nervous at the prospect of showing Ester the footage of her and April, but she no longer cares. There's nothing she can do. It's up to Ester now. And so she presses play, and the first of the images floods the screen, starting with suitcases, her own from when she was young, her school satchel with her name written on it, and the bag she took when she came to Australia, leading down to the story of all she chose to keep from her past when she began her new life here.

It wasn't much.

Clothes, a diary, two novels, and a camera.

Cracked leather, frayed cotton, yellowed paper, and a hard Bakelite shell.

She stands, washed out by white sunlight, hair like fairy-floss in the stiffness of the sea breeze, that camera pressed to her eye.

And the images build — negatives, prints, too many to contain, kept in files, digitised, catalogued, weightless and yet so very weighty — until, finally, they settle on a photo of Maurie, a man without suitcases or bags, just paints and pencils and turpentine, canvas and wood, colours waxy and oiled, palettes overrun with hues, splattered floors and walls, and paintings stacked up against walls, in storage, digitised, catalogued, and valued.

Hilary glances across at Ester, who is leaning forward, listening to her mother's narrative, her voice weaving a tale of a life, of all that is amassed in such a short period of time, all that is purchased, created, swapped, gifted, lost, and forgotten.

And now the sisters sleep — two young girls, one dark, one fair, lying next to each other in a hammock by the river. Hilary would like to touch the downy hair on those legs again, feel the curl of a small, sticky finger in her own, and breathe in the sugary sweetness of milk teeth and plump cheeks.

They are older now, in dress-ups from one of the suitcases, dancing on the verandah of the river house, behind them a hazy drone of insects buzzing in the grass and the sky, everything wilting under the summer heat.

Suitcases again — dress-up clothes tumbling out across the floor, and the images melt into carefully folded pants and shirts, jackets, ties and sweaters, shoes in rows, socks curled into each other, underpants; the sadness of clothes without flesh. Hilary puts them all into garbage bags, talking to the camera the whole time, saying that this is not what she wants to hold onto. Not at all. And then she sits there on the empty bed, her hands open on her lap. She has nothing she can grasp.

The footage shifts now to other tales, memento mori, keepsakes — dandelion wisps of hair in lockets, pressed flowers, jewellery, even a clipping about a woman who kept fur from each of her cats. Slowly, these images dissolve to the floor of the river shack, belongings spread out across the bare boards.

Hilary has filmed herself packing up.

She glances across at Ester now, who is still watching, chin cupped in one hand, eyes focused. Hilary knows Ester has not been there since she learnt about April and Lawrence. But she does not flinch at the footage.

The camera flickers off and then on again, the images blurred by the rain that had fallen on the lens, the focus now on the swollen river seizing debris with its furious pace, the swirl and then the stillness as all the force of that water rushed up against a small dam, everything left behind as the flow moved on.

Hilary reaches for the light and then stops.

Ester has her head in her hands.

'Has it upset you?' Hilary eventually asks.

'No.' Ester looks at her mother. 'It's a beautiful film. The best you've made. You should be very proud of it.' She picks up her empty glass and turns it around in her hands. 'You're not really elderly.' Her words are slow, considered. 'You're only seventy — and look at your work.'

In the darkness of the studio, Hilary doesn't move.

Ester turns on the desk lamp, a pale pool of golden light spilling across the room. *She has on that face*, Hilary thinks, *that therapist face*.

'Is everything all right?' Ester asks.

Hilary stands up briskly and comes over to the computer, leaning forward to log off. 'Absolutely fine.'

'I know it's been some time since Maurie died.' Ester's words are hesitant. 'But you know people can be depressed after the loss of a partner … well, for many years.'

Her head hurts and she does not want to snap, each word slapping the next towards an argument. 'I'm not depressed,' she replies. And then she tells Ester that they should get inside to the warmth. 'You'll need to get going. For your date.'

Fortunately, this is enough to distract Ester from the conversation she has been attempting.

'I'm glad you showed me,' she tells Hilary.

The air is sweet outside, damp and cool, a scattering of crushed leaves and twigs and petals covering the path from the front door. Hilary throws her head back. 'Sometimes I think how extraordinary it would be to be a dog — to be led by scent.' She picks up a small branch of red-and-gold eucalyptus, astringent and cold, and inhales deeply.

'I'm fine,' she tells Ester, who is still looking at her.

Ester's gaze stays fixed for a moment longer, and then she lets it go. 'Wish me luck.'

'I wish you all the luck and wonder and beauty in the world.' Hilary holds her close, breathing her in, warm and soft, the dampness of her hair, the faint perfume of her lipstick, the musty smell of rain on clothes, all of it, and then because she is terrified of letting go, she laughs with a little too much gaiety, and steps back into the emptiness of her house. 'I love you,' she tells Ester. 'With all of my heart.'

Her declaration floats off into the night, unheard by her daughter who is already out on the street.

Ester raises her hand. 'I'll ring you tomorrow.'

'Look forward to it,' Hilary replies.

It was an ordinary hour together, she thinks. Which is what it had to be.

All of her is stretched, taut. She looks down at her arm, the flesh and muscle, the living, breathing being that she is, warm blood pumping, pumping. Her own heart too loud. Her head thumping. And so she closes the front door, standing pressed against the wall until she is steady again, steely inside and out, focusing only on the alternative, because the horror of *not* doing what she has resolved to do is all she has left to propel her forward.

IT IS TEN O'CLOCK.

April was right. There are so many ways in which Lawrence could respond. He could fight, lie, and cheat, wait until Edmund has written to Paul and then deny everything, say that Edmund is going through a personal crisis, perhaps a mental illness. He could go public, be loud about all that is wrong with surveys, polls, focus groups, be the rebel she laughingly urged him to be. Or he could just confess in an email to Paul. A message that isn't long or difficult to compose. He altered the results. Not significantly. But the fact remained that he had done this. There were a number of reasons why. He was happy to explain, if Paul were interested in hearing, but at this stage all he wanted to do was tell him the truth. He wished him luck with the robo polls. He had enjoyed the work they had done together.

Perhaps not that last sentence. He won't lie. He deletes it, writing his name before raising his glass to his own reflection. 'To Hilary,' he whispers, pressing 'send' before he can change his mind.

And so he is done. Ruined. Fucked.

Tomorrow, Paul will ring him and ask him what in God's name he thought he was doing. Perhaps he will think Lawrence's email is some kind of drunken joke in response to his contract ending, perhaps he'll delete it before he even reads it.

He forwards a copy to Edmund with one word in the subject line: *Done*.

The response is almost immediate: Edmund is glad Lawrence has confessed, he hopes this will represent a fresh start in his life, the first steps towards being a better person. He has every confidence it will.

Lawrence deletes it.

Outside, it is silent, quiet after hours and hours of rain. The peace wraps around, soft and heavy, and Lawrence sits with it, the bottle of whiskey by his side. Somewhere in the distance, he hears a car alarm, and then a harsh beep, followed by voices, the sound of people saying farewell, laughter, and a door slamming shut. He wonders about topping himself — isn't this what people do, professional suicide followed by the real thing? He contemplates the quietness of this moment: he hasn't lied to cover it up, or gone down screaming dragging others with him, he hasn't been a rebel. He has simply confessed and said he is sorry. And he feels nothing.

Paul will bury it. No one will know. And life will carry on, with him doing shitty jobs for not much money, never quite becoming the better person he could be. *That's the truth of it*, he thinks, and he reaches for his glass, warm to the hold now, all the ice long since melted, and drinks — water with just an insipid touch of alcohol. And so he stands to pour himself another, surprised that he is slightly unsteady on his feet because he usually holds his booze with the practiced skill of a seasoned drinker.

The bottle is empty.

Outside the girls' room, he presses his ear to the door, wanting to hear their breathing, and then he slowly turns the handle.

They lie side by side in the bottom bunk, pale hair knotted, cheeks waxy, Lara's eyes closed, Catherine's open. She does this sometimes — sleeping like she is wide awake — and he bends down and shuts her eyelids gently, fingers light on the smooth skin, not looking because he has always found it disconcerting, too like the sleep of the dead.

'I love you,' he whispers, but she doesn't stir.

She hasn't spoken to him all night. And he knows he is going to have to talk to her about the kiss with April, somehow resolve it in her mind, make it seem like nothing and yet also make her realise she shouldn't tell Ester. How, he doesn't know.

Back in the lounge room, he shuts his laptop. Lawrence the pollster is done. Tomorrow he will be Lawrence the guardian of the dead, the keeper of a promise. Hungover on the job, but true to his word.

How can she bear it? Will she be lying there awake, knowing that this is it?

Against this, all the rest is just noise.

He has had too much alcohol. He knows that, but in the midst of the haze there is a clarity, and he acts on impulse, picking up his phone and ringing Ester, the switch to message bank quick.

No need to call me, he texts. *Girls are fine. Just thinking of you, and wanting all the best for you.*

She will think he is drunk — which he is — but he is glad he sent it. Tomorrow he will call her, and his heart sinks with the weight of the news he will bear.

THE RESTAURANT THEY are in is crowded, their table right at the back, out of the worst of the noise but still loud enough for them to need to lean close. Ester's knee occasionally touches his, and she can see the veins on the inside of his wrist as he reaches for the water.

Can I just kiss you? This is what she'd like to say. *Can I just take you home now?*

But of course she doesn't; she is telling Steven about her mother's films, the strange, ordered chaos of them, the beauty of the images she chooses, the way in which she weaves a story from a seemingly random selection of ideas, and, as she speaks, she is enjoying this moment of being new to someone, a whole lifetime of tales that have not been told, each one shiny and unsullied, ready to be unwrapped and marvelled at.

'I'll have to look at them,' he tells her, and he offers her some of his meal.

She shakes her head, too nervous to trust herself with the simple act of taking his fork and getting it to her mouth without spilling the lot. It is ridiculous. And then she knocks her knife to the ground, only just managing to stop her wine from toppling in the process. She laughs as she looks at him.

'I'm a klutz when I'm nervous,' she confesses. 'It's my curse. You'll just have to excuse me in advance for the many accidents that may occur before dinner is finished.'

He grins. 'Fortunately, I'm a sucker for slapstick.'

It is then that she feels her phone in her pocket, and she apologises for quickly checking. 'Just in case it's the kids.'

But it isn't. It's Lawrence.

She shakes her head in wonder at his timing.

And then puts the phone away immediately.

'It's nothing,' she says.

Steven is asking her about her sister now, and it takes a moment before Ester answers. 'I have a complicated relationship with her,' she eventually says. 'It's not great.' She looks at him, grimacing slightly. 'You might have to wait a while before I go into the details.'

He tells her he had a brother. 'My twin.' He pauses for a moment here. 'We're identical, but there was an accident during the birth. For some reason, he didn't breathe for a while. He was on life support. And there was some trauma. In any event, he had a lot of problems.'

Ester is not sure if he is going to continue. She sits back a little.

'He killed someone.'

He utters the words without stumbling, his voice remaining even, but as he swallows, she can see how hard it was to say out loud.

'So I guess I know about complex sibling relationships.' His smile is tight.

She asks whether he ever sees this brother, if they have stayed in touch.

He shakes his head. 'I did for a while. He's in a psych ward. It's so difficult. I used to try and tell myself he couldn't be held completely accountable for his actions. He's struggled with psychosis and addiction — but in the end I just didn't know what I thought. I still don't. And I stopped seeing him.'

She is about to speak, but he cuts over her.

'It was a brutal crime.' He narrows his eyes in shame, and then meets her gaze. 'And I guess I just don't know if he has ever felt that what he did was wrong. Not that I am his judge.' He looks down at the table. 'We had a difficult history, and it was just too painful.'

She waits for a moment longer, but he is finished now.

'I can't imagine,' she eventually says.

He waves his hand. 'Maybe we should move on from siblings. I'm sorry if I was clumsy in telling you this. I suppose I felt it was important for you to know.' Steven nods as the waiter offers him another glass of wine. 'Perhaps there's something about him being my twin that makes me feel responsible.'

Ester puts her hand over her glass as the waiter offers her the bottle.

'I'm a cheap drunk,' she tells Steven. 'Particularly after a day of clients.' She shifts slightly in her chair, awkward now. 'I appreciate you telling me,' she says. She looks at him directly. Her mouth is dry, but she wants to speak. 'I've been by myself for a while now — and I mean really by myself.' She bites on her top lip, barely daring to keep her gaze fixed on him. 'I don't want to drink any more because I fear I'll just make a fool of myself. I have a tendency to just crash out on alcohol.'

'We can't have that,' he winks.

She picks up her napkin and glances across to where the waiter stands, ready to come over and ask if they want dessert. 'Can we skip the next course?' she asks.

'And go home together?'

She nods.

And he leans across the table and kisses her, red wine lips, his hand on hers.

APRIL SITS UNDER the open window, face turned to the night sky, and plays her guitar softly, teasing out a combination of other people's melodies and her own.

On the wall behind her, she has tacked up Catherine's drawing: a deep swirl of black, streaked with colour.

'It's called "Joy",' she'd said when she'd finished. 'It's for you.'

She has never regretted not having children, and supposes she still could if the urge overwhelmed her, but the truth is she's never wanted it enough.

But she loves those girls.

She remembers Lara singing this afternoon, and she smiles.

Picking up the phone, April calls Hilary without checking the time. She does this often, oblivious to the fact that it may be late.

Hilary answers, wide awake. 'I knew it was you,' she says. 'You do realise it's almost eleven?'

April apologises.

'It doesn't matter. I couldn't sleep,' Hilary confesses.

'I saw the twins today,' April tells her. 'It was so lovely. Like there'd been no time apart. They're beautiful girls.'

Surprisingly, Hilary doesn't ask if Ester knew, or how the visit came to pass. She doesn't want details, she just agrees. 'They look like you did when you were their age,' she says. 'Golden, a streak of sunlight. You were such a treasure.'

'Not always,' April adds.

'Nobody said anything about always,' Hilary agrees.

'I'm going to talk to Ester,' April tells her. 'I miss them, I miss her, I hate that we can't all be together. It's enough. Surely there has to be an end to punishment.'

Hilary is silent for a moment. When she speaks, her voice is soft. 'Oh, my brave one,' she says.

The slight slur in Hilary's voice makes April wonder whether she has been drinking. 'Are you okay?' she asks.

Hilary tells her it is the painkillers she takes. 'I've been getting headaches, I haven't been well …'

'Have you been to a doctor?'

'I've been,' Hilary says.

April switches back to Ester. 'I've decided I'm just going to go round there. Maybe tomorrow. I will stay at the door until she talks to me. I'll camp there,' she laughs. 'Maybe even take placards and a tent. A camp cooker and a stool.'

Hilary is silent.

'I'll call you tomorrow,' April says.

'I'm going to the river,' Hilary reminds her.

'When you get back. I'll let you know how I went. Sleep well,' she adds, hanging up and standing by the open window.

She thinks about going out. She can see the first of the stars, a smattering in the one patch of clear sky. She could walk down to the wine bar on the corner, she might see someone she knows. She looks around the lounge room, wondering where she left her bag, and then she changes her mind. She will try to sleep. Face Ester tomorrow with a clear head.

She stands tall, breathes in deeply, and wishes herself good night, her voice clear and sweet as she replies with a grin. 'A very good night to you, too,' she says. 'I'll see you in the morning.'

But it is just her and her reflection in the darkness of the glass doors that divide the living room.

THE DAY AFTER

THIS IS IT.

Hilary drives with complete focus on the road, aware that the painkillers have made her slow, her vision slightly blurred. She has all the windows down, the freshness of the afternoon streaming in, each leaf, each blade of grass, each particle of air washed clean and new.

She does not stop until she reaches the turn-off that leads to the top of the river, pulling over where the orchard flats stretch under the sunlight, rows and rows of glossy-leaved orange trees pressed close to each other.

This is what she wants. To smell an orange.

Leaning over the fence, she reaches into one of the branches, through the mass of foliage, and plucks a perfectly formed navel. The peel is waxy, its scent sweet and sharp. She closes her eyes and breathes it in, breaking through the rind with her thumb, the juice cold.

'This is private property.'

The harshness of the voice makes her jump, and she apologises. 'They just looked so beautiful.'

He continues to glare at her.

She holds the orange out to him, but he doesn't take it.

'I'm dying, you know.' She utters the words without thinking. 'I wanted to smell one of these before I …' At a loss for words, she shrugs. 'Get to the other side.'

She is just a loony old bat. She can see it in his eyes. And in a strange way, it is a relief.

'Well, now you have.'

She nods at him, and walks to the car without looking back.

He'll feel like shit, she thinks, *when he hears about them finding me*, and she almost turns around to tell him not to feel bad, that it's okay, but the exuberance of the moment is rapidly fading. She needs to get back into the car and drive, to keep propelling herself forward before her nerve fails and she collapses, weak, pain-riddled, and at the mercy of others.

The rains have been here, too. When she reaches the low wooden bridge that takes her onto the last stretch of road, she sees the swollen down-flow rushing over the boards, dirty brown and fast. Strange how she pulls up to see whether it is safe to cross — but then to be swept away, injured and even worse off than she is now, is not a possibility she wants to bring into this very small orbit she is spinning around in. She leans out and looks closely at the depth.

Maurie wouldn't have paused.

There had been times late at night when she'd told him it wasn't safe, when she'd insisted he let her and the girls out.

He never did.

She follows his lead, foot steady on the accelerator, the rush of water spraying up against the side of the car and through the window, icy on her arms, smelling of dirt and leaves, both rotten and sweet.

On the other side, the road pulls steeply upwards beneath overarching branches, patches of washed blue sky like tattered holes in fabric.

She drives until she reaches the gate, the 'For Sale' sign hanging off the wire, one end loose, the lock rusty.

At the bottom of the dip she can see the house, the crazy angles of the roof and the golden, dappled sway of the new leaves on the poplars beyond the clearing. Her heart lifts, beating too fast, as she looks down.

This is the place she has loved more than any other, she realises. This is Maurie, and the girls, and the sweetest moments of life.

She is here.

In her bag is the white powder.

She runs her fingers over the plastic.

First, she will swim in the river.

Under the shade of the desert oaks, Hilary takes off all her clothes.

Strange, this body of hers. Old now. Knotted veins on her legs, a stomach that droops, small breasts, pale skin. She unties her hair, white-grey, like wool, and lets it loose. Her feet sink in the cold sand, and the touch of the water is like an ice grip, solid around her ankles.

She has had a good life, she thinks, and she lets herself sink down, her breath caught tight in her chest as the chill takes hold. A good life. Floating past her. The girls in the river, her and Maurie drifting on their backs under the light of the full moon, making love on one of the small islands, the grit of the sand against her legs, the sweat on his skin, and she scoops up a mouthful of the water, pure and sweet, and drinks it down, eyes closed to the darkening sky, skin alive to the cold.

Oh God, she whispers.

Perhaps she could just stay here forever, naked in this water, the cold slowly squeezing the life out of her. She looks up now, inhaling deeply as she does.

Her clothes are in a bundle, and she dresses slowly. She does not want to be found naked, and she smiles at her own vanity, her hands shaking as she tries to clasp her bra. Smoothing down her hair, she ties it back again, and then she begins the walk back up to the house, feet slipping in the mud, hands grasping for branches, using her arms to haul herself up to where the grass stretches, pale and long beneath the poplars, crumpled leaves of bronze and gold and silver scrunching underfoot.

Maurie once painted this grove, the metallic lines of the trunks slashed across the canvas. She has filmed it. She remembers the footage — the girls are skipping beneath one of the trees — but she doesn't think she ever used it. Why not? She shakes her head. It doesn't matter.

The verandah boards are rough beneath her feet, scattered with twigs and dirt, dry and swollen; they creak beneath her, and she sits for a moment, trying to breathe calmly.

All around her it is quiet and still. *It is that hour*, she thinks. Where day turns to night.

Her bag is on the ground where she left it. The white powder still inside.

She has written letters. She has told her daughters she loves them. She has urged them to make up. She has told the twins that they are beautiful and special and she adores them. She has asked them all not to be angry with Lawrence, but to remember that he is just respecting her wishes, and that she is grateful to him, more grateful than she was able to allow herself to express at the time. She wrote with her black Artline pen, her script round and clear; words, words, and more words.

Here, far from them all, it no longer matters. In another place, April is standing on Ester's doorstep, knocking until she is let in; or perhaps she is already inside and they are talking, really talking; or maybe she is at home, her courage having failed her. Ester is smiling; it is her best self she is showing to someone, a man Hilary has never met and will never meet, it is all her hope and promise and goodness unfurling once more. And the girls, those girls; they will live and stumble and fall, and pick themselves up and shine.

The strangeness of imposing last words of advice and wishes now seems ludicrous. At most, her letters will give them some ease about her decision.

She has the spoon, the needle, a cigarette lighter, and the heroin.

Henry has shown her what to do.

As the daylight slides away, Hilary picks up her phone, the text written: *I've gone*, the message reaching Lawrence, who is driving to be with her, behind him a mauve light, deepening like a bruise, the cold breath of the wind a low moan in his ear as he heads out along the highway, on the road already because he knew she wouldn't falter, and he, too, didn't want to falter, but to be there, just as he'd promised he would be.

ACKNOWLEDGEMENTS

Thank you to all the team at Scribe, and particularly Marika Webb-Pullman. Your work on this book was so much appreciated. I'd also like to thank John Stirton for sharing his years of polling experience with me.

This book is dedicated to the four people whom I hold most dear in my heart: Rosie, Anne, Odessa, and Andrew. You have provided joy, counsel, and love, and I am blessed to have had you in my life.